★

s h

o

square

t

h

r

e e

edited by albert.

manguel
three
bloomsbury

First published 1990

Bloomsbury Publishing Ltd, 2 Soho Square, London W1V 5DE

A CIP catalogue record for this book
is available from the British Library

ISBN 0 7475 0716 3

Jacket illustration by Jeff Fisher
Designed by Jeff Fisher
Printed in Great Britain by Butler & Tanner Ltd, Frome and London

Cynthia Ozick's piece appeared in The American Poetry Review; *Grace Paley's in* Seven Days; *Margaret Atwood's in* The Michigan Quarterly Review. *Some of the translated texts were previously published in their original language.*

Contents

ALBERTO MANGUEL Introduction 7
CYNTHIA OZICK Helping T.S. Eliot Write Better 10
GÜNTER GRASS The Lefthanders 20
JORGE LUIS BORGES 8 August 1946 28
JORGE LUIS BORGES The Rose of Paracelsus 32
RICHARD OUTRAM Two Poems 38
JULIO CORTÁZAR A Rejected Chapter from *Hopscotch* 50
JULIAN BARNES Dirty Story: the Making of Madame Bovary 62
MARGARET ATWOOD The Female Body 68
MARGUERITE DURAS The Slut of the Normandy Coast 74
ANNE SZUMIGALSKI Two Poems 80
ROSE TREMAIN Over 84
TIMOTHY FINDLEY Parcel Post 90
MICHAEL COREN H.G. Wells and the Mask of Biography 100
JOSEPH ROTH Goethe's Oak in Buchenwald 106
YVES BONNEFOY All Night Long 110
GUILLERMO CABRERA INFANTE The Unknown Political Prisoner 112
TOMÁS ELOY MARTÍNEZ The End 118
MARQ DE VILLIERS A White Tribe's Dream 124
ANITA DESAI A Reading Rat on the Moors 130
LILIANA HEKER Early Beginnings or Ars Poetica 136
FRIEDRICH DÜRRENMATT Document 142
FRIEDRICH DÜRRENMATT The Sausage 148
MARY MORRISSY Rosa 152
BONNIE BURNARD Deer Heart 160
ALEJANDRA PIZARNIK Four Poems 170
URSULA K. LE GUIN Texts 174
IZAAK MANSK Genesis According to Leon Hartman 178
ROHINTON MISTRY The Scream 182
JANE URQUHART The Inner Landscape of Saint Kathleen 194
HARUKI MURAKAMI A Perfect Day for Kangaroos 202
JOHN HAWKES Sire 208
DAVID BROOKS The Wood 216
ROBERT BRINGHURST All the Desanctified Places 224
JOSEPH SKVORECKY from *The Miracle Game* 230

ISABEL HUGGAN End of the Empire 236
DON COLES Three Poems 244
MARY FLANAGAN Not Quite Arcadia 248
GRACE PALEY Three Days and a Question 252
RONALD WRIGHT Crossroads 256
AMPARO DÁVILA Welcome to the Chelsea 264
SUSAN SWAN Meeting Your Reader 270
UMBERTO ECO Tales From the Past 276
ROBERT FULFORD Gotcha! The Literary Imagination in Our Time 280

Illustrations

JORGE LUIS BORGES (aged four) 30, 31
CHRISTINA BRIMAGE 134, 135, 268, 269
BENOÎT JACQUES 71-73, 176, 177, 180, 181, 213, 214, 215, 278, 279
MICHAEL LEVINE 116, 117
KEN NUTT 169
MICHAEL LEUNIG 122, 123, 262, 263
OSKI 48, 49
CHARLIE PATCHER 88, 89
TONY URQUHART 194-201
BRIAN WEBB 206, 207, 251, 283
WENDY WORTZMAN 82, 83, 140, 141
All other illustrations by JEFF FISHER

Photographs

RAFAEL GOLDCHAIN 26, 27, 108, 109
ROBERT READ 201

Introduction

Like the precious mirror of wind-and-moon in *The Dream of the Red Chamber*, like Li'l Abner's kind schmoos who granted humankind any wish whatsoever, like (according to partisan slogans) Evita Perón, like Venice, like St Paul, the ideal magazine should be all things to all people. More modestly, this editor has chosen to please no one except himself in the hope that what one reader enjoys in good conscience will in good conscience be enjoyed by his *semblables*, his *frères*.

Being asked to edit a magazine, being asked to compile an anthology, simply exaggerates the natural impulse every reader has to bring a beloved author, a lovely text, to someone else's attention. As a method, it is politer than nudging with an elbow, and safer than lending the books from one's own library. It also gives one the exultant feeling of pulling rabbits out of hats.

I decided at once that my rabbits would be international. Being a foreigner almost by profession, having chosen to live in Canada, a country whose identity is increasingly defined by its reaction to a hundred different immigrant nationalities, nothing (except my ignorance and my personal taste) has limited my selection for *Soho Square*. While histories of literature and literature professors insist on keeping books in tidy geographical and chronological hutches, every reader knows that literature follows only the vagaries of one's own reading. In mine, Borges comes before Plato, John Hawkes and Haruki

Murakami share the same shelf, Liliana Heker and Margaret Atwood are citizens of the same vast republic, and a number of celebrated authors are unwelcome strangers. My rabbits have hutches too, but at least I admit that these hutches are my own invention.

I have said that ignorance and my own taste have formed this selection: that's not entirely true. Financial considerations (the publisher's limited budget) have restrained me from commissioning certain texts which I imagine as perfect. I would have liked to have sent Ronald Wright to Paraguay, to write about the Guaraní Indians; I would have asked Julian Barnes to interview Mrs Thatcher; I would have financed an expedition for Richard Outram to describe the fauna of Madagascar and another for Ursula K. Le Guin to chronicle a season in Antarctica . . .

The order in which the pieces appear is one of more or less fortuitious association. I knew I wanted to begin with Cynthia Ozick's essay, making mine her indictment of the editor as busybody. I was brought up in a language in which 'editor' means 'publisher', and 'author' the person responsible for every word in the text to him or her attributed, and still feel uneasy with the notion of a professional who feels entitled to fiddle with another person's writing. In spite of the forseeable 'would that he had', this editor has not blotted out a single line belonging to someone else. I wanted to end with Robert Fulford's piece on the literary imagination of our time because I know of no other statement that so clearly expresses my belief in the necessity of literature. The pieces in between form a pattern in my mind which, I hope, will lead the reader on an unguided tour of some of my favourite writers.

May you enjoy the voyage as much I did.

Alberto Manguel *Toronto, 1990*

CYNTHIA OZICK

Helping T. S. Eliot Write Better
(Notes Towards a Definitive Bibliography)

It is not yet generally known to the world of literary scholarship that an early version of T. S. Eliot's celebrated poem, 'The Love Song of J. Alfred Prufrock', first appeared in *The New Shoelace*, an impoverished publication of uncertain circulation located on East 15th Street. Eliot, then just out of Harvard, took the train down from Boston carrying a mottled manila envelope. He wore slip-on shoes with glossy toes. His long melancholy cheeks had the pallor associated in those days with experimental poets.

The New Shoelace was situated on the topmost floor of an antique factory building. Eliot ascended in the elevator with suppressed elation; his secret thought was that, for all he knew, the young Henry James, fastidiously fingering a book review for submission, might once have entered this very structure. The brick walls smelled of old sewing machine oil. The ropes of the elevator, visible through a hole in its ceiling, were frayed and slipped occasionally; the car moved languidly, groaning. On the seventh floor Eliot emerged. The deserted corridor, with its series of shut doors, was an intimidating perplexity. He passed three with frosted glass panels marked by signs: BIALY'S WORLDWIDE NEEDLES; WARSHOWER WOOL TRADING CORP.; and MEN. Then came the exit to the fire escape. *The New Shoelace*, Eliot reasoned, must be in the opposite direction. MONARCH BOX CO.; DIAMOND'S LIGHTING FIXTURES – ALL NEW DESIGNS; MAX'S THIS-PLANET-ONLY TRAVEL SERVICE; YANKELOWITZ'S ALL-COLOUR BRAID AND TRIM; LADIES. And there, at the very end of the passage, tucked into a cul-de-sac, was the office of *The New Shoelace*. The manila envelope had begun to tremble in the young poet's grip. Behind that printed title reigned Firkin Barmuenster, Editor.

In those far-off days, *The New Shoelace*, though very poor, as its shabby furnishings readily attested, was nevertheless in possession of a significant reputation. Or, rather, it was Firkin Barmuenster who had the reputation. Eliot was understandably cowed. A typist in a fringed scarf sat huddled over a tall black machine, looking rather like a recently oppressed immigrant out of steerage, swatting the keys as if they were flies. Five feet from the typist's cramped table loomed Firkin Barmuenster's formidable desk, its surface hidden under heaps of butter-spotted manuscript, odoriferous paper bags, and porcelain-coated tin coffee mugs chipped at their rims. Firkin Barmuenster himself was nowhere to be seen.

The typist paused in her labours. 'Help you?'

'I am here,' Eliot self-consciously announced, 'to offer something for publication.'

'F. B. stepped out a minute.'

'May I wait?'

'Suit yourself. Take a chair.'

The only chair on the horizon, however, was Firkin Barmuenster's own, stationed forbiddingly on the other side of the awe-inspiring desk. Eliot stood erect as a sentry, anticipating the footsteps that at last resounded from the distant terminus of the corridor. Firkin Barmuenster, Eliot thought, must be returning from the door marked MEN. Inside the manila envelope in Eliot's fevered grasp, 'The Love Song of J. Alfred Prufrock' glowed with its incontrovertible promise. One day, Eliot felt sure, it would be one of the most famous poems on earth, studied by college freshmen and corporate executives on their way up. Only now there were these seemingly insurmountable obstacles: he, Tom Eliot, was painfully young, and even more painfully obscure; and Firkin Barmuenster was known to be ruthless in his impatience with bad writing. Eliot believed in his bones that 'Prufrock' was not bad writing. He hoped that Firkin Barmuenster would be true to his distinction as a great editor, and would be willing to bring out Eliot's proud effort in the pages of *The New Shoelace*. The very ink-fumes that rose up out of the magazine excited Eliot and made his heart fan more quickly than ever. Print!

'Well, well, what have we here?' Firkin Barmuenster enquired, settling himself behind the mounds that towered upwards from the plateau of his desk, and reaching into one of the paper bags to extract a banana.

'I've written a poem,' Eliot said.

'We don't mess with any of those,' Firkin Barmuenster growled. 'We are a magazine of opinion.'

'I realise that,' Eliot said, 'but I've noticed those spaces you sometimes leave at the bottom of your articles of opinion, and I thought that might be a good place to stick in a poem, since you're not using that space for anything else anyhow. Besides,' Eliot argued in conciliatory fashion, 'my poem also expresses an opinion.'

'Really? What on?'

'If you wouldn't mind taking half a second to look at it –'

'Young man,' Firkin Barmuenster barked rapidly, 'let me tell you the kind of operation we run here. In the first place, these are modern times. We're talking 1911, not 1896. What we care about here are up-to-date issues. Politics. Human behaviour. Who rules the world, and how. No wan and sickly verses, you follow?'

'I believe, sir,' Eliot responded with grave courtesy, 'that I own an entirely new Voice.'

'Voice?'

'Experimental, you might call it. Nobody else has yet written this way. My work represents a revolt from the optimism and cheerfulness of the last century. Dub it wan and sickly if you will – it is, if you don't mind my blowing my own horn' – but here he lowered his eyes, to prove to Firkin Barmuenster that he was aware of how painfully young, and painfully obscure, he was – 'an implicit declaration that poetry must not only be found *through* suffering, but can find its own material only *in* suffering. I insist,' he added even more shyly, 'that the poem should be able to see beneath both beauty and ugliness. To see the boredom, and the horror, and the glory.'

'I like what you say about the waste of all that white space,' Firkin Barmuenster replied, growing all at once thoughtful. 'All right, let's have a look. What do you call your jingle?'

'"The Love Song of J. Alfred Prufrock."'

'Well, that won't do. Sit down, will you? I can't stand people standing, didn't my girl tell you that?'

Eliot looked about once again for a chair. To his relief, he spied a high stool just under the single grimy window, which gave out on to a bleak airshaft. A stack of back issues of *The New Shoelace* was piled on it. As he gingerly removed them, placing them with distaste on the sooty sill, the cover of the topmost magazine greeted Eliot's eye with its tedious headline: MONARCHY VS. ANARCHY – EUROPE'S POLITICAL DILEMMA. This gave poor Tom Eliot a pang. Perhaps, he reflected fleetingly, he had brought his beloved 'Prufrock' to the wrong crossroads of human aspiration? How painfully young and obscure he felt! Still, a novice must begin somewhere. Print! He was certain that a great man like Firkin Barmuenster (who had by then finished his banana) would sense unusual new talent.

'Now, Prudecock, show me your emanation,' Firkin Barmuenster demanded, when Eliot had dragged the stool over to the appropriate spot in front of the editor's redoubtable desk.

'Prufrock, sir. But I'm Eliot.' Eliot's hands continued to shake as he drew the sheets of 'Prufrock' from the mottled manila envelope.

'Any relation to that female George?' Firkin Barmuenster free-associated companionably, so loudly that the fringed typist turned from her clatter to stare at her employer for a single guarded moment.

'It's *Tom*,' Eliot said; inwardly he burned with the ignominy of being so painfully obscure.

'I like that. I appreciate a plain name. We're in favour of clarity here. We're straightforward. Our credo is that every sentence is either right or wrong, exactly the same as a sum. You follow me on this, George?'

'Well,' Eliot began, not daring to correct this last slip of the tongue (Freud was not yet in his heyday, and it was too soon for the dark significance of such an error to have become public knowledge), 'actually it is my belief that a sentence is, if I may take the liberty of repeating myself, a kind of Voice, with its own suspense, its secret inner queries, its chancy idiosyncrasies and soliloquies. Without such a necessary view, one might eunuchise, one might render neuter –'

But Firkin Barmuenster was already buried in the sheets of 'Prufrock'. Eliot watched the steady rise and fall of his smirk as he read on and on. For the first time, young Tom Eliot noticed Barmuenster's style of dress. A small trim man lacking a moustache but favoured with oversized buff teeth and grizzled hair the colour of ash, Barmuenster wore a chequered suit of beige and brown, its thin red pinstripe running horizontally across the beige boxes only; his socks were a romantic shade of robin's egg-blue, and his shoes, newly and flawlessly heeled, were maroon with white wing-tips. He looked more like a professional golfer down on his luck than a literary man of acknowledged stature. Which, Eliot mused, was more representative of Barmuenster's intellectual configuration – his sartorial preferences or the greasy paper bags under his elbows? It was impossible to decide.

Firkin Barmuenster kept reading. The typist went on smacking imaginary flies. Eliot waited.

'I confess,' Firkin Barmuenster said slowly, raising his lids to confront the pallid face of the poet, 'that I didn't expect anything this good. I like it, my boy, I like it!' He hesitated, gurgling slightly, like a man who has given up pipe-smoking once and for all. And indeed, Eliot spied two or three well-chewed abandoned pipes in the tumbler that served as pencil-holder; the pencils, too, were much bitten. 'You know our policy on fee, of course. After we get finished paying Clara and the rent and the sweeping up and the price of an occasional banana, there's not much left for the writer, George – only the glory. I know that's all right with you, I know you'll understand that what we're chiefly interested in is preserving the sanctity of the writer's text. The text is holy, it's holy writ, that's what it is. We'll set aside the title for a while, and put our minds to it later. What's the matter, George? You look speechless with gratitude.'

'I never hoped, sir – I mean I *did* hope, but I didn't think –'

'Let's get down to business, then. The idea is excellent, first-rate, but there's just a drop too much repetition. You owned up to that yourself a minute ago. For instance, I notice that you say, over here:

In the room the women come and go
Talking of Michelangelo,

and then, over *here*, on the next page, you say it again.'

'That's meant to be a kind of *refrain*,' Eliot offered modestly.

'Yes, *I* see that, but our subscribers don't have *time* to read things twice. We've got a new breed of reader nowadays. Maybe back, say, in 1896 they had the leisure to read the same thing twice, but our modern folks are on the run. I see you're quite a bit addicted to the sin of redundancy. Look over here, where you've got:

'I am Lazarus, come back from the dead,
Come back to tell you all, I shall tell you all' –
If one, settling a pillow by her head,
Should say, 'That is not what I meant at all;
That is not it, at all.'

Very nice, but that reference to the dead coming back is just too iffy. I'd drop that whole part. The pillow, too. You don't need that pillow; it doesn't do a thing *for* you. And anyhow you've said 'all' four times in a single place. That won't do. It's sloppy. And who uses the same word to make a rhyme? Sloppy!' Barmuenster iterated harshly, bringing his fist down heavily on the next banana, peeled and naked, ready for the eating. 'Now this line down here, where you put in:

No! I am not Prince Hamlet, nor was meant to be,

well, the thing to do about that is let it go. It's no use dragging in the Bard every time you turn around. You can't get away with that sort of free ride.'

'I thought,' Eliot murmured, wondering (ahead of his time) whether banana-craving could somehow be linked to pipe-deprivation, 'it would help show how Prufrock feels about himself –'

'Since you're saying he *doesn't* feel like Hamlet, why put Hamlet *in*? We can't waste words, not in 1911 anyhow. Now up here, top of the page, you speak of:

a pair of ragged claws
scuttling across the floor of silent seas.

Exactly what kind of claws are they? Lobster claws? Crab? Precision, my boy, precision!'

'I just meant to keep it kind of general, for the atmosphere –'

'If you *mean* a crustacean, *say* a crustacean. At *The New Shoelace* we don't deal in mere metonymy.'

'Feeling is a kind of meaning, too. Metaphor, image, allusion, lyric form, melody, rhythm, tension, irony, above all the objective correlative –' But poor Tom Eliot broke off lamely as he saw the older man begin to redden.

'Tricks! Wool-pullers! Don't try to tell Firkin Barmuenster about the English language. I've been editing *The New Shoelace* since before you were born, and I think by now I can be trusted to know how to clean up a page of words. I like a clean page, I've explained that. I notice you have a whole lot of question marks all over, and they go up and down the same ground again and again. You've got *So how should I presume?* and then you've got *And how should I presume?* and after that you've got *And should I presume?* You'll just have to decide on how you want that and then keep to it. People aren't going to make allowances for you for ever, you know, just because you're painfully young. And you shouldn't put in so many questions marks anyhow. You should use nice clean declarative sentences. Look at this, for instance, just look at what a mess you've got here:

I grow old . . . I grow old . . .
I shall wear the bottoms of my trousers rolled.

Shall I part my hair behind? Do I dare to eat a peach?
I shall wear white flannel trousers and walk upon the beach.
I have heard the mermaids singing, each to each.

That won't *do* in a discussion of the ageing process. There you go repeating yourself again, and then that question business cropping up, and 'beach' and 'each' stuck in just for the rhyme. Anybody can see it's just for the rhyme. All that jingling gets the reader impatient. Too much baggage. Too many *words*. Our new breed of reader wants something else. Clarity. Straightforwardness. Getting to the point without a whole lot of nervous distraction. Tell me, George, are you serious about writing? You really want to become a writer some day?'

The poet swallowed hard, the blood beginning to pound in his head. 'It's my life,' Eliot answered simply.

'And you're serious about getting into print?'

'I'd give my eyeteeth,' admitted Tom.

'All right. Then you leave it to me. What you need is a good clean job of editing. Clara!' he called.

The fringed typist glanced up, as sharply as before.

'Do we have some white space under any of next issue's articles?'

'Plenty, F.B. There's a whole slew of white at the bottom of that piece on Alice Roosevelt's new blue gown.'

'Good. George,' the editor pronounced, holding out his viscid hand in kindness to the obscure young poet, 'leave your name and address with Clara and in a couple of weeks we'll send you a copy of yourself in print. If you weren't an out-of-towner I'd ask you to come pick it up, to save on the postage. But I know what a thrill real publication in a bona fide magazine is for an aspiring novice like yourself. I recollect the days of my own youth, if you'll excuse the cliché. Careful on the elevator – sometimes the rope gets stuck on that big nail down near the fifth floor, and you get a bounce right up those eyeteeth of yours. Oh, by the way – any suggestions for the title?'

The blood continued to course poundingly in young Tom Eliot's temples. He was overwhelmed by a bliss such as he had never before known. Print! 'I really think I still like "The Love Song of J. Alfred Prufrock",' his joy gave him the courage to declare.

'Too long. Too oblique. Not apropos. Succinctness! You've heard of that old maxim, "So that he who runs may read"? Well, my personal credo is *So that he who shuns may heed*. That's what *The New Shoelace* is about. George, I'm about to put you on the map with all those busy folks who shun versifying. Leave the title to me. And don't you worry about that precious Voice of yours, George – the text is holy writ, I promise you.'

Gratefully, Tom Eliot returned to Boston in high glee. And within two weeks he had fished out of his mailbox the apotheosis of his tender years: the earliest known publication of 'The Love Song of J. Alfred Prufrock'.

It is a melancholy truth that nowadays every company president can recite the slovenly unedited opening of this justly famous item:

Let us go then, you and I,
When the evening is spread out against the sky
Like a patient etherised upon a table;
Let us go, through certain half-deserted streets,
The muttering retreats
Of restless nights in one-night cheap hotels, etc.

– but these loose and wordy lines were not always so familiar, or so easily accessible. Time and fate have not been kind to Tom Eliot (who did, by the way, one day cease being painfully young): for some reason the slovenly unedited version has made its way in the world more successfully during the last seventy years than Barmuenster's conscientious efforts at perfection. Yet the great Firkin Barmuenster, that post-*fin-de-siècle* editor renowned for meticulous concision and passionate precision, for launching many a new literary career, and for the improvement of many a flaccid and redundant writing style, was – though the fact has so far not yet reached the larger reading public – T. S. Eliot's earliest supporter and discoverer.

For the use of bibliographers and, above all, for the delectation of poetry lovers, the complete text of 'The Love Song of J. Alfred Prufrock' as it appeared in *The New Shoelace* of 17 April 1911 follows:

THE MIND OF MODERN MAN
by
George Eliot

(Editor's Note: A new contributor, Eliot is sure to be heard from in the future. Out of respect for the author's fine ideas, however, certain purifications have been made in the original submission on the principle that, in the Editor's words, GOOD WRITING KNOWS NO TRICKS, SO THAT HE WHO SHUNS MAY HEED.)

On a high-humidity evening in October, shortly
after a rainfall, a certain nervous gentleman
undertakes a visit, passing through a bad section
of town. Arriving at his destination, the unhappy
man overhears ladies discussing an artist well known
in history (Michelangelo Buonarroti, 1475-1564, Italian
sculptor, painter, architect, and poet). Our friend
contemplates his personal diffidence, his baldness, his
suit and tie, and the fact that he is rather underweight.
He notes with some dissatisfaction that he is usually
addressed in conventional phrases. He cannot make a
decision. He believes his life has not been well spent;
indeed, he feels himself to be no better than a mere
arthropod (of the shelled aquatic class, which includes
lobsters, shrimps, crabs, barnacles, and wood lice). He has
been subjected to many social hours timidly drinking tea, for,
though he secretly wishes to impress others, he does not know
how to do so. He realises he is an insignificant
individual, with a small part to play in the world.
He is distressed that he will soon be eligible for
an old-age home, and considers the advisability of a
fruit diet and of permitting himself a greater

relaxation in dress, as well as perhaps covering his bald spot. Thus, in low spirits, in a markedly irrational frame of mind, he imagines he is encountering certain mythological females, and in his own words he makes it clear that he is doubtless in need of the aid of a reliable friend or kindly minister. (As are, it goes without saying, all of us.)

— Кто включил мой телевизор и сломал его?!

Художник Ю. Денисов

НОЯБРЬ ПОНЕДЕЛЬНИК

☉

Восх. 8.19
Зах. 16.12
Долгота дня 7.53

—326

1917

21

○

Полнолуние 23 ноября
Зах. 5.12
Восх. 14.41

+40

1988

GÜNTER GRASS
The Lefthanders

Eric watches me. Nor do I look away from him, not even for a second. Both of us hold weapons in our hands, and it has been decided that we are to use these weapons and wound each other. Our weapons are loaded. We point at one another pistols tried out during lengthy exercises, carefully cleansed after the exercises, while the cold metal slowly grows warm. After a time, weapons like these behave in a seemingly harmless manner. Because don't we hold in exactly the same fashion a pen, a heavy key, make a faint-hearted aunt scream by pointing at her a black leather glove, separating the thumb and the index finger?

I must not even begin to imagine that Eric's weapon may be unloaded, may be harmless, a toy. I also know that neither will Eric hesitate to recognise the seriousness of my own weapon. Furthermore, barely half an hour ago we took the pistols apart, cleaned them and reassembled them, loaded them and unfastened the catch. We're not playing a game. As site for our unavoidable purpose we chose Eric's weekend cottage. As this ground-plan building is more than one hour's walk from the nearest train station – and therefore quite secluded – we can rest assured that any undesirable ears, in the truest sense of the word, will find themselves at a fair distance from the shot. We cleared the living-room and took the pictures off the walls – most of them hunting scenes and still lifes with game. The shots are not intended for the chairs, for the warmly glowing chest-of-drawers and the richly framed paintings. Neither do we wish to destroy a mirror or ruin a porcelain knick-knack. We have agreed only to shoot at one another.

We are both lefthanders. We met at the club. It is a well-known fact that the lefthanders of this city, just like any other group stigmatised by a common handicap, have founded a club. We meet regularly and try to teach our comrades a certain manoeuvre, albeit a clumsy one. For a time, a kind righthander gave us lessons. But, much to our regret, he no longer comes to teach us. The gentlemen on the board of directors criticised his teaching methods and resolved that from then on the members of the club should only be instructed according to their individual abilities. We therefore prepare, effortlessly and only among ourselves, parlour games which wc have invented and which comprise several tests of dexterity, such as threading a needle with the right hand, sewing, buttoning up and unbuttoning an article of clothing. Our statutes establish that we shall not rest until right is as left.

For all its vigour and beauty, this statement is nevertheless a colossal absurdity. We will never succeed in this, and the extremist wing of our club has been demanding for a long time now that this motto be eliminated and that in its place be written: 'We want to be proud of our left hand and not feel ashamed of our congenital natural talents.'

Of course, this other motto isn't accurate either, and only its emphasis and a certain generosity of feeling led us to choose these words. Eric and I, both of whom consider ourselves part of this extreme wing, know full well how deep the roots of our shame are. Our father's house, our school and later our military service proved themselves incapable of teaching us a posture that would enable us to bear with decorum our insignificant defect – insignificant compared to other, more generalised anomalies. This began with simple handshakes in childhood. Those aunts, uncles, mother's friends, father's colleagues; that dreadful family photograph, impossible to overlook, which darkened the horizon of our early days. And everyone had to be given an outstretched hand. 'No, not the naughty hand, the good one. You must always give your good hand, intelligent hand, capable hand, the only true hand, the right hand.'

I was sixteen when I first touched a girl. 'Oh no, you're lefthanded!' she cried out, disillusioned, and moved my hand away from her blouse. Memories like this one linger on and if, in spite of everything, we still want to subscribe in our statutes, in exactly those same words, the new motto – Eric and I devised it – then it should be considered as no more than an ideal which certainly will never be reached.

Eric has tightened his lips and squints. I do the same. Our cheek muscles contract, the skin across the forehead tautens and our noses contract. Right now Eric resembles a film actor whose features are familiar to me because of the many times I've watched him in adventure movies. Must I admit that I also carry about me that fatal resemblance to one of those ambiguous heroes of the screen? Maybe we seem ferocious; I'm glad that there is no one around to see us. That undesirable eyewitness – would he not perhaps suppose that we were two young men, romantically inclined, about to engage in a duel? Maybe he'd imgine that we share the same wanton girlfriend, or he might suppose that one has offended the other in some particular way. A family feud dragged across generations, a matter of honour, a cruel game. This is how adversaries look upon one another. Those thin, discoloured lips, those noses that could only belong to a couple of irreconcilable beings. How these two sanguinary creatures brood over their hatred!

We are friends. Even though our professions are vastly different (Eric is the department head of a store; I chose the well-paid job of a precision mechanic), we can list as many common interests as those required for a lengthy friendship. Eric has over me the advantage of seniority at the club. Well do I recall the day on which, shy and dressed too solemnly for the occasion, I entered the premises of the association of 'unilaterals'. Eric came forward to meet me and pointed out – to me, to the uncertain one – where the coat rack was, observed me prudently but without bothersome curiosity, and then addressed me in his own particular kind of voice. 'No doubt you wish to join us. Cast your inhibitions aside. We are here to help you.'

I've said 'unilaterals'. This is the official denomination we have chosen for ourselves. But this denomination, like most of the statutes, seems to me infelicitous. The name doesn't express with adequate clarity the thing that should unite and strengthen us. No doubt we would be better known if we were simply called 'the lefthanders' or, if one wished for something more high-falutin, 'the brotherhood of the left'. You will of course have guessed the reasons we renounced to register with these titles. Nothing would have been more incorrect and at the same time offensive, as comparing ourselves to those creatures, certainly pitiful, whom Nature has deprived of the only human possibility of satisfying a thirst for love. On the contrary, I must say that we constitute an association in which our women have over the righthanders the advantage of being more beautiful, more graceful and better mannered. If we were to compare them carefully, we would come up with an image of such morality as the one a pastor, preoccupied with the salvation of the soul of his flock, would use from his pulpit. 'Ah, if we were all lefthanders!'

That fatal name given to our association! Even our first president, a man of somewhat patriarchal ideas and unfortunately a high official in the municipal administration, land register office, is forced to recognise, from time to time, that our name is not heartily accepted by all, that the word 'left' is missing, that we are not 'unilaterals', that we do not think, feel or act in a unilateral fashion.

Of course, there are also political reasons for declining better denominations and for calling ourselves that which we should never have called ourselves. Given that the members of the club lean to either one side or the other, and that the chairs in the house are placed in such a manner that this same arrangement betrays the political situation of our country, it has become customary to attribute a dangerous radical point of view to any piece of writing or any speech in which this little word 'left' appears more than once. Well, in that respect there is nothing to worry about. And if in our city there is one association that exists without political ambitions and whose only purpose is to help and support fellow members, that association is our association. And to eliminate for ever all suspicion of erotic connotations, let it be said in passing that among the girls in our youth group I met my bride-to-be. As soon as an apartment is vacated, we shall be married.

When, at long last, the shadow cast over my soul by that first encounter with the opposite sex vanishes, I will thank Monica for this act of kindness.

Our love has had to overcome not only the problems known to every couple and described in many books: it also has had to overcome and transfigure our manual shortcomings in order to turn them into an intimate bliss. After trying in the first and understandable confusion to be loving to one another with our right hand, and realising how insensitive this, our deaf side, was, we caressed one another adroitly – that is to say, as God made us. I will not reveal too much, I hope I am not being indiscreet, if I mention here the fact that it was always Monica's beloved hand which gave me strength to persevere and maintain my promise. After our first time together at the movies, I had to promise her that I would respect her virginity until the moment of placing the rings on the right-hand finger – unfortunately giving way to the clumsiness of an inborn tendency, and even making it stronger. In the Catholic countries of the South, the golden symbol of marriage is worn on the left-hand finger, because in those sunny regions the heart rules more firmly than inexorable Reason. Perhaps to show their feminine stubbornness, and demonstrate the unmistakable manner in which women can argue when their interests seemed threatened, during laborious evening hours the young ladies of our society embroidered the following motto on our green banner: 'The Heart Beats to the Left'.

Monica and I have frequently discussed the moment of exchanging rings, and nevertheless we always reach the same conclusion: we cannot afford the luxury of appearing, in the eyes of an ignorant and frequently malicious world, as a couple engaged to be married, when for a long time now we have been a couple whose union has already taken place and who shares everything, the little things and the big things. Very often Monica weeps because of this question of the rings. As much as we plan to be happy on that day, a veil of sadness will be cast upon the presents, the richly laid-out tables and the celebrations.

Once again, Eric shows his kind and normal face. I also give in, but for a long time I still feel tenseness in the jaw muscles. Also, the tremor in the temples persists. No, no doubt about it, these grimaces do not suit us. Our eyes meet serenely and for that very reason look braver. We aim. Each one of us reflects upon the other's steady hand. I am convinced I shall not fail, and I can also trust in Eric. We practise a great deal, spending every free moment we have in an abandoned gravel pit on the outskirts of the city, so that we won't fail today when the stakes are so high.

One could say, This verges on sadism! No, this is self-mutilation, and we know all these arguments. Nothing, there is not a single misdemeanour for which we don't blame ourselves. This is not the first time we find ourselves in this empty house. Four times we have faced one another armed as we are today, and four times, frightened by our purpose, we let drop the hand bearing the pistol. But today we have managed to see things clearly. The latest events in our personal life, as well as those of a public nature, confirm our decision. We must do it. After long and careful thinking, we began by questioning the association, then the decisions of the right-wing faction, and finally we took up the weapons for the last time. However regrettable this action may be, we can no longer take part in the strife. Our conscience demands that we distance ourselves from our comrades at the club. Sectarianism has taken root there, and the ranks of those with more sensible convictions have been invaded by dreamers, even by fanatics. Some see Heaven on the right, others swear by the left. I would never have believed it: they shout slogans from table to table, they preserve the abominable custom of hammering down nails with their left fist, a gesture representing an oath of such importance that many board meetings resemble orgies during which the violent and obsessive hammerings lead to ecstasy. Even though no one voices it out loud, and up to now those who evidently have succumbed to the vice have been immediately expelled, it is no longer possible to deny that the – in my eyes – abhorrent and incomprehensible love between homosexuals has also found followers in our midst. And to state the worst, my relationship with Monica has also suffered. She sees too much of her girlfriend, a whimsical and unstable creature. Frequently she accuses me of procrastination and lack of courage regarding the question of the rings, as if to help me believe that the same trust still exists between the two of us, that she is still the same Monica I've held in my arms – certainly less and less.

Eric and I breathe calmly. The more we are in agreement on this, the more certain we are that our actions are guided by the right sentiments. Let no one believe that we are moved by the word of the Bible advising the refusal of anger in cases such as these. Rather it is the ardent and constant wish to see clearly, even more clearly, that which is taking place around me – to see whether our fate is irrevocable or whether the decision of intervening and giving our lives a normal orientation lies in our own hands. Enough of asinine prohibitions, restrictions and other schemes! We wish to act adroitly, with free will, and start again with nothing to keep us away from the common folk and from the use of a felicitous hand.

Now we both breathe in unison. Without any sign, we both fire at exactly the same time. Eric has hit the mark, and I have not disappointed him either. As we had foreseen, each one of us has cut the primordial tendon in such a way that the pistols could no longer be held upright and have fallen to the ground. Thus a second shot has become useless. We laugh, and we begin the great experiment of applying emergency bandages, now that we have been left to the mercy of our right hand only.

Translated by Alberto Manguel

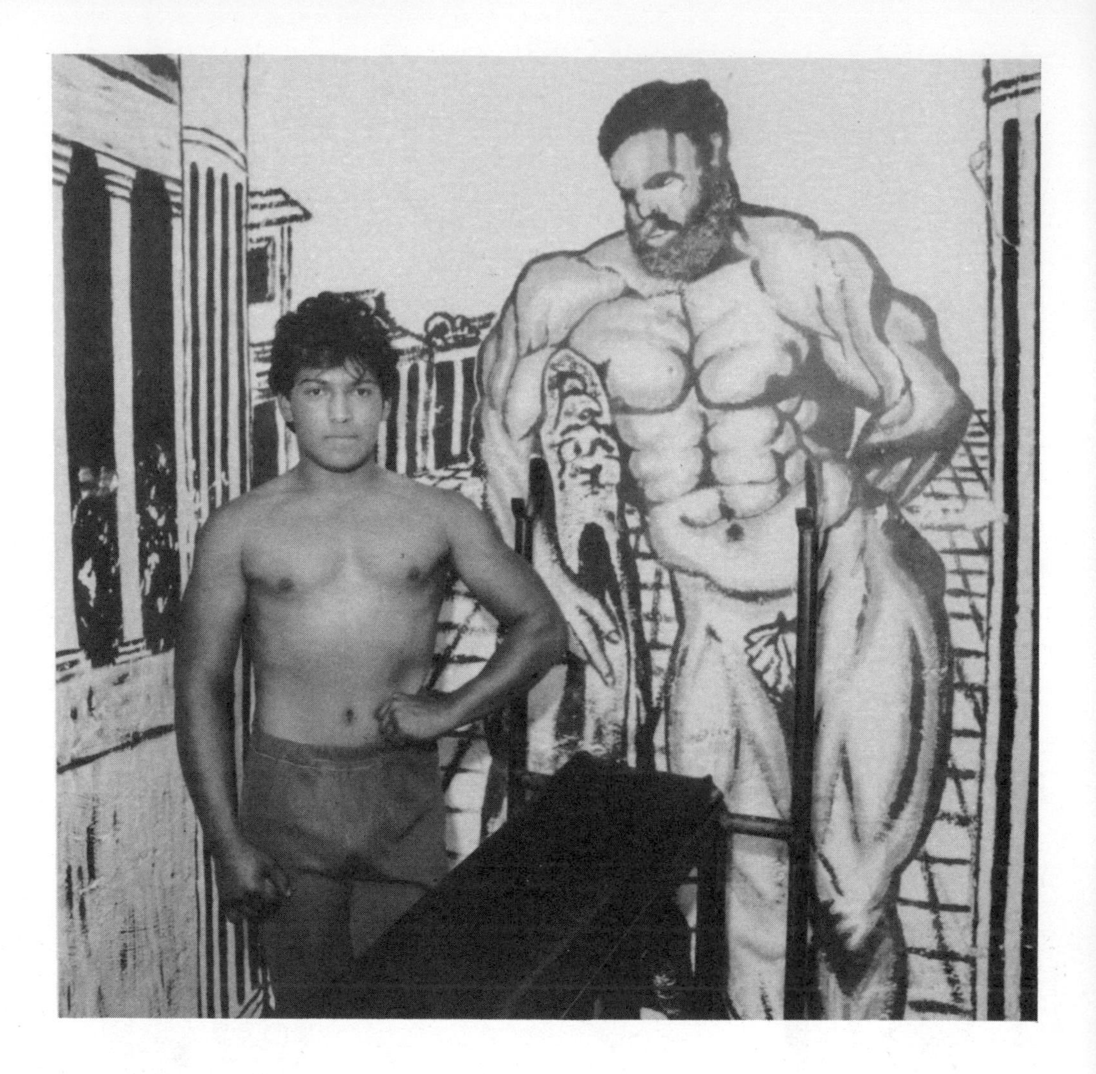

JORGE LUIS BORGES
8 August 1946

In 1946, the Perónist government forced Borges to resign by demoting him from his post in a small municipal library to rabbit and poultry inspector at a neighbourhood market. A group of writers organised a dinner in Borges' honour and Borges thanked them with the following speech, later published in Victoria Ocampo's magazine Sur.

A day or a month or a Platonic year ago (so intrusive is oblivion, so insignificant the event I am about to recall) I held, however unworthy, the post of assistant clerk in a municipal library of the southern suburbs. For nine years I went to work at that library, nine years that will become in my memory a single afternoon, a monstrous afternoon during which I classified an infinite number of books, and the Reich devoured France, and the Reich did not devour the British Isles, and Nazism, expelled from Berlin, sought out new regions. During a moment's break in that single afternoon, I fearlessly signed a certain democratic declaration; a day or a month or a Platonic year ago, I was ordered to serve in the municipal inspection police. Marvelling at this administrative avatar, I visited City Hall. There I was told, in confidence, that this metamorphosis was a punishment for having signed the declaration. While I was listening to this information with the interest it deserved, I was distracted by a sign which decorated the solemn office. It was rectangular and laconic, and of a considerable size, and held the interesting epigram: *Go on – Go on.* I don't remember the face of the person who spoke to me, I don't remember his name, but until the day of my death I shall remember the outlandish inscription. *I'll have to hand in my resignation*, I repeated as I walked down the steps of City Hall, but my own fate concerned me less than that symbolic sign.

I don't know up to what point the episode I've described is a parable. I suspect, however, that memory and oblivion are gods who know what they're doing. If they have lost the rest and retained this absurd legend, some justification must assist them. This is how I formulate it: dictatorships breed oppression, dictatorships breed servility, dictatorships breed cruelty; more abominable is the fact that they breed stupidity. Badges that stammer orders, effigies of leaders, foreseeable 'up withs' and 'down withs', walls adorned with names, unanimous ceremonies, mere discipline taking over the role of lucidity . . . To battle against these sad monotonies is one of the writer's many tasks. Must I remind the readers of *Martin Fierro* and *Don Segundo Sombra* that individualism is an old Argentinian virtue?

I also want to tell you how proud I am because of this multitudinous night and this active friendship.

Translated by Alberto Manguel

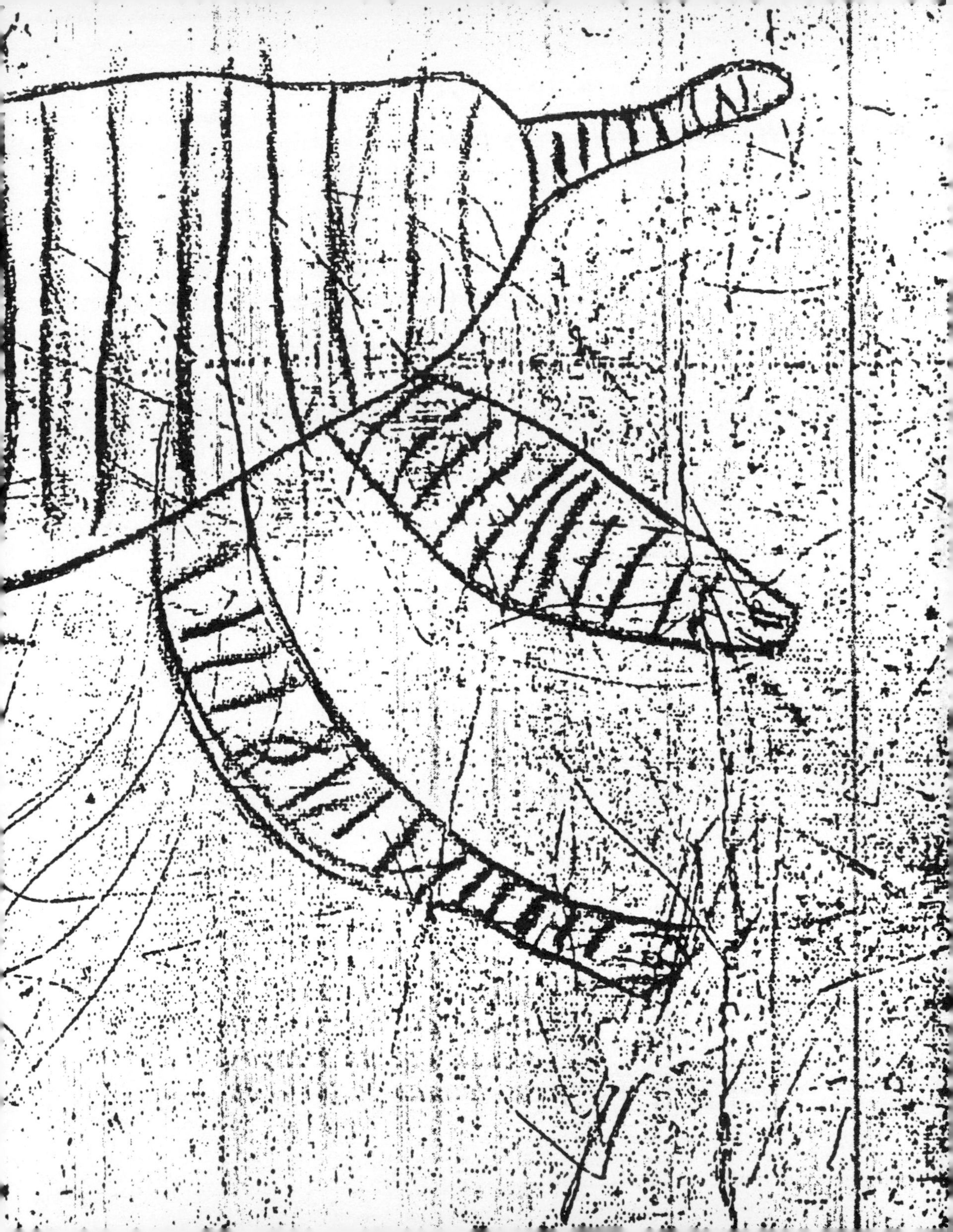

JORGE LUIS BORGES

The Rose of Paracelsus

De Quincey: ***Writings, XIII, 345***

In the laboratory, which occupied the two rooms of the basement, Paracelsus asked his God, his indeterminate God, any God, to send him a disciple. It was growing dark. The meagre fire in the hearth cast irregular shadows. Lifting himself to light the iron lamp would have required too great an effort. Paracelsus, distracted by his weariness, forgot his prayer. Night had blotted out the furnace and the dusty alembics when a knock was heard on the door. Drowsy, the man stood up, laboriously climbed the short spiral staircase, and half opened the double door. A stranger entered. He also seemed very tired. Paracelsus offered him a stool: the other sat down and waited. For a while neither said a word. The master was the first to speak.

'I remember faces from the East and faces from the West,' he said, not without a certain intensity. 'I cannot recall yours. Who are you and what do you want from me?'

'My name is of no importance,' the other answered. 'I have walked for three days and three nights to reach your house. I wish to become your disciple. I have brought you all I possess.'

He pulled forth a bag and turned it out on to the table. The coins were many and of gold. He did this with his right hand.

Paracelsus, in order to light the lamp, was forced to turn his back on him. When he faced him again, he noticed that in the stranger's left hand was a rose. The rose made him uneasy.

He bent over, joined his fingertips, and said, 'You believe me to be capable of making the stone that turns the elements into gold, and you offer me gold. It is not gold I am after, and, if it is gold you care for, you will never be my disciple.'

'I do not care for gold,' the other answered. 'These coins are nothing but a proof of my willingness to learn. I want you to teach me the Art. By your side, I want to take the road that leads to the Stone.'

Paracelsus said slowly, 'The road *is* the Stone. The point of departure *is* the Stone. If you cannot understand these words, you have not yet begun to understand. Every step you take is the goal.'

The other looked at him with a diffident air. He said, with a clear voice, 'But does the goal exist?'

Paracelsus laughed.

'My detractors, who are no less numerous than stupid, maintain the contrary, and accuse me of being an impostor. I do not agree with them, but it is not impossible that I labour under a delusion. I *know* a road exists.'

There was a pause; then the other said, 'I am ready to explore it with you, even if we must travel for many years. Let me cross the desert. Let me see, even from afar, the promised land, even if the stars will disallow my entrance. But before undertaking the journey, I want a proof.'

'When?' asked Paracelsus anxiously.

'Immediately,' answered the disciple with sudden determination.

They had begun the conversation in Latin; now they spoke in German.

The young man lifted up the rose.

'They say,' he continued, 'that you can burn a rose and make it rise again from its ashes by the art of your magic. Let me bear witness to this miracle. This is what I ask from you: after that, my life will be your own.'

'You are credulous,' said the master. 'I have no use for credulity; I demand faith.'

The other insisted. 'It is because I am credulous that I want to see with my own eyes the destruction and resurrection of the rose.'

Paracelsus had taken it in his hand and was toying with it while he spoke.

'You are credulous,' he repeated. 'Are you saying that I am capable of destroying a rose?'

'No one is incapable of destroying it,' answered the disciple.

'You are mistaken. Do you believe that anything can be reduced to nothing? Do you believe that the first Adam in Paradise was able to destroy a single flower, a single leaf of grass?'

'We are not in Paradise,' the young man said obstinately. 'Here, beneath the moon, everything is mortal.'

Paracelsus had risen to his feet.

'And where are we now if not in Paradise? What was the Fall if not ignoring that we are in Paradise?'

'A rose can burn,' said the disciple in defiance.

'There is still fire in the hearth,' Paracelsus answered. 'If you were to throw this rose on the embers, you would believe that the flames had consumed it and that the ashes were real. I tell you that the rose is eternal and that only its appearance can change. I would need but a word to make you see it again.'

'A word?' said the disciple with amazement. 'The furnace is dead and the alembics are covered in dust. What would you do to bring the rose back to life?'

Paracelsus looked at him sadly.

'The furnace is dead,' he repeated, 'and the alembics are covered in dust. At this point in my long day I use other instruments.'

'I dare not ask which,' said the other with humility or malice.

'I mean that which the divinity used to create Heaven and Earth, and the invisible Paradise in which we find ourselves and which was hidden by original sin. I mean the Word that is taught to us by the science of the *Kabbalah*.'

The disciple said with no emotion in his voice, 'I beg of you the grace to show me the disappearance and appearance of the rose. Little do I care if you achieve this by the Word or by the alembics.'

Paracelsus thought for a moment. Then he said, 'If I did it, you would say it was an image forced upon your eyes by magic. The miracle would not give you the faith you seek. Therefore, forgo the rose.'

Still diffident, the young man looked up at him. The old man raised his voice and continued. 'And, furthermore, who are you to enter the house of a master and demand that he produce a miracle? What have you done to deserve such a gift?'

The other answered, trembling, 'I know well that I have done nothing. I beg of you, for the sake of the many years during which I intend to study in your shadow, to show me first the ashes and then the rose. I will ask for nothing else. I will believe whatever my eyes witness.'

Suddenly he grasped the rose that Paracelsus had left on the lectern and threw it into the flames. The colours faded and only a few ashes remained. For an infinite instant he waited for the words and for the miracle.

Paracelsus had remained impassive. He said with strange simplicity, 'All the doctors and apothecaries of Basilea say that I am a hoaxer. Perhaps they are right. Here lie the ashes that were a rose and that will never be one again.'

The young man felt full of shame. Paracelsus was a charlatan or a simple visionary, and he, an intruder, had crossed his door and was now forcing him to admit that his famous magical arts were futile. He knelt down and said, 'I have behaved in an unforgivable manner. I have lacked the faith that the Lord demands of all believers. Let me look once more at the ashes. I will return when I am stronger and I will be your disciple and at the end of the road I will see the rose.'

He spoke with true passion but his passion was the pity inspired by his old master, so venerated, so dedicated, so famous and yet so empty. Who was he, Johannes Grisebach, to discover with a sacrilegious hand that behind the mask was no one?

To leave the golden coins would have been like leaving alms. He picked them up on his way out.

Paracelsus accompanied him to the foot of the stairs and told him he would always be welcome.

Both knew that they would never see each other again.

Paracelsus stood there, alone. Before extinguishing the lamp and sitting in the worn-out chair, he collected in the palm of his hand the small fistful of ashes and in a low voice uttered a single word. The rose appeared.

Translated by Alberto Manguel

A man saw a lea

t believe his luck

of an aeroplan

ey formed some

ing an aeropla

There was a

still life.

bird. He couldn
He saw parts
Together th-
approach-

RICHARD OUTRAM

Two Poems

Tradecraft

Goes with the territory, fireman (Save my Babe!)
which ain't, we are advised, the bleeding map.
Ask any pavement artist in the sanguine field:
none does offend. All my own work, I can ask one
condign in bastardy to tell me who I am, but not
on pain of suffering a fate far worse than life
(lace-curtain jobs are not for your timid souls)
demand a candid answer, daughter, to thy *quis*
custodiet . . . it's Ms Fallacious on the blower
for you, Dad, expressing sympathy. Let's not
forget the possible improbable in Art, or craft,
in an Election year. Get thee glass eyes.

Wrangler, wrangler, where have you been?
I've been engrossed in what meaning might mean.
Wrangler, wrangler, what did you there?
I deciphered a little fact from Dzerzhinsky Square.

It's still a jungle out there, Evie baby; he/
she had devised, however, found, or been vouchsafed
the perfect drop: a burly guardsman's busby,
housing each evening a murmuration of stares,
directly in front of palatial Buckingham Palace,
folks; also the ideal fall-back: Home Sweet Home,
with a hunk of Mom's how-do-you-like-them rotten
disbranched apples pie left simmering on the hob,
say cheese; they may be late about this business.
For there is conjuring abroad, no less nor more.

Listener, listener, where have you been?
I've been in the back room for what I can glean.

Listener, listener, what did you there?
I gathered a little fact out of the blare.

Having befriended a scrumpy-hound, gone pong,
dossed down rough on the Embankm ent overnight,
a genuine piss-artist, ex-BBC, in drag,
who in the bitter morning was revealed to be
one of the lesser Deities, now into tares,
the Ritual Ablutions and the staff canteen,
he had been granted a miraculous four-piece
Holy City suit that rendered him invisible.
In which he could tail assets forth and back
for ever without backup; and could not for love
hee-haw! nor money hee-haw! himself be tailed.

Housekeeper, housekeeper, where have you been?
I've been on a paper chase serving the Queen.
Housekeeper, housekeeper, what did you there?
I enabled a little fact to split a hair.

He quailed in his own presence, and had come
to obviate all contact with his mirrored eye;
In the mysterious West despite his better self
embraced a martial art the juju Master deemed
so formy-dabluh, with rosette and jaded belt,
that like old Stompin' Tennessee Tom Yahweh
it cannot be named, lest Cosmos self-destruct.
And qualified as lethal weapon, Mark whatever
X. Was designated henceforth simple minder and
best British baby-sitter. Registry, who knows
when one is dead and when one lives was chuffed.

Flutterer, flutterer, where have you been?
I've been in a snarl with my silken machine.
Flutterer, flutterer, what did you there?
I sifted for fictions, fact being rare.

Well junk indeed; but Waldorf, would you buy

a rusted, used and long-discarded sunbeam
flivver from this con-man much dismissed? Age
should bring you Nunc (*bibendum est*) to some
late understanding of this common stage of fools.
Th'insurance once laid on, the kickshaw laced,
the nasty capsule by tame fangmonger set hid
in the back molar, the salvific coup disguised
as a swig of Geritol, this is revealed as naught.
Egregious Ludwig laid it down, misunderstood:
all that is necessary strictly is to silent fall
never to speake againe. For nothing *will* come
of nothing (voices, ranting, off) O mad bon moT.
Chancery is said to be rethinking the whole
vexed expensive question of garrulous Seniors.

Gorilla, gorilla, where have you been?
I've been up to Lubianka to play it obscene.
Gorilla, gorilla, what did you there?
I sweated a little fact out of its lair.

What can man disregard? We have not learned;
the history of Buncombe County still not writ
and having rote moves on to dusty wawl and cry.
The Antichrist, or at least *their* Antichrist,
(with Casement at Iquitos, for starters, chum)
if seldom oracular in hallways and hullabaloo
of smoke and mirrors, recks and reveals thuswise:
when invoking the inessential need to know, for
the censor there is no repeat no discernible difference whatsolutely abever between God's anagogic
disinformation and for-Your-eyes-only. This is
classified Bottom Secret and shredded after death.

Coat trailer, coat trailer, where have you been?
I've been masquerading to see if you're keen.
Coat trailer, coat trailer, what did you there?

I honeyed a little fact for a Red Bear.

Put paid to persiflage, stout Watson, kindly lend
your strict attention to the matter; one will ask
grave questions later. Now of lendings learn
(see Fawn: *On Anticryptic and Procryptic Habit*);
Jake was trained and made, not born chameleon.
There is, so it would seem, a bloody proclamation
always to escape. One looks for usual shoes.
Your issue anorak reverses; the swift switch,
Dodger, of titfers, Bevan's peepers, branded bags;
but subject's boots that very Dogges disdain'd
are always so-to-speak dead giveaways, my Son.

Heeltapper, heeltapper, where have you been?
I've been up my own backside to keep myself clean.
Heeltapper, heeltapper, what did you there?
I passed by a little fact with headroom to spare.

Disheartening in the extreme, no virile bod
of any adoptive gender, colour, class or creed
whatever inducement presents itself desires
to do the act of darkness with his pusser mother.
Which is not just beige cashmere twin-sets, pearls,
the lingo studiously clipped, the set blue rinse
(they are full-fed with fresh grass from the waist),
but (sob) the end of Classicism as we have known it.
And in that general collapse, high-flying sixth-
former, scent the genesis of incest. Prick an ear!

Honey-trap, honey-trap, where have you been?
I've been up to London to screw a Marine.
Honey-trap, honey-trap, what did you there?
I burned a little fact that now we all share.

Go tell it juggins to the judge. Well said or no,
we will not hear of worthy Pioner, that can'st

work i'th ground. No shade on leathern wing,
buster, and he shall batten on the body politic
. . . now, in the much-meandered ornament about
the lapidary text, the limned initial Word
of What's-her-face, embowered on the page
we have our rubric, and our guttered beasts . . .
it is that Basilisk again, come back to haunt.
Excess of cunning damnable, their turning our
redoubled triple agent once again will cause
(the cry resounds still silver in the quad,
that offers, *pace* Hume et al, the promise of
material, efficient, formal and at longing last
but no mean least your final-type causation)
tenacious groper Mouldwarp, overly adored
since infancy for there is *nothing* absolutely
nothing (let's be blunt). As simply messing
about in holes now is there Ratty my old Soul-
mate to sequester his beloved self snugged up
his own U-fundamental aura po-face. S'trewth!

Finger man, finger man, where have you been?
I've been up on the rooftops waiting unseen.
Finger man, finger man, what did you there?
I whistled a little lead fact through thin air.

You will be happy with the news: who munches here
on cow-dung sallets does so from a proper desire
of rousing other men into a perception (so we have
it from the Cousins-germaine) of the infinite.
Now there's relief! What's more, both nuts and bolts
and stinks-and-bangs (trust me friends) concur:
the microdot contains the text that doth contain
a microdot the which contains a text that must
perforce contain a microdot O friends it is facile
to write etc. etc. and yes it is (the very truth
be mustered, sized and formed two-deep, my Sahib)

turtles turtles turtles all the way down. This does
obtain, if withered now as William oft had hoped
to Truth, despite the promulgations of the Raj.

Shoemaker, shoemaker, where have you been?
I've been transmogrifying a Duke to a Dean.
Shoemaker, shoemaker, what did you there?
I altered a little fact with loving care.

She rides sidesaddle and must not be spooked.
Our fesnyng was put in and ravening missed
but one, not bad; a perfect purloined bug
inserted as a deaf-aid in her dexter ear
(a print by Hockney, never well received,
but sent to embassies wherever). Did connect
by taught string to an emptied can of worms
in darkest Moscow. And she come in ugly, Love!
He, sloven else, makes that and th'action fine.

Burrower, burrower, where have you been?
I've been in the realms of dark Archive's demesne.
Burrower, burrower, what did you there?
I chevied a little fact out into the glare.

He came of another generation that relied
on Orders, bisque strokes, green baize and book codes.
Once one could rest assured, in one's old school
pyjamas, each agent at his left hand handy had
his dog-earedeyednosedthroated and inscribed
prize-day *Crockford's* in yapped vellum, gilt.
Or if to interface with our spread-eagled Cousins
who would durst turn a blind eye on it all
obtain by stealth H. Alger's *Bound to Rise.*
State-Of-The-Art and nowadays the random bitch
scribbles on one-time pads her one-time poems.

Scalphunter, scalphunter, where have you been?
I've been abroad to bite cords a-twain.

Scalphunter, scalphunter, what did you there?
I infected a little fact to your disrepair.

Safe? Safe as houses! As the three-doored house,
where he is beat about with bladders on a stick
bow wow bow woe who sometime cringing comes,
sometimes, obeyed in upstart office, bites.
The art of our necessities is passing strange
where there are many mansions to be scrounged,
so enter here, to find straw kindly strewn;
a frypan for the kindred chop; the purling loo;
the curtained window that must not be twitched;
the baubl'd goggle box to kill the mortal time;
the telephone as scrambled as Nunc's yolky yegg
(sad, sad Saint Peteman peters out, still stoned)
for She attends ensilvered in the promised main
of light that skulking notwithstanding comes.

Deskman, deskman, where have you been?
I haven't been anywhere, that's where I've been.
Deskman, deskman, what did you there?
I did nothing to nobody nowhow nowhere.

You see, Control broke down, and unrepentant wept.
O Soul flesh out the thing itself, inhuman res!
He/she had once been summoned to rememberance,
that we might prophesy the scattering of guise.
There is no patience liken unto that displayed,
if thus bereft, by our pale Lady Minim at the top-
left of your screen, My Dear; and loveless swear
it is because (no cause no cause what final price
is fortune's fool full circle) she is on the blink
we say because same cursor is Her eyelid as yet un-
identified officially we say but Ile kneele downe
and aske of Angels recognised as Neither-Nor
and come and take upon's the mystery of things . . .

The Flight out of Egypt

I

I will tell you a story. Or I will not
tell you a story. That once upon a time
I tried to respond in kind to the mute universe.

Here was the ocean fumbled at endless length
over the rocks. The world will come to an end,
of course. There is hope, said Kafka; but not for us.

One distant intricate ship sank with the sun,
quenched, with all souls presumably lost. Or we
did not find them the following morning with the usual

resurrection of fire, of stained flame spread
along the fine-crimped wire of the horizon. No,
though the sun rose, bearer of tales of other fires.

II

In the absence, not of God, but of the prophetic,
with Phoenix ash, pumice-fine, everywhere sifted,
it became our very onus to harrow our whereabouts.

But outline was lost. Mass, massive, massy,
the oceans rolled, heaved with a sick slick
on to the vague land, so far and no further,

withdrew as usual, leaving its wrack-lines
of interwoven foreboding staining the formerly
gold sand. We bowed, but translation escaped us

until, inland, beyond the slashed rain forest,
the insatiable fire-fledgling screamed again and again
with primitive rage. Once, once was enough.

III

To tell you of death. At full noon the youth,
all of his father's promise, his mother's grief,
fell like a fleshstone down from the topmast

crosstree, plunged through the hatched shrouds,
the necessary rigging, the parti-coloured sails
to smash on the seamed deck. Parlous, a sudden

vast fist had canted our vessel, nearly careened
us in mid-ocean, here, halfway from there to there.
Caught unawares, still staggered, aghast, we stared

in dumb conjecture at the unbelievable bright blood
slow-spread on the commonplace holystoned planks:
an antipodal sun continued elsewhere to rise and set.

IV

As we say. Once, in chosing a sacramental stone,
one of the burnished plenitude strewn at my feet,
I threw it as far as I might out into the hugely

indifferent ocean. At once the barely discernible
rings started to spread outward. Love, it is that
when they reach the rare bound of the universe of words

(we have contrived just such stringent myths
in fictions sans Gods or beasts or withered heroes
or mazarined maidens or bloodwine or sacred leaven

or the least promise of valour) becomes my prayer:
that they will in the new-sanctioned order of things
curve and return upon us shrived in this telling.

JULIO CORTÁZAR

A Rejected Chapter from **Hopscotch**

I know perfectly well the traps and snares of memory, but I think that the story of this 'suppressed chapter' (number 126) is approximately as follows:

Hopscotch was born from these pages; born as a novel, as the intention of a novel, because several short texts already existed (like those which later became chapters 8 and 132), texts that were trying to cluster around a story. I know I wrote this chapter in one go, and it was followed immediately and with equal violence by the one that would eventually be called 'the title chapter' (number 41 in the book). In this way there first was a kind of early core in which the images of Oliveira, Talita and Traveler became defined; suddenly the lurch subsided, there was a painful pause, until with the same initial violence I understood that I had to leave it all and wait and go back through a plot of which I knew next to nothing, and write, using the short texts mentioned as a point of departure, the whole of the Paris section.

From that 'other side' I jumped effortlessly to 'this side', because Traveler and Talita had stayed there as if waiting, and Oliveira simply went to meet them, in exactly the way it is told in the book. And then one day I finished writing. I re-read the mountain of papers, I added the host of elements that need to be included after a second reading, and I started to make a clean draft of the whole. It was then, I think, that I discovered that this initial chapter, which had set the novel itself in motion, was *superfluous.*

The reason was simple and yet mysterious. I had not realised, two years into the novel, that, at the end of the book, Horacio's night in the mental institution took place within a make-believe equivalent to that of this first chapter; there, as well, someone was tying threads from one piece of furniture to another, from object to object, in a ceremony as inexplicable to Oliveira as it was to me. Suddenly the now old first chapter became repetitious, even if in fact it was the opposite. I realised that I had to eliminate it, overcoming the unpleasant task of having to pull away the cornerstone of the entire building. There was something like a feeling of guilt in that necessary act, something like ingratitude; that is why I began by looking for a possible solution, and when I wrote the clean draft I eliminated the names of Talita and Traveler – the main characters in the chapter – thinking that the faint enigma which would then surround them would deaden the flagrant parallel with the asylum chapter. An honest re-reading was enough to understand that the threads had not moved an inch, that the ceremony was analogous and recurrent, and with no further thought I pulled out the cornerstone, and as far as I know the house has not tumbled down.

These pages can't add (or take away, I hope) anything from a book that embodies me as I was then, at a time of change, of search, of birds in flight.

started because after gulping down the last of the coffee, he signalled but stared at him blankly and went to get the paper to read the obituary column as is only proper after coffee. waited for a moment and then said he would make some more coffee because he still felt like drinking real coffee and not the whitish juice made with the excuse that there was no ground coffee left in the blue tin. To this answered with an equally whitish look, and, when made the sign again, her eyes allowed themselves to be lowered and began to search (in a morning paper) for Juan Roberto Figueredo, r.i.p., passed away peacefully on 13 January 195 – , with the blessing of the Church and the benefit of last rites. His wife, et cetera. Isaac Feinsilber, r.i.p., et cetera. Rosa Sánchez de Morando, r.i.p. No one she knew, not today, not even one name that sounded like someone she knew and would allow the doubt and the genealogy.

came back with the coffee pot and started by spooning a good amount of sugar into 's cup who wasn't looking, deep in the paper, reading about Remigio Díaz, r.i.p. He then poured the coffee up to the rim of her cup, and filled his own, while with the free hand he took out a packet of cigarettes and put it to his mouth as if he were about to bite it, but it was only dexterously to extract a cigarette without touching the others with his lips.

'I'm very sleepy,' said after ten minutes.

'With the kind of news you read,' said who had been waiting for those words and was beginning to get seriously worried.

yawned delicately.

'Take advantage now that the bed isn't made,' said . 'You'll save yourself work afterwards.' looked at him as if she hoped he would do his signalling again, but had begun to whistle with his eyes glued to the ceiling, and more precisely on a cobweb. Then thought was miffed because she had not answered his signalling with the expected answer (passing her hand over her left ear as a sign of tenderness and compliance) and went off to take her nap, leaving the table with the remains of a splendid casserole.

waited three minutes, took off his pyjama top and entered the bedroom. was fast asleep, on her back. As it was hot, she had taken the blanket off as well as the top sheet; it was exactly what wanted, and also the fact that should have nothing on except the nightdress in which she had got up that morning. The blue dressing-gown was lying at the foot of the bed, covering her feet, and hooked it on his slipper and kicked it into a corner. He missed his shot and the dressing-gown almost flew out of the window, which would have been a nuisance.

Out of the left pocket of his trousers took a tube of Secotine glue and a ball of black thread. The thread was shiny and rather thick, almost like wrapping-string. Carefully, put his hand inside the right pocket of his trousers and took out a razor blade wrapped up in a piece of toilet paper. The toilet paper was torn and one could see the blade's edge. Sitting on the bed, began to work while loudly whistling a bit from an opera. He was certain she would not wake up, because large quantities of coffee always made her sleep profoundly, and also he would have been very surprised if she did wake up, considering the penumbrate of oxtaline he had slipped in with the sugar. On the contrary, 's sleep was quite extraordinary; she huffed to take the air in, so that every five seconds her upper lip would blow up like the frill of a curtain, while the air blew underneath it in a noisy puff. used this as a pacemaker to carry on whistling the opera while cutting the black thread, after calculating approximately how much he needed.

A tube of Secotine glue is opened by taking out the round-headed pin that serves both to cover and uncover it, a detail that gives one an idea of the maker's ability. Once the pin is out, it is more than likely that a drop will appear on the tip of the tube, a drop of a rather revolting substance, with its already famous smell and certified mucilaginous properties. Very carefully, and while he embroidered variations on *Bella figlia dell'amore*, wet the tip of the black thread with Secotine and, leaning over , pressed the wet tip in the middle of her forehead, leaving his finger in place long enough for the thread to stick to the forehead without sticking to his finger, that is to say, about four seconds more or less. He then climbed on a chair (after placing the tube, the pin and the ball of thread on the chest-of-drawers) and stuck the other end of the thread to one of the cut-glass prisms of the chandelier that hung over the bed and that had refused to throw out of the window in spite of his (now past and not repeated) pleading.

Satisfied that the thread remained sufficiently tense, because he loathed sagginess in any human creation, placed himself on the left side of the bed armed with the razor blade, and cut with a single stroke 's nightdress beginning with the armpit. Then he cut the turn of the sleeve, and did the same on the other side. The sleeves fell like snakeskins, but proceeded with a certain solemnity when he came to lifting the front of the nightdress, leaving stark naked. There was nothing on 's body that could be unknown to him, but the sudden contemplation of her body always dazzled him, although the Great Custom always managed to stale the effect. 's navel, more than anything else, made him giddy at first glance; it had something of confectionery, of failed transplant, of a pillbox thrown into a drum. Every time he saw it from above, felt the urgent desire to fill his mouth with saliva, very white and very sweet, and delicately spit on the navel, filling it to the rim with warm birthday lace. He had done so many times, but now was not the right moment, so he turned to look for the ball of thread and began cutting threads of different lengths, first measuring out certain distances. The first piece of thread (because the one leading from the forehead to the chandelier was like a previous pledge that could not be taken into account) he stuck on the big toe of 's left foot; this piece went from the toe to the bathroom doorknob. The second piece of thread he stuck to the second toe and also to the doorknob; the third, to the third toe and also to the doorknob; the fourth, to the fourth toe and to a carving in the shape of the horn of plenty on the oak chest-of-drawers, split in three parts; the fifth thread was drawn from the little toe to another cut-glass prism of the chandelier. All this on the left side of the bed.

Satisfied, stuck another piece of thread to 's left knee and fixed it to the top of the window frame that looked out on to the hotel courtyard. At precisely that moment an enormous bluebottle fly flew in through the open window and began to buzz over 's body. Without paying any attention to it, stuck another thread to 's groin, at the top of her left thigh, and also to the upper rim of the window frame. He thought for a moment before making up his mind, and then took the tube of Secotine and squeezed it against 's navel till it was full. He immediately stuck six threads there and fixed them on to five cut-glass prisms hanging from the chandelier, and on to the window frame. This did not seem enough, so he stuck eight more pieces of thread to the navel, which he stuck to seven more prisms and to the window frame. Stepping back two feet (he was somewhat cornered between the bed, the window and the pieces of thread that led from to the window frame), gave the finished work an appreciative look and found it satisfactory. He took out another cigarette and lit it with the butt that was already burning his lips. Suddenly he cut another half-dozen more pieces of thread, and stuck one to 's left nipple, another among the hairs of the left armpit, another to the earlobe, another to the left corner of the mouth, another to the left nostril and another to the corner of the left eye. The first three he stuck to the cut-glass prisms of the chandelier, and the others to the window frame, with a great deal of difficulty because he hardly had any room to move. After doing this, he stuck pieces of thread to each and every finger of the left hand, to the elbow and to the shoulder on that same side. Then he put the lid back on the Secotine with the pin provided for that purpose, wrapped the razor blade in the piece of toilet paper he had carefully kept in the hip pocket of his trousers, and tucked away both things and the ball of thread in the left pocket of the above-mentioned article of clothing. Bending over very carefully so as not to touch the threads which looked amazingly tense, he crept under the bed until he came out on the other side, completely covered in fluff and dust. He shook himself against the window that opened on to the street, took out once again his working utensils, and cut a number of pieces of thread that he stuck successively to different parts of the right side of 's body, in general keeping a symmetry with the left side but allowing himself certain variations; for instance, the piece of thread corresponding to the right earlobe was drawn between the earlobe and the bathroom doorknob; the thread leaving the corner of the right eye was stuck to the window frame opening on to the street. Finally (even though he was under no obligation to finish that task in a hurry), cut a fair number of pieces of thread, put a good quantity of Secotine on them, and plunged into a vehement improvisation, spreading them among 's hair and eyebrows, and sticking most of them to the cut-glass prisms of the chandelier, and yet keeping some for the window frame opening on to the street, the bathroom doorknob and the carved horn of plenty.

Sliding under the bed, after putting away the tube, the razor blade and the ball of thread in his trousers, dragged himself along till he came out at the foot of the bed, and kept sliding till he came to the bathroom door. Very slowly, so as not to touch any of the threads that led to the doorknob, he stood up and admired his work. Through the windows came a yellowish, rather dirty light, like the reflection of the peeling wall opposite that still held on to the remains of a painting depicting a baby sucking on something with a delighted look on his face; but the paint had come off in strips, and instead of a mouth the baby had a kind of purplish sore that seemed a poor recommendation for the nutritive product praised below in rather stuttering letters. The street was immensely narrow and the windows on one side were no more than five feet away from the other side. At that time not one window was open, except 's, but would probably not be there at that time, or would be napping. The fly began to bother intensely, and he would have liked to shoo it out of the window, but in order to do this hc would havc had to step forward to the foot of the bed and wave his hand next to the chandelier, which would have been impossible due to the large quantity of threads stretched in that direction.

'It's hot,' thought   , wiping his forehead with the back of his hand. 'It's really terribly hot.'

On the one hand he would have liked to close the blinds, but quite apart from the fact that it was difficult to wind one's way through the threads, he would not have had enough light to see with the perfect clarity he needed   's body.   's nakedness seemed cut out against the background, not so much because she lay on her back on the bed, but because the black threads seemed to converge from everywhere and fall upon her. Had they not been that tense, the overall effect would have been completely bungled, and   congratulated himself on his dexterity, even though his naturally demanding spirit led him to notice that the thread that led from the window frame to the corner of the right eye was slightly slack. For a moment he thought that   had moved, altering the general balance of tensions, but it was enough for him to eye the total array of threads to dismiss that possibility. Furthermore, the amount of sleeping powder he had put into   's coffee would not have allowed   even to blink.   thought of sliding down to the slackest thread and tightening it, but he would probably have spoiled some of the threads that met with this one on the window frame. He concluded that all in all the work was fine, and that he could allow himself a rest and another cigarette.

Eight minutes later he threw the butt out of the window into the street, and took off his clothes without moving from where he was. His tall, thin body seemed to have come out of an engraving (a frequent opinion of   's). Even though   could not see him, he gave the convened signal, and waited for an answer for about thirty seconds. Then he began to draw nearer the bed, avoiding little by little, with infinite care, the threads that led to the bathroom doorknob. To do this he bent down and then stood up every time it was necessary, until he was standing exactly at the foot of the bed, closing a triangle formed by   's two feet and his own body. He waited a while, until   opened her eyes and stared at him. As soon as he was sure that she could see him (because sometimes the state of unconsciousness lasted a few minutes after waking up) he lifted a finger and pointed to one of the threads.   's eyes began to wander up and down the threads, beginning by the ones that sprang from her eyebrows and the corners of her eyes, and following the entire length of her body. They rose to the cut-glass prisms of the chandelier and back to their starting-point; they left again, travelling to the window that looked on to the courtyard, and then returned to fix themselves to a knee or a nipple; they followed the black track to the window that opened on to the street, and returned to the groin or to the toes. was waiting with his arms crossed, identical to a painting of the blue period.

When finished reconnoitring the threads, something like a sigh lifted her chest and projected her lips forwards. Cautiously she moved her right arm, but she stopped when she heard the cut-glass prisms of the chandelier tinkle. The bluebottle fly flew heavily, slid among the threads, swirled around 's stomach and was about to land on her mount of , but then it ascended to the ceiling and stuck to one of the mouldings. and followed its flight with exasperated attention; they did not look at each other until they were sure that the fly had settled down on the ceiling with every intention of staying there.

Putting one knee down on the edge of the bed, bent his head and began leaning forwards towards , who stared at him, motionless. The other knee appeared on the edge of the bed, while the torso advanced horizontally and one of the hands tried to grip the mattress, exactly in between 's legs. The pieces of thread surrounded him, but his movements were so precise that he did not so much as touch one when he lifted a knee and put it on the mattress; then the second knee together with the other hand, and remained on bent knees, completely arched between 's legs, breathing heavily because the manoeuvre had been slow and difficult, and his calves hurt him, still perched as he was on the edge of the bed.

Lifting his head, looked at . Both were sweating, but while the sweat wrapped in a fine mesh of transparent droplets, had both her face and shoulders sodden, even though her breasts and stomach were dry.

'One makes the signal, but the other plays with the clouds,' said.

'Clouds are also an answer,' said.

'A borrowed phrase.'

'Exactly what you deserve.'

waited.

'You did it, at last,' said . 'You've been preparing me for months for this. First with your obsession with teaching me to recite filth, to dance like a Tibetan woman, to eat like an Eskimo, to make love like a dog. Then you forced me to cut my nails, you threw me into the street that day when it was hailing, you locked me in a wooden box with an infrared lamp, you bought me a stamp album. All that was nothing.'

'You know how much I love you,' said in a voice so low that opened her eyes as if in surprise. 'My love is held tight in this fist, crumpled and broken till it becomes a screeching ball, a portable star that I can take out of my pocket and put next to your body, to burn it, to tattoo it. Every time I signal you, you don't answer, and the star fries my legs, runs over my ribs like a storm in the Sargasso Sea, that inexistence where the Kraken floats, where the jellyfish couple in thousands, slowly turning in the night, in a bath of phosphorus and plankton.'

'And is all that my fault?'

'You'll move the threads,' said . 'When you move your mouth, two of the threads change position.'

'So what, the threads?' said .

'What do you mean, so what the threads?' said . 'It took me half an hour's work, I'm covered in dust and fluff. You never sweep under the bed. Even worse, you sweep the room and then hide the rubbish under the bed. I've just found out. My love is also like that, bits and pieces that come together and join and merge and stick on to one another. But I sweat, which rubbish doesn't.'

'It seems as if I've slept for a hundred years,' said . 'How long did I sleep, ?'

'A hundred years,' said .

'That's a lot, a hundred years.'

'For the one who stays awake.'

'You must have been terribly bored.'

'Exactly,' said . 'When you fall asleep you take the world away with you, and I am left in sort of nothing crossed by lines of perspective. After a while it becomes boring.'

'That's why you play like this,' said , staring at the threads.

'This is not playing. To be naked looking at one another.'

'I swear,' said . 'I think I didn't see the signal.'

'Of course you saw it.'

'Had I seen it I would have answered it. I'd rather be awake, with you.'

'Explanations never suckled bees,' said .

'Maybe I saw it and didn't answer it, but that was because of the heat and because after all I'd have had to do the dishes before coming to bed.'

'First the dishes,' said . 'An excellent motto. At the bottom of how many knifings lies this excuse that no judge would accept. You'd lick the dirty dishes rather than lick my chest like an industrious little snail. Leaving a track in the shape of a four or an eight. Or better still, a seven, a number drunk in sacredness. But no, first we'll lick the dishes, as Queen Victoria would say. First we'll lick the dishes.'

'But they're so filthy, ,' said . 'It's been fifteen days since we've washed anything in the kitchen. You noticed we had our lunch on dirty dishes, we can't go on like this.'

'You're disturbing the threads,' said

'And if now you'd signal to me, if even now you'd . . .'

A whistle was heard, in the shape of an S. It came in through the window that opened on to the street.

'It's ,' said . 'Calling me.'

'Put something on before leaning out,' said . 'You always forget you're naked.'

'I'm always naked. You are the one who forgets that.'

'Fine,' said . 'But at least put the pyjama pants on. And till when do I have to stay like this?'

'I don't know,' said . 'First I've got to see what wants.'

'To ask for something, I'm sure. A cigarette or matches, something like that.'

'He's an addict.'

'But you protect him.'

'Well, if you're going to protect normal people . . .'

'True,' said . 'After all, is a good guy. Listen how he whistles. It's unbelievable how he can whistle. My mouth would fall to bits if I tried.'

' is an alchemist,' said . 'He changes the air into a strip of mercury. Shit, he's fucked up.'

'Why don't you look out and see what he wants? I'm not too comfortable here with these threads.'

stood for a moment silently studying 's words.

'I know,' he said. 'What you want is that I let you go so that you can wash those dirty dishes.'

'I swear I don't. I'll stay here with you. If you give me the signal, I swear I'll . . .'

'Bitch, bitch, you bitch,' said . 'If I give you the signal, eh? Now you come making up to me with the signal. Why should I care about the signal, if I had you any way I wanted while you slept? Even now all I have to do is slide down some twenty inches, making my way like a seagull through that wonderful black web, those ropes on the mast of a galley, and enter you in one single thrust so that you scream out, because you always scream out when I take you by surprise. And you're longing for it, I've been smelling you for the past five minutes and I know you're longing for it, I could enter you like a hand into a used glove, you have the perfect level of humidity advised by the specialists in copulatory matters, you hot sea-slug.'

'Did you really do it while I slept?' said .

'I did it in the most perfect way, but you would never understand,' said , looking at the threads in profound admiration. 'Beyond the signal, beyond your dirty kitchen, and above all beyond your animal desire. Keep quiet, you're moving the threads.'

'Please,' said . 'Go and see what wants, and then close the blinds and come to me. I swear I won't move, but hurry up.'

once again studied 's words in silence.

'Maybe,' he said. 'You don't move. Do you want me to dry you a bit with a towel? You're sweating like a stoat.'

'Stoats don't sweat,' said .

'They sweat gallons,' said .

They always talked about stoats when they were making up.

'Now the problem is to see how I can get out of here,' said . 'There are so many pieces of string that I could bump into one, and when you go backwards you don't have the same clairvoyance as when you go forwards. It's incredible how man was born for going forwards. From behind we're nothing. Like driving in reverse, even the cockiest will run over a post box at the first change of gears. Guide me. First I'll take this leg out and put this knee on the edge of the bed.'

'A little further to the right,' said .

'I think I'm touching a thread with my foot,' said , looking behind him and correcting his movement.

'You hardly grazed it. Now put the other knee there, but slowly. You look beautiful, all in a sweat. And the light from the window seems to bathe you in green. You look like something rotten, I swear. I never saw you look so lovely.'

'Stop flattering me and guide me instead,' said , furious. 'You think I should put my foot down on the floor or should I slide down? I'll scrape my shins if I do that, this bed has a very sharp edge.'

'First put the right foot down,' said . 'The thing is that I can't see the floor; how can I guide you if I can't even move?'

'There,' said . 'Now I'll bend down slowly and go back inch by inch, like in 's novels.'

'Don't name that bird of ill omen,' said .

Crawling like an everglades alligator, passed little by little under the threads that led to the window frame. He did not look up at again, concentrating on the study of the chest-of-drawers' horn of plenty, and the problem of overcoming the threads that went from the horn of plenty to one of the toes, and to 's hair and eyebrows. Like that he passed under the greater part of the threads, but the last one he jumped. Only then, with his hand on the doorknob, he looked back at who seemed asleep. He realised that instead of going to the window he was standing next to the door, and that from there it was easy to reach the head of the bed without disturbing the pieces of thread. Approaching her on tiptoes, he began to blow on her hair. The threads wavered, and the cut-glass prisms tinkled.

'Come here,' said in a very low voice.

'Oh no,' said , walking away. 'I signalled you and you didn't answer.'

'Come, come here immediately.'

looked towards the door. was breathing with difficulty, as if the black threads were sucking her blood. The crystal-clear note of one last cut-glass prism was heard, and then the silence of the afternoon nap. From the house opposite came a terrible whistle, and from below it was answered by something very similar to someone breaking wind.

'They've sent him a splendid fart,' said . 'He really deserves it.'

'Please come here,' she begged. ' . It's painful to wait for you like this, I feel I'm going to die. Who'll cook your steak tonight?'

opened his arms, took a deep breath, and jumped on to the bed, sweeping the threads with a fabulous swing. The racket made by the cut-glass prisms coincided with the crash of his feet touching the floor on the other side of the bed and with 's yell, clutching her stomach with both hands. was still screaming in pain when fell on her, squashing her, weighing her down, biting her and fucking her. 'My belly-button hurts terribly,' managed to say, but could not hear her, completely on the far side of words. The air smelt more and more of Secotine, and the bluebottle fly circled around the shaken chandelier. Bits of black thread twisted like insect legs all over the place, falling from the edge of the bed, crossing over each other and tearing with tiny snaps.

had bits of thread in his mouth, under his nose, another coiled around his neck, and was moving her hands almost unconsciously, mingling caresses with desperate waves to rid herself of the threads that sprang from her everywhere. And all this seemed to last for ever, and the horn of plenty was lying on the floor broken in three pieces, one bigger and the other two almost the same, as divine proportion requires.

Translated by Alberto Manguel

JULIAN BARNES

Dirty Story: the Making of Madame Bovary

'Erection. Only use the word when talking about ancient monuments.'
– Dictionnaire des Idées Reçues

I shall get to the stage where I shall no longer dare to write a single line, because each day I feel smaller, thinner, feebler. The Muse is a virgin whose hymen is made of bronze: you would have to be a strapping fellow to . . .
17 September 1847

Oh for those good old peaceful, periwigged days! You certainly knew how to live, up on your high heels, twirling your canes! But beneath us the ground trembles. Where can we place our fulcrum, even assuming that we've got the lever? What we lack – all of us – isn't style, nor that virtuosity of bow and fingers known as talent. We have a large orchestra, a rich palette, a variety of resources. As for the tricks and ruses of writing, we know most of them, perhaps more than ever have been known before. No, what we're lacking is the intrinsic principle, the soul of the thing, the central idea of the subject. We take notes, we travel, yet these are empty procedures. We become scholars, archaeologists, historians, doctors, cobblers and persons of taste. What's the point of it all? Where is the heart, the verve, the sap? Where do we start from and where do we go to? We're good at sucking, we go in for a lot of tongue games, we play with ourselves for hours. But as for fucking! As for ejaculating and making a child!
2 June 1850

Literature is an old tart who's been screwed silly by filthy pricks. We must dose her with mercury, make her take pills, and scour out her deepest recesses.
27 June 1850

Fear of doing bad work soaks into us like a fog (one of those filthy December fogs that freezes your guts, stinks out your nose, and stabs your eyes), to the point where, fearing to go forward, we remain rooted to the spot. Don't you feel we're becoming *critics* . . . What we lack is *boldness.* Oh for those splendid days of my youth, when I could tear off a five-act play

in three days. Our scruples are turning us into the equivalent of those poor religion-haunted creatures who daren't live for fear of hell, and who wake up their confessors early in the morning to unburden their souls because they've dreamed of having a miscarriage. We shouldn't worry so much about the outcome of things. Let's fuck, let's fuck! Who cares about what sort of child the Muse gives birth to? Isn't the purest pleasure that of her embraces?
4 September 1850

Don't worry that I'll be bored on my return from Egypt. I have passed the age of boredom and left part of myself behind with it. Anyway, I'll have too much work to do to get bored. Something new is germinating inside me: a new manner, perhaps? But before too long I must give birth. I am eager to discover what I'm capable of.
14 November 1850

I played the real prude with dear old Gautier. For a long time he's been asking me to show him something I've written, and I'm always promising to. It's amazing how prudish I feel about doing this. At bottom, my aversion to being published is no more than the instinct one has to hide one's arse: a similar source of extreme pleasure.
3 April 1852

How grateful I am that I've had the good sense not to publish anything! I'm not in any way compromised! My Muse (waggle her hips as she may) hasn't yet been prostituted in any way, and I've a good idea to let her die a virgin, given all the sorts of pox there are at large in the world.
29 May 1852

I've read the Gautier volume [*Emaux et Camées*]. It's lamentable. Here and there you find a decent strophe, but never a whole poem. It's strained, contrived; he's trying all his old tricks. You have the sense of an intelligence that's been dosing itself with aphrodisiacs. It's an inferior kind of erection – the erection of a weakling.
26 July 1852

Today I got back to work on my *Bovary* . . . But it's going very slowly . . . The erections of the mind are like those of the body: they don't come when you want them to! (And then I'm such a heavy machine to get moving! I need so

many preparations and so much time to get myself going!)
17 February 1853

I have plans for writing which will last me until the end of my days, and if there are sometimes bitter moments, when I feel my impotence and weakness so strongly that I want to scream with rage, there are others when I can scarcely contain my joy. Something deep and ultra-voluptuous comes spurting out of me, like an ejaculation of the soul.
27 March 1853

This is what I think about your idea for a Review. All the Reviews in the world start off with the idea of being virtuous; none of them ever has been . . . You swear to be chaste, and you are for a day, for two days, and then . . . and then . . . Nature takes over! There are secondary considerations! The friends! The enemies! Some you have to puff, and some you have to perforate . . . A model Review would be a splendid thing, but it would require nothing less than the full time of a man of genius . . . After all, a magazine is a shop. And given that it's a shop . . . the question of getting customers sooner or later takes precedence over all other considerations. I fully realise that it's impossible to publish anywhere these days, and that all the existing reviews are filthy whores who are trying to play the coquette. Riddled with pox to the very marrow of their bones, they jib at opening their thighs to healthy creations which badly need to get in.
31 March 1853

Life is so short! I want to cut my throat when I realise that I shall never write as I want to, or produce a quarter of what I dream. All this strength you feel within yourself, which almost chokes you, will be buried with you without having been expended. It's like wanting to fuck. Mentally you lift every skirt that passes. But after the fifth go there isn't any sperm left. Blood still comes to the knob, but desire remains behind in the heart.
24 August 1853

2 a.m. I must love you to be writing to you tonight, because I'm *exhausted.* My skull feels as if it's encased in an iron helmet. I've been working on my *Bovary* since two o'clock this afternoon (except for about twenty-five minutes for dinner) . . . My knees are in agony, so is my back, and so is my head. I feel like a man who is all fucked out (excuse the expression): that's to say, in a state of rapturous lassitude.
23 December 1853

As for your magazine . . . I won't appear in it any more than in any other magazine. *What's the point?* And how would it advance my cause? If (when I get to Paris) you need me to supply you with articles, I'll do so with all my heart. But never with my byline attached. I've been guarding my virginity for twenty years now. The public will have it intact and at one go, or not at all.
23 January 1854

You're right to call me a hypochondriac . . . But how do you expect me to retain any sort of serenity or confidence after all the internal knocks (they're the worst sort) that I've suffered one after the other. Besides, isn't every book that you write like grabbing a dose of pox? I'm just now withdrawing from a long and painful copulation. I have a fine chancre on my pride: It will indurate – and so on.
16 June 1856

I am at this very moment being printed. A week on Thursday, on the first of October, I lose my virginity as an unpublished author. May *Fortuna Virilis* (she who hides from the husband the defects of the wife on their wedding-night) smile upon me! May the great public never spot in me any imperfection, like a hunch back or halitosis!
22 September 1856

MARGARET ATWOOD
The Female Body

'. . . entirely devoted to the subject of The Female Body. Knowing how well you have written on this topic . . . this capacious topic . . .'
– letter from the *Michegan Quarterly Review*

1.
I agree, it's a hot topic. But only one? Look around, there's a wide range. Take my own, for instance.

I get up in the morning. My topic feels like hell. I sprinkle it with water, brush parts, rub it with towels, powder it, add lubricant. I dump in the fuel and away goes my topic, my topical topic, my controversial topic, my capacious topic, my limping topic, my nearsighted topic, my topic with back problems, my badly behaved topic, my vulgar topic, my outrageous topic, my ageing topic, my topic that is out of the question and anyway still can't spell, in its oversized coat and worn winter boots, scuttling along the sidewalk as if it were flesh and blood, hunting for what's out there, an avocado, an alderman, an adjective, hungry as ever.

2.
The basic Female Body comes with the following accessories: garter belt, panti-girdle, crinoline, camisole, bustle, brassière, stomacher, chemise, virgin zone, spike heels, nose ring, veil, kid gloves, fishnet stockings, fichu, bandeau, Merry Widow, weepers, choker, barrettes, bangles, beads, lorgnette, feather boa, basic black, compact, Lycra stretch one-piece with modesty panel, designer peignoir, flannel nightie, lace teddy, bed, head.

3.
The Female Body is made of transparent plastic and lights up when you plug

it in. You press a button to illuminate the different systems. The Circulatory System is red, for the heart and arteries, purple for the veins; the Respiratory System is blue, the Lymphatic System is yellow, the Digestive System is green, with liver and kidneys in aqua. The nerves are done in orange and the brain is pink. The skeleton, as you might expect, is white.

The Reproductive System is optional, and can be removed. It comes with or without a miniature embryo. Parental judgement can thereby be exercised. We do not wish to frighten or offend.

4.

He said, I won't have one of those things in the house. It gives a young girl a false notion of beauty, not to mention anatomy. If a real woman was built like that she'd fall on her face.

She said, If we don't let her have one like all the other girls she'll feel singled out. It'll become an issue. She'll long for one and she'll long to turn into one. Repression breeds sublimation. You know that.

He said, It's not just the pointy plastic tits, it's the wardrobes. The wardrobes and that stupid male doll, what's his name, the one with the underwear glued on.

She said, Better to get it over with when she's young. He said, All right but don't let me see it.

She came whizzing down the stairs, thrown like a dart. She was stark naked. Her hair had been chopped off, her head was turned back to front, she was missing some toes and she'd been tattooed all over her body with purple ink, in a scrollwork design. She hit the potted azalea, trembled there for a moment like a botched angel, and fell.

He said, I guess we're safe.

5.

The Female Body has many uses. It's been used as a door-knocker, a bottle-opener, as a clock with a ticking belly, as something to hold up lampshades, as a nutcracker, just squeeze the brass legs together and out comes your nut. It bears torches, lifts victorious wreaths, grows copper wings and raises aloft a ring of neon stars; whole buildings rest on its marble heads.

It sells cars, beer, shaving lotion, cigarettes, hard liquor; it sells diet plans and diamonds, and desire in tiny crystal bottles. Is this the face that launched a thousand products? You bet it is, but don't get any funny big ideas, honey, that smile is a dime a dozen.

It does not merely sell, it is sold. Money flows into this country or that country, flies in, practically crawls in, suitful after suitful, lured by all those hairless pre-teen legs. Listen, you want to reduce the national debt, don't you? Aren't you patriotic? That's the spirit. That's my girl.

She's a natural resource, a renewable one, luckily, because those things wear out so quickly. They don't make 'em like they used to. Shoddy goods.

6.

One and one equals another one. Pleasure in the female is not a requirement. Pair-bonding is stronger in geese. We're not talking about love, we're talking about biology. That's how we all got here, daughter.

Snails do it differently. They're hermaphrodites, and work in threes.

7.

Each female body contains a female brain. Handy. Makes things work. Stick pins it and you get amazing results. Old popular songs. Short circuits. Bad dreams.

Anyway: each of these brains has two halves. They're joined together by a thick chord; neural pathways flow from one to the other, sparkles of electric information washing to and fro. Like light on waves. Like a conversation. How does a woman know? She listens. She listens in.

The male brain, now, that's a different matter. Only a thin connection. Space over here, time over there, music and arithmetic in their own sealed compartments. The right brain doesn't know what the left brain is doing. Good for aiming, though, for hitting the target when you pull the trigger. What's the target? Who's the target? Who cares? What matters is hitting it. That's the male brain for you. Objective.

This is why men are so sad, why they feel so cut off, why they think of themselves as orphans cast adrift, footloose and stringless in the deep void. What void? she says. What are you talking about? The void of the Universe, he says, and she says, Oh, and looks out the window and tries to get a handle on it, but it's no use, there's too much going on, too many rustlings in the leaves, too many voices, so she says, Would you like a cheese sandwich, a piece of cake, a cup of tea? And he grinds his teeth because she doesn't understand, and wanders off, not just alone but Alone, lost in the dark, lost in the skull, searching for the other half, the twin who could complete him.

Then it comes to him: he's lost the Female Body! Look, it shines in the gloom, far ahead, a vision of wholeness, ripeness, like a giant melon, like an apple, like a metaphor for *breast* in a bad sex novel; it shines like a balloon, like a foggy noon, a watery moon, shimmering in its egg of light.

Catch it. Put it in a pumpkin, in a high tower, in a compound, in a chamber, in a house, in a room. Quick, stick a leash on it, a lock, a chain, some pain, settle it down, so it can never get away from you again.

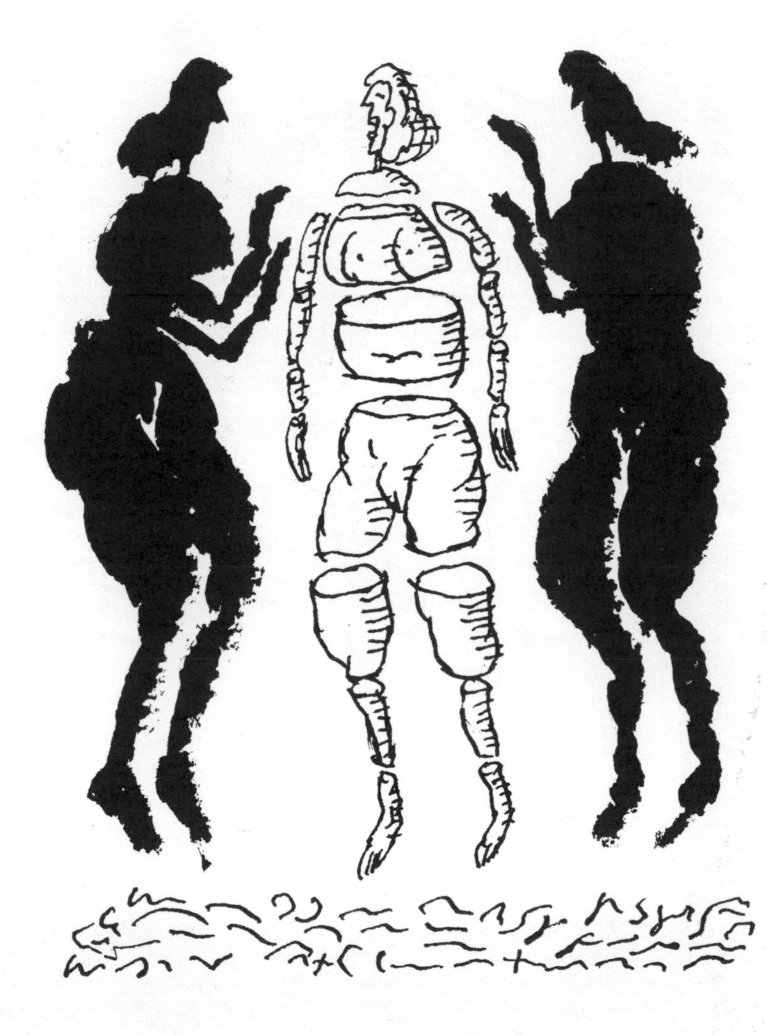

MARGUERITE DURAS
The Slut of the Normandy Coast

Luc Bondy had asked me to direct *La maladie de la mort* (*The Sickness of Death*) at the Schaubuhne in Berlin. I had accepted, but I had told him that first I'd have to adapt it for the stage, that I'd have to make a selection of the text, that it could be read but not acted. I made the adaptation. In it, the story's heroes were silent, and the actors were the ones who told their story, what they had said, what had happened to them.

All the scenes, all ten or twelve of them, were finished. They were to be read, as well as the text of the dialogue between the main characters. The woman had not been called upon in this adaptation, she had been set aside. The actors would speak to the man, but not to the woman. Two days after having sent this stage adaptation of *La maladie de la mort* to Berlin, I phoned to ask them to send it back because I was giving up on it. I told Yann. I often tell him what I do. From the very moment I severed myself from the manuscript, I realised I had made a mistake. I had done exactly what I had tried to avoid. I had gone back to *La maladie de la mort*, to its very principle of a text for three voices, to its stilted and unitary form. I had been emptied out, I had become the opposite of a writer. I was the plaything of a formal fate from which I was trying unsuccessfully to escape. I spoke of this to Yann. He didn't believe me. He had often seen me stalled in my projects, come to a halt, then begin again. Three times I started on the Berlin adaptation, the third time with a typist and a schedule. That time I dictated what I imagined to be the perfect version, but in fact it was the worst of all, pompous and artificial. Three times I tried. I would begin with *La maladie de la mort* and I would come back to it. While I was working I had no idea where I was going. I'd find myself back there, each time back to the same place in the book, huddled against it, dazed. I could no longer trust myself, I was lost. To make matters worse, it was always at the stage of typing out the final draft that I would become aware of the results. Whatever I did, it seemed that I had always to resort to a false solution: the stage. Once again I spoke to Yann. I told him it was over. I was fed up with wasting time, I was giving up the idea of adapting the text. I've said that I had discovered, once again, that *La maladie de la mort* was such an evidently ambiguous text that one had to use other methods to defeat it, that it made me feel incapable of anything. Even today, this is still all I know about the difficulties I had with that text.

And then there was that Quilleboeuf episode, to which I paid no attention at the time. Shortly afterwards I began a book which was to be called *L'homme menti* (*The Perjured Man*), but was also abandoned. And then, one day, the weather was warm, in the evening, at night. It was midsummer, in June. I began writing about the summer, about the hot evenings. I didn't know exactly why, but I carried on.

It is the summer of 1986. I'm writing the story. Throughout the summer, every day, sometimes in the evening, sometimes at night. It is then that Yann enters a period of crying out loud, of shouting. He types out the book, two hours a day. In the book, I'm eighteen, I'm in love with a man who loathes my desire, my body. Yann types as I dictate. While he types, he doesn't shout. That happens afterwards.

He shouts at me, he becomes a man demanding something, who doesn't know what that something is. So he shouts, to say that he doesn't know what he wants. And he also shouts to find out, so that, from the current of words, the knowledge of what he wants might appear on its own. He can't separate the detail of what he wants this summer from the whole of what he has always wanted. I hardly ever see him, this man, Yann. He's hardly ever there, in our apartment by the sea. He goes for walks. During the day he covers different distances, each several times. He goes from hill to hill. He visits the large hotels, he seeks out beautiful men. He meets several handsome bartenders. Also on the golf courses he seeks them out. He sits in the lobby of the Hotel du Golf and waits there, watching. That evening he says, 'I had a nice quiet time at the Hotel du Golf, I felt very relaxed.' Sometimes he falls asleep on the Hotel du Golf lounge chairs, but, as he's well dressed, very elegant, Yann, all in white, they let him sleep. He carries with him all the time a huge old blue bag, made out of cloth, which I made in case he needed it for his shopping. He keeps his money there. At night, he goes to the Melody. In the afternoons he also goes, sometimes, to the Normandy. In Trouville, he goes to the Bellevue. When he comes back, he screams, he shouts at me, and I carry on writing. Even if I say, Hello, How are you?, Have you had dinner?, Are you tired?, he shouts.

Every night, for a month, he wants the car to drive to Caen and see some friends. I refuse to give him the car because I'm afraid. So he takes taxis, he becomes the driver's chum, his best client. When he shouts, I continue to write. At first, it was difficult. I thought it was unfair, his shouting at me. That it wasn't right. And when I wrote and saw him coming and knew that he was going to shout, I could no longer write, or rather the writing stopped everywhere. There was nothing left to write, and I would write sentences, words, scribbles, to make believe that I didn't hear the shouting. I spent weeks with a jumble of different writings. Today I believe that those which seemed to me then the most incoherent were, in fact, the most decisive in the book to come. But of this I knew nothing. I wouldn't tell him that I couldn't because of his shouting, and because of what I thought was his unfairness towards me. Soon, even when he wasn't there, I was incapable of writing. I waited for his shouts, his screams, but I continued to fill the page with sentences that were alien to the book which was there, in the process of being made, in a field foreign to it, in fiction.

At last a sense of order was established, one for which I was not responsible, I who worked the writing on to the page, but for which Yann was responsible, he alone, and without putting pen to paper, without having to do anything about it, without any other intention than that of slaughtering, down to its very roots, anything that might be seen as an encouragement to live on. Of himself and of his anger he knew as little as an animal does, that is to say, nothing, not even that he shouted. That is how, a month before the date agreed upon for the delivery of the manuscript, I began the definitive book, that is to say, I began to find that man, Yann, but elsewhere than there where he found himself, looking for him in things that were alien to both him and the book – for instance, in the landscapes of the Seine estuary. Very much there. And in himself as well, in his smile, Yann's smile, in his walk, his hands, Yann's hands.

I separated him completely from his words, as if he had caught them unwittingly, and they had made him ill. And that was how I found out that he was right. That he was right to want something with such intensity, whatever that thing might be. However terrible it might be. Sometimes I would imagine that the time had come, that I was going to die. Four years ago I underwent a treatment that left me weak; since then I tend to believe that death is there, in reach of my life. He wanted everything at once, he wanted to destroy the book and he feared for the book's survival. For weeks he had typed two hours a day for me. Drafts, different stages of the book. He knew that the book was already in existence. He would say, 'What the fuck are you doing writing all the time, all day long? You've been abandoned by everyone. You're crazy, you're the slut of the Normandy coast, a fool, you're embarrassing.' After that, sometimes we'd laugh. He was afraid I'd die before the book was completed, maybe, or rather, that I'd throw the book away, once again.

I thought no longer about Quilleboeuf, but I still felt the need to go there. I would go there with friends, but I didn't know why that alien place meant so much to me; I thought it was because of the large river which ran past the square where a café stood. I thought that it was because of the sky of Siam, here yellow with petrol fumes, while Siam itself was dead.

Sometimes he would return at five in the morning, happy. I began not to ask him any more questions, not to speak to him, to say good morning just because of the pleasure of doing so. Then he became louder, he became terrible, and at times I was afraid, and believed that he was more and more in the right, but I could no longer stop the book, any more than he could stop the violence. I'm not certain against what Yann was shouting. I think it was against the book itself, real or imagined, beyond all definition, pretext, excuse, etc. It was simply that: making a book. It went beyond what was reasonable in its reasons, and what was unreasonable in those same reasons. It was like a goal: kill it. I knew that. I knew more and more things about Yann. In the end, it was like a race. Run faster than him in order to finish the book, so that he would not stop it completely. I lived with this throughout the summer. I also must have expected it. I would complain to people, but not about the essentials, not about what I am writing now. Because I thought that they would not be able to understand. Because there had been nothing in my entire life as unlawful as our story, Yann's and mine. It was a story that meant nothing outside our space, there where we stood.

It's impossible to speak of how Yann spent his time, his summer – it's impossible. He had become illegible, unforeseeable. One could say that he had become fathomless. He went in all directions, to all those hotels, to search beyond the beautiful men, the bartenders, the husky bartenders of foreign lands, of Argentina or Cuba. He spun in all directions. Yann. All directions met in him at the end of the day, at night. They met in the mad hope that a scandal might occur, an absolutely commonplace scandal centred around my own life. In the end, it might have become comprehensible. We had reached a place where life was not totally absent. Sometimes we received signals from it. It, life, strolled along the seaside. Sometimes it crossed through town, in the cars of the Morality Squad. There were also tides, and then Quilleboeuf, of which one became aware in the distance, as everpresent as Yann.

When I wrote *La maladie de la mort*, I did not know how to write about Yann. That I know. Here, the readers will say, What's got into her? Nothing happened, since nothing takes place. When in fact what took place is what happened. And, when nothing else takes place, then the story is truly beyond the reach of both the writer and the reader.

Translated by Alberto Manguel

MODERN OBSER

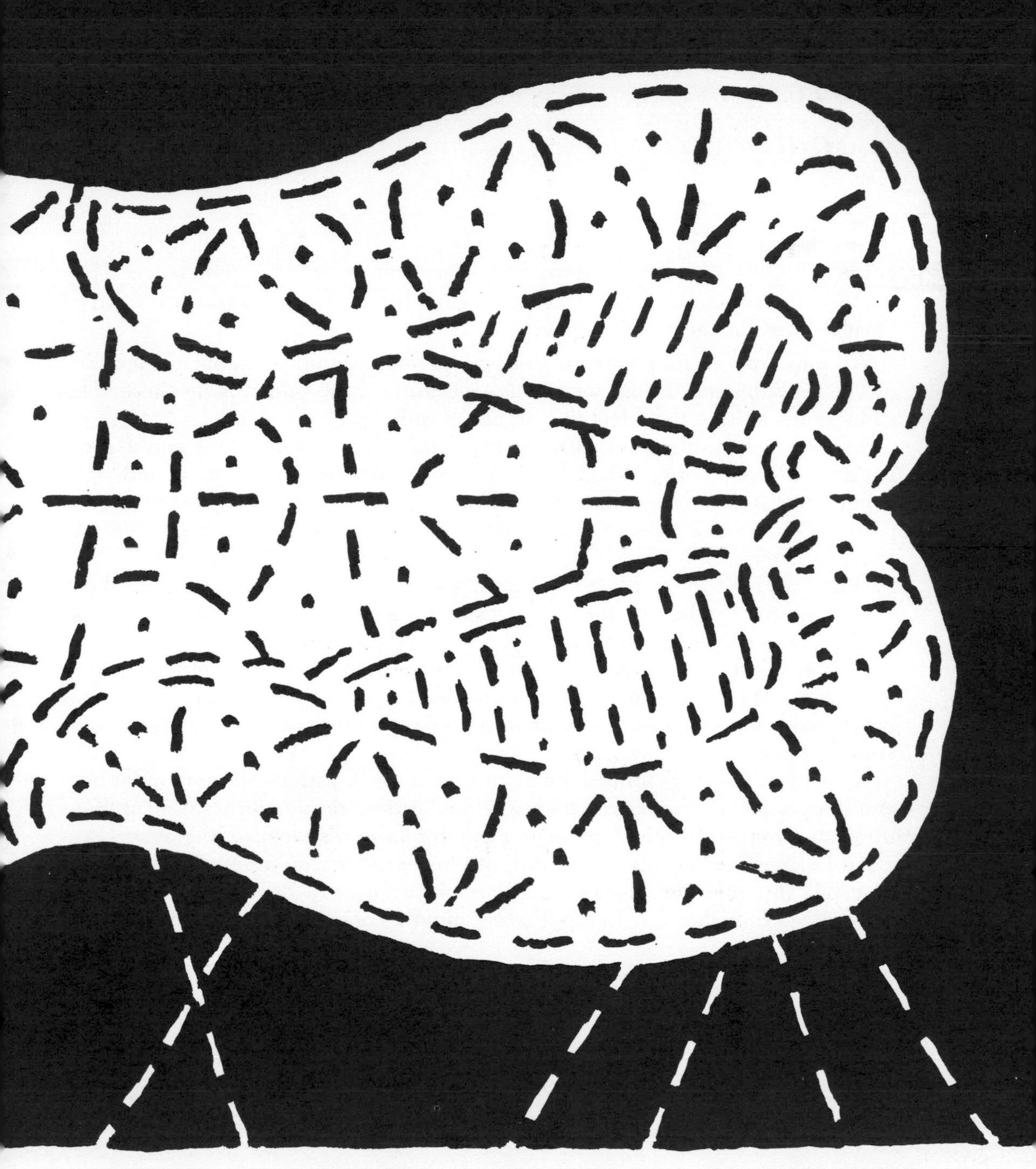

VATION BALLOON

ANNE SZUMIGALSKI

Two Poems

A Sanctuary

There are women living in a house on the mountain, a house that sticks to the rocks as tightly as lichen. At dawn they come out on the bluestone ledge. They stand in lines, a choir singing us awake. Their high voices in unison are a sort of shriek, hard for the teeth to bear.

We look up and they look down upon us poor primitives in our deep valley not yet enlightened. Look, we say to each other, how cold it is up there. The snow scuds around their feet like an ankle veil.

Snow which hardly ever falls in our valley. If we wanted we could grow potatoes all year long. When it's a bit chilly we chop down trees and light small fires. A few snowflakes fall into the flames and sizzle to nothing. And perhaps our smoke rises to those holy nostrils, and perhaps it brings tears to those holy eyes.

When we have too many girl children we send a few babies by rope to those women above. We bundle the little ones in quilted bags for we don't want them bruised as the sisters haul them up the broken face of the rock.

They say that on the mountain no one has teeth, for there is nothing whatever to chew up there. Ground bones of their dead is what they eat, and sometimes powdered reindeer moss. It's rumoured they suck these delicate meals through straws of ice.

None of us has ever climbed the mountain to speak with these women, for how could we hope to comprehend their wisdom? But we do sometimes stare at them through a makeshift telescope, trying to tell one nun's face from another.

And sometimes a lowly farmer will put his ear to the mountainside, straining to catch the voice of his lost child in prayer as she kneels in her granite cell whispering through her puckered mouth cool words of separation and of grace.

Jesus

A child sees Jesus coming towards her through the glass of the nursery door. When his reflection fades she turns around and there he is standing right behind her. She knows him by his beard, by his pierced hands, by his bare feet cold on the linoleum. He bends down to kiss her, and she notices that his halo stays there on the wall above him empty, waiting for his head to fit back in.

She's pleased with the visitation, of course, but she'd much rather he'd sent an angel with long feathered wings to lift her up and fly with her over the tops of trees, over oceans full of rocky islands with seabirds nesting on them.

Her mother has warned her that he's simply a man, with all the things a man has: bristly chin, hairy knees, bony feet, this and that. Sooner or later, her mother has said, he will come for you and take you on a long journey.

The child glances outside, and sure enough there is a very old donkey with downtrodden hooves tethered in the garden. The scruffy-looking thing is chewing on some lilies in the perennial border. Spotted orange petals and black-tipped stamens are scattered about on the grass.

Jesus has his arm around her now and is urging her through the door and down the path towards the back gate. Panic, like a long-necked bird, is opening and closing its beak in her throat. Nothing comes out, not even the crumbly hiss of a murrh.

She looks back at the house, at the nursery door still standing a little open. I should go back and shut it, she says to the man who is squeezing her shoulder with large possessive fingers. He doesn't answer but points with his other hand towards the road where she sees her mother getting into her small yellow car. She has on her big straw hat, the one she wears for picnics. Her father is already sitting in the passenger seat. He has taken off his glasses and is breathing on them, first one side and then the other. Just as the car moves off, he holds them up to the light and begins polishing the lenses with his large white pocket-handkerchief.

2.5 ON THE RICHTER SCALE

360 DEGREES

ROSE TREMAIN
Over

Waking is the hardest thing they ask of him.

The nurse always wakes him with the word 'morning', and the word 'morning' brings a hurting into his head which he cannot control or ameliorate or do anything about. Very often, the word 'morning' interrupts his dreams. In these dreams there was a stoat somewhere. This is all he can say about them.

The nurse opens his mouth, which tastes of seed and fills it with teeth. 'These teeth have got too big for me,' he sometimes remarks, but neither the nurse nor his wife replies to this just as neither the nurse nor his wife laughs when from some part of his ancient self he brings out a joke he did not know he could still remember. He isn't even certain they smile at his jokes because he can't see faces any longer unless they are no more and no less than two feet from his eyes. 'Aren't you even smiling?' he sometimes shouts.

'I'm smiling, Sir,' says the nurse.

'Naturally, I'm smiling,' says his wife.

His curtains are drawn back and light floods into the room. To him, light is time. Until nightfall, it lies on his skin, seeping just a little into the pores yet never penetrating inside him, neither into his brain nor into his heart nor into any crevice or crease of him. Light and time, time and light lie on him as weightless as the sheet. He is somewhere else. He is in the place where the jokes come from, where the dreams of stoats lie. He refuses ever to leave it except upon one condition.

That condition is so seldom satisfied, yet every morning, after his teeth are in, he asks the nurse: 'Is my son coming today?'

'Not that I know of, Sir,' she replies.

So then he takes no notice of the things he does. He eats his boiled egg. He pisses into a jar. He puts a kiss as thin as air on his wife's cheek. He tells the nurse the joke about the talking dog. He folds his arms across his chest. He dreams of being asleep.

But once in a while – once a fortnight perhaps, or once a month? – the nurse will say as she lifts him up on to his pillows: 'Your son's arrived, Sir.'

Then he'll reach up and try to neaten the silk scarf he wears at his throat. He will ask for his window to be opened wider. He will sniff the room and wonder if it doesn't smell peculiarly of water-weed.

The son is a big man, balding, with kind eyes. Always and without fail he arrives in the room with a bottle of champagne and two glasses held upside down, between his first and second fingers.

'How are you?' he asks.

'That's a stupid question,' says the father.

The son sits by the bed and the father looks and looks for him with his faded eyes and they sip the drink. Neither the nurse nor the wife disturbs them.

'Stay a bit,' says the father, 'won't you?'

'I can't stay long,' says the son.

Sometimes the father weeps without knowing it. All he knows is that with his son here, time is no longer a thing that covers him, but an element in which he floats and which fills his head and his heart until he is both brimming with it and buoyant on the current of it.

When the champagne has all been drunk, the son and the nurse carry the father downstairs and put him into the son's Jaguar and cover his knees with a rug. The father and the son drive off down the Hampshire lanes. Light falls in dapples on the old man's temples and on his folded hands.

There was a period of years that arrived as the father was beginning to get old when the son went to work in the Middle East and came home only once or twice a year, bringing presents made in Japan which the father did not trust.

It was then that the old man began his hatred of time. He couldn't bear to see anything endure. What he longed for was for things to be over. He did the *Times* crossword only to fill up the waiting spaces. He read the newspaper only to finish it and fold it and place it in the waste paper basket. He snipped off from the rose bushes not only the dead heads but the blooms that were still living. At mealtimes, he cleared the cutlery from the table before the meal was finished. He drove out with his wife to visit friends to find that he longed, upon arrival, for the moment of departure. When he made his bed in the morning, he would put on the bedcover then turn it down again, ready for the night.

His wife watched and suffered. She felt he was robbing her of life. She was his second wife, less beautiful and less loved than the first (the mother of his son) who had been a dancer and who had liked to spring into his arms from a sequence of three cartwheels. He sometimes dismayed the second wife by telling her about the day when the first wife did a cartwheel in the revolving doors of the Ritz. 'I've heard that story, darling,' she'd say politely, ashamed for him that he could tell it so proudly. And to her bridge friends she'd confide: 'It's as if he believes that by rushing through the *now* he'll get back to the *then*.'

He began a practice of adding things up. He would try to put a finite number on the oysters he had eaten since the war. He counted the cigarettes his wife smoked in a day and the number of times she mislaid her lighter. He tried to make a sum of the remembered cartwheels. Then when he had done these additions, he would draw a neat line through them, like the line a captive draws through each recorded clutch of days, and fold the paper in half and then in quarters and so on until it could not be folded any smaller and then place it carefully in the waste paper basket next to the finished *Times*.

'Now we know,' the wife once heard him mutter. 'Now we know all about it.'

When the war ended he was still married to the dancer. His son was five years old. They lived in a manor house with an ancient tennis court and an east-facing croquet lawn. Though his head was still full of the war, he had a touching faith in the future and he usually knew, as each night descended, that he was looking forward to the day.

Very often, in the summer of 1946, he would wake when the sun came up and, leaving the dancer sleeping, would go out on to the croquet lawn wearing his dressing gown and his slippers from Simpson's of Piccadilly and stare at the dew on the grass, at the shine on the croquet hoops and at the sky, turning. He had the feeling that he and the world made a handsome pair.

One morning he saw a stoat on the lawn. The stoat was running round the croquet hoops and then in and out of them in a strange repeated pattern, as if it were taking part in a stoat gymkhana. The man did not move, but stood and watched. Then he backed off into the house and ran up the stairs to the room where his son was sleeping.

'Wake up!' he said to the little boy. 'I've got something to show you.'

He took his son's hand and led him barefoot down the stairs and into the garden. The stoat was still running round and through the croquet hoops, jumping twice its height into the air and rolling over in a somersault as it landed, then flicking its tail as it turned and ran in for another leap.

The boy, still dizzy with sleep, opened his mouth and opened wide his blue eyes. He knew he must not move so he did not even look round when his father left his side and went back into the house. He shivered a little in the dewy air. He wanted to creep forward so that he could be in the sun. He tiptoed out across the gravel that hurt his feet on to the soft wet lawn. The stoat saw him and whipped its body to a halt, head up, tail flat, regarding the boy. The boy could see its eyes. He thought how sleek and slippery it looked and how he would like to stroke its head with his finger.

The father returned. 'Don't move,' he whispered to his son, so the boy did not turn.

The father took aim with his shotgun and fired. He hit the stoat right in the head and its body flew up into the air before it fell without a sound. The man laughed with joy at the cleanness and beauty of the shot. He laughed a loud, happy laugh and then looked down at his son to get his approval. But the boy was not there. The boy had walked back inside the house, leaving his father alone in the bright morning.

OVER

What is the Queen watching? Draw it.

TIMOTHY FINDLEY
Parcel Post

My memory keeps delivering the past in brown paper parcels done up with string and marked 'address of sender unknown'. One such parcel arrived the other day. Winter. Early evening. Not quite dark, but dark enough to turn on lights.

I had gone upstairs. The parcel was in my bedroom – waiting to surprise me. Not by saying 'boo' and flinging itself at my feet . Nothing like that. It was a gentle, undemonstrative surprise.

I don't know how it arrived – I don't know why. But slowly, as I moved about the room adjusting lamps and thermostats, I was gradually overwhelmed by a certainty that someone was about to speak.

The noise, my dear. And the people . . .

The words were only in my mind, but the voice was very clear – distinct as any living voice.

Ernest Thesiger – wraithlike enough while still alive – pulled in and out of focus as I closed my eyes and tried to conjure him. *Ernest, tied with string and wrapped in brown paper.* Where was he coming from? Why was he being delivered now?

The noise, my dear. And the people . . .

This was Ernest's best-known pronouncement, his reply when – returning from Flanders in 1917 with his hands so badly mangled it was thought they must soon be amputated – he was asked to describe the horrors of the battlefield.

The noise, my dear. And the people, he said.

But why had I thought of that now?

I hadn't seen Ernest Thesiger for over thirty-five years – and he'd been dead since 1961.

Ernest Thesiger. Actor. Eccentric. Friend.

Well. What else was in the package?

I sat on the bed and lit a cigarette. Outside, the sky had almost completely blackened. A wind had risen – cold and menacing, promising snow. The world was disappearing, whiting-out in the dark.

Moscow. That was it. Part of it.

I had gone to Moscow with Ernest Thesiger in 1955. We had arrived there long after nightfall, in a blizzard. The storm had been so bad and our landing had been delayed so long that the plane was running out of fuel. We thought for certain we would be killed. And, out of the silence created by our fearfulness, Ernest had asked in an offhand manner, *Does anyone remember the Russian word for ambulance?*

He made us all laugh.

He always could – if he wanted to.

Christmas was not far off, and I realised with pleasure that Ernest would soon begin turning up again on the television screen, making his annual appearance in *Scrooge*. I mean in the best of all possible versions – the one with Alastair Sim. Thesiger plays the conniving undertaker, plotting the acquisition of Scrooge's possessions after Ebenezer 'dies' in one of his nightmares. It is delightful. The undertaker's role gives him an opportunity to put on display what might be called 'the essential Thesiger'. Swathed in scarves and dressed in black, with his hands in fingerless gloves, he gives the impression of a cadaver's cadaver just as, in life, he was an actor's actor.

I hadn't thought of Ernest Thesiger in such a long while. It was a comfort, sitting there in the lamplight, bringing him back into focus. I had been aware of him long before we met – aware of him even before I knew his name. His most famous role, perhaps, was in *The Bride of Frankenstein*, where he played Doctor Pretorius. And, of course, you thought of him ever afterwards as Pretorius – not as that actor *what's-his-name*. Ernest was the actor whose appearance always made you smile with anticipation: something interesting was bound to happen if he turned up. His appearance had the same effect as a music cue.

Often, what happened was sinister. For instance, if it was a 'costume film', the minute Ernest turned up, you knew the hero was about to be caught in a diabolical trap. Whereas, if the setting was contemporary, the presence of Ernest Thesiger signalled comic complications. He was rarely sinister in modern dress – and I've no idea what that meant, except to say it must have had to do with his physical appearance. Robes and ruffles gave him somewhere to hide – a business suit could not begin to hide him. Hidden, he could be frightening – but revealed, he caused a riot. Ernest Thesiger was a *provocateur* – in life as well as his career.

Tucked in the parcel of memories beside him, there was a ring, an autograph, a sewing needle and a bicycle.

I recognised them instantly. These were Ernest's signs and symbols; his accumulation, over time, of the keys to his personality; his signature.

The bicycle on which, in his youth, he had ridden to Tite Street and tea with

Oscar Wilde had become the symbol of his destiny. The sewing needle was a sign of patience. The autograph was his signature imposed on yours – and the ring was his symbol of disguise.

There was always a sense, in Ernest's company, of being drawn into a charming conspiracy. The autograph game was his way of introducing himself.

Give me your signature, he would say. *Put it on a large sheet of paper.*

Once you had complied, Ernest would stare at your name for a moment, in much the same way a medium would stare at whatever talisman you might have handed her in order to acquaint her with your *karma*. He would turn the autograph upside down and sideways – hold it up against the light and run his eye up and down its shape. Then he would say, *Most interesting* . . . as if your name had spoken.

You would watch all this with growing fascination. His own concentration augmented yours and, this way, he could create an alarming sense of tension. *What was he going to find in what you had written?*

Then, with pursed lips, he would say to you, *Give me your pen*. And he would begin to mark your autograph with what, at first, appeared to be hieroglyphs and runes. But they were not.

When he was finished, he would hand you back your pen and the sheet of paper on which *you* had written and *he* had drawn – and, instead of your signature, there would be a human figure or a tree, a vase of flowers or a gargoyle. Mine was a young Edwardian dandy – wearing a boater and sporting a walking stick. *That's you*, he said. *Or one of you . . .*

He had not known that I had played such a character on Canadian television long before I had gone to England and longer still before I had met him.

I have said that Ernest's hands were all but destroyed in the First World War. They were crushed when a building he was hiding in was blown to pieces during a bombardment. A whole wall fell on Ernest, smashing his hands and almost tearing his arms from his body. 'I lay there, waiting for rescue, almost all of one day,' he said. 'I could not see my arms or my hands – and the only thing that informed me I had not lost them was the pain. I was almost reassured by this, until I dimly remembered what friends had said to me when they had lost their legs and arms – which was that you go on feeling as if they were still with you, long, long after they have gone. *Ghost pains*, they call this. I got in a dreadful panic then, and prayed that I would die. I could not imagine, you see, my life without arms. I had wanted to be an artist and an actor – and how could I be either one without my arms?'

The noise, my dear. And the people . . .

His arms and his hands were saved – but it took a great, long while for

Ernest Thesiger to recover their use. This is where needlework entered his life – as a therapeutic activity by which he could regain control of his dexterity. It is also where the ring, as a symbol of disguise, took its place in Ernest's consciousness.

His hands, as he found them even after two or three years of therapy, had not recovered their 'beauty'.

'Very ugly, they were,' he said – and held them out for me to see. 'Worse than you see them now. I could not bear to look at them. They made me weep.'

Until the day of his death, it is true, his hands – in repose and stripped of gloves and other masquerades – were not the best a person could hope for. The fingers were delicate and bent and the knuckles as bony as those of any victim of arthritis. Still, he had beautiful fingernails and skin and he hid what he could of the wounds with rings.

Silver rings were his favourites. Never gaudy and always intriguing, each ring had a story. One I remember in particular. It was shown to me on a winter evening in 1955 – much like the evening thirty-five years later on which I had been ambushed so unexpectedly by Ernest's ghost in its brown paper wrappings.

The ring was one of the many Ernest wore – a heavy silver ring with an opal set in lion's claws. He showed it to me at his flat in London, after we had returned from Moscow. He was giving a cocktail party on a Sunday afternoon – the favoured day for actors' parties – and we sat on a blue velvet sofa under lamplight.

Ernest's voice, as I remember it, crackled and wavered somewhere between his nose and the back of his throat. He always seemed to be about to expire. It was a quavering voice with amazing strength . . .

'This ring,' he said – and he held it under the lamplight – 'belonged to Lucretia Borgia . . . '

I asked if I could touch it and he said, 'You may, but not before I show you something. Here – look at this . . . '

He placed the ring on the little finger of his left hand, removing another ring in order to do so.

'Give me your drink,' he said.

I gave him my Martini.

He placed the glass on a small round table between our knees and waved both hands above it – the right hand touching the left hand for the briefest moment.

'There,' said Ernest, sitting back and smiling invitingly. 'Take it now and see what you think.'

I lifted the glass and drank. My Martini was suddenly inexplicably sweet. I made a face.

Ernest laughed.

'You're dead,' he said. 'I've poisoned you!'

'You've also ruined my drink,' I said.

'It's only sugar,' Ernest explained. He removed the ring and showed it to me again – giving the opal a gentle tap with his fingernail. 'The poison goes in here, beneath the stone, you see.' He pushed against the opal, revealing a tiny compartment underneath. 'I fill it with sugar from time to time, for amusement's sake,' he said. His eyes were shining. 'I poisoned the Prince of Wales with it once,' he told me. 'It was quite a triumph!'

Ernest lifted another Martini from a passing tray and gave it to me. 'Whenever I dined with the Prince of Wales after that, he used to inspect my rings before we sat down. It became our joke. He asked me, once, if I would lend it to him, but I told him, *Not, sir, unless you tell me who the intended victim is going to be.* My brother, George, he said – meaning the late Duke of Kent – and I said, *Oh, sir, you cannot want to kill the Duke of Kent!* And he said yes, because he has more fun than I do . . .'

Ernest became quite suddenly serious.

'You know,' he said, 'the strangest expression came into the Prince's eyes when he told me that. He was joking. Of course, he was joking. But . . . a look of anguish – of *sadness* – overcame him – just for a moment – and he could not prevent it. Poor man. Deep inside, he really did feel trapped, I think. And the Duke of Kent – *well, he . . .* ' Ernest laughed. ' . . . *was another story!* The Prince of Wales was right. Quite right! His brother George had a great, *great* deal more fun than *any*one!'

We looked again at Lucretia Borgia's ring.

'Put it on,' he said. 'Go ahead.'

But I had lost – I don't know why – my desire to wear it.

'No,' I said. 'Thank you.'

Ernest looked at me.

He could see that his story had sobered me, as perhaps he had intended. Hidden inside what appeared to be a harmless anecdote about regal foibles, there had been a tender message of sympathy. He had seen in me a young man who shared the same crises and misgivings that he had endured when he was young. Ernest had found his courage long before Flanders, when his mentor, Oscar Wilde, had been humiliated, arrested and sent to gaol – losing everything in one rash gesture. We never spoke of these things in so many words. But much was implicit through various other words and gestures. Ernest, in spite of public mockery, had gone on to become, most emphatically and fearlessly, himself – and he was always urging me to do the same.

It wasn't easy.

None the less, when he heard me say that I no longer wanted to wear Lucretia Borgia's ring, he looked at me carefully before he spoke – and then he said, 'Never mind, never mind.'

Then he put the ring away.

'But I was so looking forward to hearing about your intended victim!' he said.

His empathy could be wicked.

The only time I worked with Ernest Thesiger was in a production of *Hamlet* in which I played Osric. All through rehearsals, I was tormented by the director, Peter Brook, who had decided – for reasons of his own I will not go into – that I was this year's whipping boy. He would simply not let me rehearse. Every time we came to Osric's entrance, he would say, *Stop! May we have the next scene, please.*

It all began about one week in, when, moments after I had made my first entrance, Peter Brook called from the darkness. 'Mr Findley – what do you think you are doing?'

These words were said with a chilling glaze of illogical anger. Hearing them, you might have thought I had come on riding a bicycle and juggling oranges.

Well – it got worse. Since I really hadn't done anything other than what we had so far decided I should be doing, both I and everyone else on stage knew perfectly well what was happening. I had been chosen. The knife had fallen and it was lodged in me.

I had seen this happen to other actors in other productions. It is just the way some directors are. Even the greatest of them – as with Peter Brook – may need, for whatever reason, to put someone away. They never fire you, under these circumstances. And your resignation would not be accepted. The whipping boy must stand his ground and make his way alone.

In the long run, the other actors and I worked out our own blocking and simply got on with the scene by rehearsing it, during breaks, in dressing rooms and corridors. Peter Brook didn't even let us do the scene at the cue-to-cue rehearsal when we first got on to the set – nor at the dress rehearsal. The first time I actually played it on the set was opening night in Brighton.

Some weeks later, we all flew to Moscow – where the production was a huge success. This was in 1955 and it was an auspicious occasion. Stalin had only been dead for two years – Burgess and Maclean had defected in the relatively recent past – and the Cold War was at its height.

Ours was the very first visit of any British company of actors since the Revolution of 1917. Hamlet was played by Paul Scofield, Gertrude by Diana Wynyard, Claudius by Alec Clunes and Ophelia by Mary Ure. Ernest played Polonius. All these actors, except Paul Scofield, are now dead – wrapped in their own brown paper parcels – but Ernest was my favourite. When we got, at last, to Moscow, he had to be restrained. He was determined that he was going to sneak out one night from our hotel across the road from the Kremlin and write – in chalk – on its historic walls: BURGESS LOVES MACLEAN!!!.

I wish he had.

Kenneth Tynan once described Ernest Thesiger as a 'praying mantis'. It was an apt description. He often held his hands before his breast with just the fingertips touching and all the rings showing nicely. He marcelled his hair and tinted it. The length of his nose, which was immense, was often powdered to hide its redness. He was something of a fashion plate. His clothes were always impeccably cut and he wore them always with a sense of style. He favoured Prussian-blue ties with polka dots – and sometimes wore a handkerchief neatly tucked into his sleeve . . .

The brown paper package is nearly completely undone – its strings are lying untied on the floor.

Ernest's final symbol was a sewing needle. Under the tutelage of his therapists, he had become so proficient in needlepoint that, less than twenty years later, he was one of Queen Mary's favourite sewing partners. She and Ernest would sit at either end of the carpet she was making and stitch away whole afternoons and mornings. Ernest, by the way, began to dye his hair around the time of the carpet – a time when he was also severely depressed and it turned, in Oscar Wilde's words, *quite gold with grief!* In the long run, Ernest Thesiger and Queen Mary began to look like one another – and, over the years, as the ageing dowager explored other colours, other rinses, so likewise did Ernest. By the time I knew him in the mid-1950s, soon after Queen Mary's death, his 'grief' was tinted blue. 'She was, in many ways, my dearest friend,' he told me. 'I sensed that her silence was made of the same ingredients as mine. She endured a kind of private mourning, from time to time. And so did I. It had to do with the lives we would have preferred to live, but could not because of who we were.' He thought about this for a moment – then he added, 'I do not mean who we were when we were born. I mean the people we became by necessity, rather than by desire . . . '

The wind blows, now – the sky is black – the snow arrives. My windows – unshaded – are filled with reflections of the lamplighted room. I think of Ernest's wondrous, crazy face and his broken hands and I think: *It is true that beauty is only skin deep.* But Ernest's lack of it cut to the marrow of his heart. Not, of course, that he ever said so. It was just the way he survived it: smiling.

He used to come, every night, dressed as Polonius, his needlework held in his hands, and he would stand in the wings and watch as I went out to play Osric. All through the sequence, he would stand there – every night for weeks, in all the towns we played in England – and in Moscow – and, finally, in London. Watching – just watching – saying nothing.

At last, the scene began to play and, in spite of all the problems it had presented, it became a joy to go on stage. One night, just as I made my exit, there came a round of applause. That had never happened to me before, under any circumstance. I was stunned.

Ernest, in the wings, was beaming.

He put out one hand and took my arm.

He didn't say a word. When we came to his dressing room, he went inside, turned around and said, *Thank you.*

Upstairs, in my own dressing room, I cried. Not because there had been applause – but because I was overwhelmed all at once with the knowledge that Ernest had stood in the wings all those weeks to show me that in spite of Peter Brook he had believed in me. And he stayed there until I got it right. Until I believed in myself. After that, he never appeared in the wings again.

As I go to the window, it seems that all I can see is the darkness outside and a few reflections. But way off – out beyond the reach of any normal light that any normal lamp can throw – I can just discern the shape of Ernest on his bicycle – making his way, aged seventeen, along the Chelsea Embankment until he comes to Tite Street, where Oscar Wilde has invited him to tea.

Ernest is about to discover the importance of being oneself – no matter what.

He arrives at Oscar's door on a day long before my parents are born – before

I am even thought of. And yet, I see him standing there. And, in between that day and this . . .

The noise, my dear. And the people . . .

I wave – and he is gone.

But not for ever. Other parcels will arrive, in time. In time, I will remember more.

MICHAEL COREN
H. G. Wells and the Mask of Biography

There is an anecdote concerning H. G. Wells which has escaped all biographies of the man, and yet exemplifies his character with more vibrancy and verisimilitude than a dozen Fabian memories. The bar of a London theatre in the 1920s. Herbert George Wells, a literary doyen of the greatest celebrity – when authorial fame was genuinely important – sips a blended brandy. A breathless young student approaches Wells, holds out his greeting hand and exclaims, 'Mr Wells, you probably don't remember me . . . ' 'Yes, I bloody do,' replies Wells, and runs from the theatre. Why has the tale not seen the light of biographical revelation in the twenty or so works on Wells and the Wellsians since his death in 1946? The sham and shame of the story is that H. G. Wells has been served very well indeed by his Boswells, and the subjective school of history has sold itself, at a pathetically low price, to the anti-Semitism, galloping misogyny, racial pomposity and emetic social engineering policies of a plump, gifted writer from Kent. Biography and authenticity deserve better; H. G. Wells deserves worse. While writers such as G. K. Chesterton choke in a miasma of misconception and sheer inaccuracy – Chesterton's alleged antipathy towards the Jews was mostly the stuff of canard, and was expunged by his early passion against Nazi anti-Semitism, yet he suffers still from the accusation; Wells's constant and consistent polemics against the Jewish people, for which he never made amends, are virtually ignored – the privileged Wells bathes in the glow of hagiography and the triumph of reputation over reality.

That reputation is solid: a radical, avuncular advocate of free love, female emancipation, social justice and rational progress, who wrote scientific fantasies and delightful, autobiographical novels of coastal romance and oracular morality. A munificent parvenu. A diminutive man of gigantic stature. A man on the side of the angels. 'Multiply the total by ten; square the result,' George Bernard Shaw wrote of Wells's petulance and selfish irresponsibility. 'Raise it again to the millionth power and square it again; and you will still fall short of the truth about Wells – yet the worse he behaved the more he was indulged; and the more he was indulged the worse he behaved.' Shaw, however, was a friend who killed with kindness. Hilaire Belloc, that deliciously extreme knight errant of Catholicism, possessed no qualms about fraternity. 'Mr Wells means to say all that is in him,' he shouted during one of his crippling bouts of vituperation, 'and, if there is not very much in him, that is not his fault.'

The inexorable hostility of Belloc is hardly surprising; the inexorable admiration of contemporary and later feminists is extremely so. Wells's ostensible championing of the emancipation movement in the Edwardian years and the 1920s manifested itself in his novels such as *Ann Veronica*, in pamphlets and political struttings. This was not a banal case of a man preaching liberalism, performing reaction and parading behind literature. Wells's personal and private actions reached far beyond the realms of hypocrisy.

'The thing to do is to go out into the world; leave everything behind, wife and child, and things; go all over the world and come back experienced,' he announced to a gathering of friends one bucolic summer evening. What would happen to the said wives? an incredulous critic enquired. 'The wives,' he replied, 'will go to heaven when they die.' The statement echoes Wells's own domestic arrangements. When Amy Catherine Robbins married Herbert George Wells, convention and decade demanded that she change her family name to that of her husband. But this was insufficient. Neither Amy nor Catherine was acceptable to the author, and it was decided his wife would be known as Jane. Acquiescence was tinged with the instinct of survival. Jane Wells was conscious of her husband's promiscuity, and acutely aware that demands for monogamy would provoke separation. She became a factotum, a perverse hybrid of secretary, home-maker, occasional lover, and the sometime referee between rivals for the position of her husband's official mistress. She represented stability, a port of succour and security when the fires of extra-marital romance became untidy and invariably unpleasant cinders. Even when Wells returned to his first wife, and pleaded with her to run away with him and rekindle their former love, the long-suffering Amy Catherine remained taciturn and resigned. She was a tangible martyr for her gender. Wells could, and would, criticise morality from the standpoint of the libertarian, condemn immorality from the point of view of the puritan, and continue to have and eat his proverbial confectionery.

Wells's mistresses fared little better. The celebrated Rebecca West was a sufficiently purposeful character to inflict as much anguish on Wells as he did on her; not so the wretched Hedwig Verena Gatternigg, who attempted suicide by slashing at her throat and wrists, or the flaccid Amber Reeves or the coterie of young women with whom Wells conducted affairs. The children of these encounters were seldom treated with anything approaching paternal devotion, reflections of the statement in Wells's hubristic but candid autobiography, in which he explained, 'For all my desire to be interested I have to confess that for most things and people I don't care a damn.'

He did care about the 'problem' of the Jews. 'I met a Jewish friend of mine the other day,' wrote Wells, 'and he asked me, "What is going to happen to the Jews?" I told him I had rather he had asked me a different question, What is going to happen to mankind?. "But my people –" he began. "That," said I, "is exactly what is the matter with them."' The anecdote is soaked in suburban smugness. At no time did Wells make the leap of empathy towards understanding Jewish anxieties – to be proved so tragically correct during his lifetime – and instead compounded ignorance with aggression. 'Throughout those tragic and almost fruitless four years of war, the Jewish spokesmen were most elaborately and energetically demonstrating that they cared not a rap for the troubles and dangers of English, French, Germans, Russians, Americans, or of any other people but their own. They kept their eyes steadfastly upon the restoration of the Jews.'

It was pointed out to Wells that the first volunteer for the American forces in Europe was Jewish, that there were numerous German-Jewish winners of the Iron Cross and that Jews died for every combatant nation in the war. His response was sullen dismissal, followed by further attack. 'There was never a promise; they were never chosen; their distinctive observances, their Sabbath, their Passover, their queer calendar, are mere traditional oddities of no present significance whatsoever.' Jew and Gentile responded with noble alacrity. Eleanor Roosevelt scolded Wells as a naive, tedious gamin; Leon Gelman, President of the Mizrachi Organisation of America, alleged that, 'H. G. Wells is brazenly spreading notorious lies about the Jews. His violent language betrays a streak of sadism that is revolting. If any man who professes to be an enlightened human being can preach such heinous distortions, then mankind is doomed to utter darkness.'

The irony of the scenario is that Wells was obsessed with the fate of mankind, claiming to understand the roads towards light and darkness with a monomaniacal clarity, where others could only perceive compromise, doubt, ambivalence. His philosophy was embedded in structure and certainty. The world was improving, morally and intellectually. The inevitability of socialism was not in question, and the men of the early twentieth century were immeasurably more able and suited to introduce it than were the men of the eighteenth and seventeenth; similarly, those of the twenty-first century would be still more qualified and redoubtable.

This dictatorship of chronology left no room for variation, possessed no defence against the genius of medievalism's Aquinas, or the pellucid ethical superiority of a past age over a recent one. Wells propounded his theories in *A Modern Utopia* and *Anticipations*. The existing structure, social and economic, would collapse, and from the violent catharsis a new order would be established, the denizens of which would be 'people throughout the world whose minds were adapted to the demands of the big-scale conditions of the new time . . . a naturally and informally organised educated class, an unprecedented sort of people'. The perverse recipe of Calvinistic claptrap and Marxian confusion went further. There were those who would be dissident, unacceptable to the revolutionary system. For the 'base', the class at the bottom of the scale, 'people who had given evidence of a strong anti-social disposition', fate would be unkind. 'This thing, this euthanasia of the weak and the sensual, is possible,' wrote Wells. 'I have little or no doubt that in the future it will be planned and achieved.' He took pride and comfort in the image of 'boys and girls and youth and maidens, full of zest and new life, full of an abundant joyful receptivity . . . helpers behind us in the struggle'. The manic sting at the end of the tale and tail was as predictable as Wells's later breakdown and mental instability. 'And for the rest, these swarms of black and brown and dingy white and yellow people who do not come into the needs of efficiency . . . I take it they will have to go.'

In the light of Wells's attitudes towards social engineering it is hardly surprising that Stalin extended his interview with the British thinker. George Orwell saw through the façade, particularly after Wells had accused him of attempted poisoning. *New Statesman* editor Kinsley Martin sheltered doubts, pained at being addressed as 'Dear Judas Martin' following a lambasting review of one of Wells's volumes in his magazine. Wells should have expected negative criticism, because in spite of comic masterpieces such as *Kipps* and *The History of Mr Polly*, or perceptive literary caveats including *The War of the Worlds* and *The Time Machine*, a combination of financial necessity and tendentious logorrhoea did produce a pack of baleful works. Indifferent product from a man of occasional genius may be forgiven; dishonest and parasitic scholarship mayn't be dismissed. Wells's *The Outline of History*, a massively successful and lucrative enterprise, was researched by a team of amanuenses working out of Wells's Essex home. During the composition of the history Wells delivered a public lecture to a group of young people. One of them enquired about a folder of papers in Wells's car. 'Today I've motored from Stonehenge, and you may care to know that I polished that off in forty minutes.' The neophyte expressed scepticism, arguing that the phenomenon had perplexed antiquaries for a thousand years. 'Very likely, but anyhow I've settled it to my satisfaction,' responded the splenetic Wells. 'I've left a couple of experts behind, they have a fussy kind of knowledge that looks well in a footnote.'

It is that very fussy knowledge that shapes and excoriates figures of the past. H. G. Wells successfully blackened the white sepulchres of pre-war England; since his death his own legacy and life has been transformed into another variety of shrine, apparently immune from the mud and dirt of accusation.

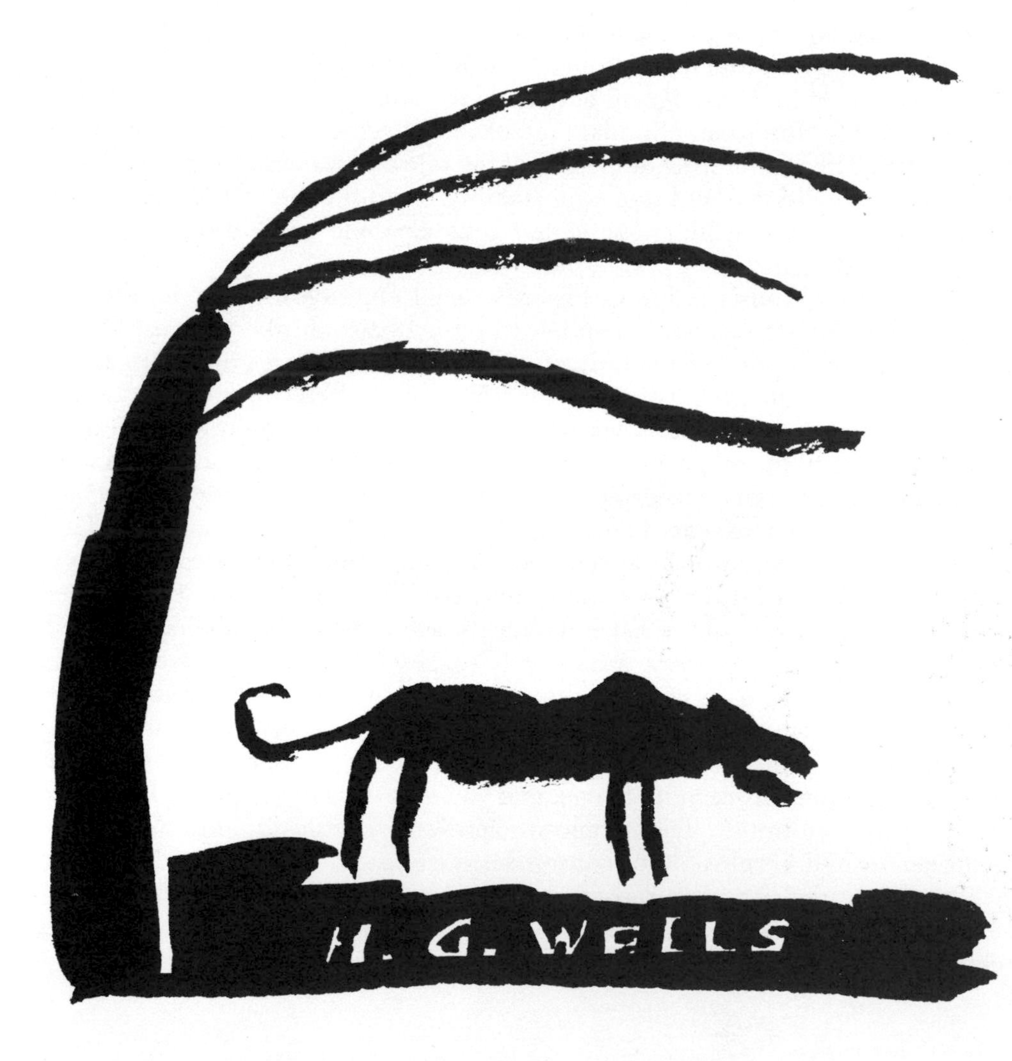

JOSEPH ROTH

Goethe's Oak in Buchenwald

(Dictated on his death bed, Monday, 22 May 1939, in Paris)

Let us give truth its due! Misinformation is being spread concerning the Buchenwald Concentration Camp – horror stories, one might say. It seems to me that the time has come to put things in the right perspective.

First of all, Buchenwald did not always bear that name, but another: Ettersberg. At one time, this was a name well known to students of literary history. It was here that Goethe used to meet Frau von Stein, under a beautiful oak tree. As it happens, this tree is covered by the so-called 'Nature Protection Act', so that, as people began to clear away the forest at Buchenwald – or rather, at Ettersberg – in order to build a kitchen to the south and a laundry to the north, for the use of the concentration camp inmates, the oak was left standing: Goethe's oak, Frau von Stein's oak.

In the past, symbolism didn't come as cheap as it does today. It has become almost child's play to write what are known as 'symbolic fables'; everyone receives them, free of charge, delivered directly from World History, at home, fed into one's pen or one's typewriter. It is indeed a modest enterprise for a writer today to produce an allegory on the Third Reich. Look: the German oak under which Goethe sat with Frau von Stein has remained standing, thanks to a 'Nature Protection Act', between the concentration camp's kitchen and the laundry. That is to say, between the 'Nature Protection Act' passed years ago, and the *Un-natural Act* of recent years (or, to put it in modern German terms, between the laundry and the kitchen) stands Frau von Stein and Goethe's 'Nature Protection' oak tree.

Every day, the inmates of the concentration camp walk by and around the oak tree; that is to say, they are made to walk by there. Indeed! Misinformation *is* being spread about the Buchenwald Concentration Camp – horror stories, one might say. It seems to me that the time has come to put things in the right perspective. Until now, not a single inmate of the concentration camp has been strapped to the oak tree under which Goethe and Frau von Stein sat, and which is still alive, thanks to the 'Nature Protection Act'. Certainly not: they have been strapped to other oaks, of which there is no shortage in this forest.

Translated by Craig Thomas and Alberto Manguel

YVES BONNEFOY

All Night Long

All night long the beast moved around in the room
What is this road that won't come to an end
All night long the raft sought the shape of the shore
What are these absent friends who wish to return
All night long the sword studied the open wound
What is this anguish that cannot find its grip
All night long the beast has whimpered in the room
Bloodied and denied the candles in the room

What is this death that will not mend or heal?

Translated by Alberto Manguel

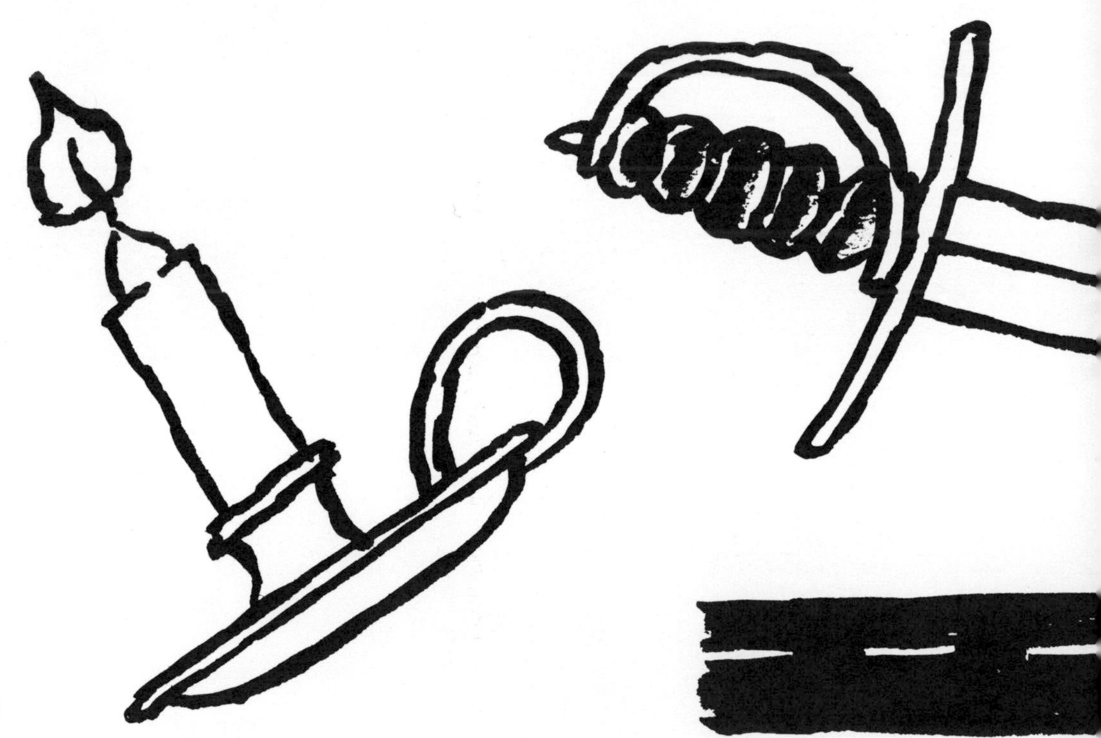

GUILLERMO CABRERA INFANTE

The Unknown Political Prisoner

Since 3 October 1965, when I left Cuba, never to return until this very day, I've been concerned with the fate of many Cuban political prisoners. I've never forgotten that I could have been one of them, and that my present endeavours could be on my own behalf. That is how I came to interview several Belgian socialists in power at the time, and several Spanish socialists who had recently risen to power (one of them directed me to a certain Spanish foundation whose name I mistook for that of a fashionable pop star, and the mistake was thought to be a pun when in fact it was nothing more than my shock in the face of power). Many of my letters, written since 1969, are in the archives of Amnesty International, several addressed to a number of English politicians. Even the American Ambassador to the United Nations, on her way through London, agreed to see me, this time on behalf of a single political prisoner.

But it was a well-known American publisher, a man of impeccable left-wing credentials, with whom I had lunch in Manhattan, who enlightened me in an unexpected way: my task was useless – and not because I was concerned with one or more political prisoners in Cuba. I was discussing one particular political prisoner, and the man sitting in front of me had accomplished the remarkable feat of literally extraditing a poet from my island. My host, whom I shall call a man of letters – even though he has never written a single line – listened to me with great interest and respect, and said in a languid yet concerned manner, oblivious to his meal, 'And your man, what is he? A poet? A writer? A musician? Or is he a scientist?' He knew there were openings for all these vocations. There was even a Cuban philosopher who was struggling to be released from prison and to leave the island. 'No,' I was obliged to answer. 'He's nothing. He's only a human being.' My host, who was Jewish and must have known about prisons and repression, said with a sigh, 'In that case, I'm afraid we won't be able to do anything for him.'

The political prisoner for whom I was pleading with the publisher (I would never have lunched with him were it not for my request) had been, to tell the truth, crucial in my life. I owe him not only my freedom to roam around the world, but also these very pages I am now writing. But that is another story. In this instance, he had become a tool of knowledge. I had even written several articles about his life, about his inhuman and above all unjust prison sentence, trying to get people to request his freedom, when in fact his freedom should have been demanded. My articles were published as a serial in the Spanish press, in Mexico, in Venezuela, in Colombia, and they were even translated into English and published in the United States. In Washington, a certain institute for human rights republished them in a brochure illustrated with a photograph of the man in his happy days as a diplomat: no greater sorrow . . . But nothing happened. The publisher was right: nothing could be done for this eminent political prisoner who was no one, was nothing.

It was then that I asked myself, And what happens to a political prisoner who doesn't have someone who will write in his name to the press, someone who will publicise his case, who will trouble friends and enemies and those indifferent to him, all terribly busy with everyday life, someone who will trouble these people's work or their leisure with a tale of woe? What happens to the prisoner who knows no one, who has never been anyone and who now is nothing but a number and a cell in a prison, or an inmate in a concentration camp? What can be done for the political prisoner whom nobody knows? How can we free the unknown political prisoner?

A case taken from history shows us a figure laden with political crimes, whom we know to be innocent because his actions, in a democracy, are no more than part and parcel of the political game. In war there are always soldiers whom no one identifies, disfigured beyond recognition, lacking medals and a name tag. He is the so-called unknown soldier exalted in cenotaphs. Politics, as we know, is war by another means, and totalitarian politics is total war which, like the other, takes its prisoners. And there must be, in that perennial war, an unknown man whom no one can identify, whom no lawyer will defend, to whom no mother, girlfriend, sister, will ever write. He is the unknown political prisoner. I don't propose a monument for him, because literature has already achieved that; other writers have exalted his life in everlasting prison.

One of these authors, Sidney Dark, an author who must be kept in the mystery of his name, wrote, 'There is no doubt about the real existence of the Man in the Iron Mask, whose identity has been discussed over the past two centuries. In the year 1698, Monsieur de Saint Mars, Governor of the prison on the Isle of Sainte-Marguerite, was named Governor of the prison of the Bastille. He took with him one mysterious prisoner, seen by many during the voyage: a tall, white-haired man whose features were hidden behind a black mask. The following entry was made in the King's Lieutenant's logbook at the Bastille:

On 19 November 1703, the unknown prisoner who has always worn a black velvet mask and who was brought here by Monsieur Saint Mars, Governor of Isle of Sainte-Marguerite, where he had been a prisoner for some time, having felt unwell on the previous day after mass, died in the night at about ten o'clock, without ever having been ill before. This unknown prisoner, who had been in custody for so long, was buried on Tuesday, 20th November in the cemetery of Saint Paul's Church, in this parish. In the registry of deaths he was listed as 'Name Unknown'.

The registry of the Bastille chapel mentions, in passing, the name of a certain Marchioly, a name everyone takes to be a *nom de prison*, quite common at the time, and states that the prisoner's age is 'close to forty-five,' which is, no doubt, an impossibility or a mockery. As usual in documents that wish to appear as truthful, signatures riddle the page – this one by the hands of the Chief Surgeon and of the Commander of the Bastille.

Dark writes:

These documents provide us with practically everything that is known up to this day about one of the foggiest mysteries in human history ['human history' is, I believe, one of the ironies Mr Dark bestows upon us]. And yet, one other fact is known. So great was the wish to hide the prisoner's identity for all time that, on the day of his death, his underwear, his only suit, his mattress, his bed, and the chair on which he sat were fed to the flames. The walls and ceiling of his cell were scrupulously scraped, and the tiles removed from the floor.

According to Alexandre Dumas, it was expressly forbidden, under pain of death, that the prisoner lift 'the iron visor which covered his face for life'. The period in which the Man in the Iron Mask lived was the golden age of Louis XIV. The man in the iron mask (to whom history would grant capital letters) died exactly twelve years before the King. Versailles, where perhaps they had once lived together, survived them both. *Homo fugit, domus manet.*

The *Encyclopaedia Britannica*, less dark than Dark, suggests other mysteries, or perhaps the same mystery behind another mask: the iron mask was in reality a velvet hood. Its owner is one of the great puzzles of modern history. The prisoner arrived at the Bastille, masked, on 18 September 1698, and died there on 9 November 1703. Everything is known about his life in prison – except, of course, his identity. He was registered in the fortress under the name Marchioly; it was Voltaire who put forward the theory that he must have been an illegitimate brother of Louis XIV. Voltaire, ironic as usual, described the mask as 'a machine with iron hinges'. The *Britannica* assures us that this description is inexact, but it captured the imagination of many writers, among them Alexandre Dumas in *Vingt ans après*, translated into English as *The Man in the Iron Mask.* Dumas also accepted the theory of the royal half-brother. (Dumas, not without reason, considered history a famous fiction.) Among other solutions to the mystery of the veiled political prisoner appear the names of Louis de Bourbon, Count of Vermandois and son of Louis XIV and Louise de la Velière; of Ercole Matthioli; of Nicolas Fouquet, Louis XIV's Finance Minister; and, more astonishing, the name of Molière, imprisoned by the Jesuits as a reprisal for his *Tartuffe.* Together with that of Matthioli, the name of Eustache Dauger has been suggested. Dauger was Fouquet's valet, and he was taken into care after his master's death. Matthioli is an impossible candidate: he died on the Isle of Sainte-Marguerite in 1694, nine years after the masked prisoner. Dauger was only the valet (and perhaps the *confidant*) of Fouquet. The *Britannica* accepts the Dauger hypothesis, but offers a final thought that makes one pause to think:

> The enigma would be resolved (with Matthioli's death) as far as the identity of the prisoner is concerned. However, the reason for his arrest and thirty-four years of prison remains a mystery.

The only proposition that includes all others is that the man in the iron mask was a political prisoner, and that the order for his senseless arrest and trial-less prison (as Lewis Carroll suggested, 'Sentence first – verdict afterwards') is typical of the totalitarian state. Our nameless subject and his terrible sentence (the mask, the perpetual Bastille) are the monument to the unknown political prisoner.

Translated by Alberto Manguel

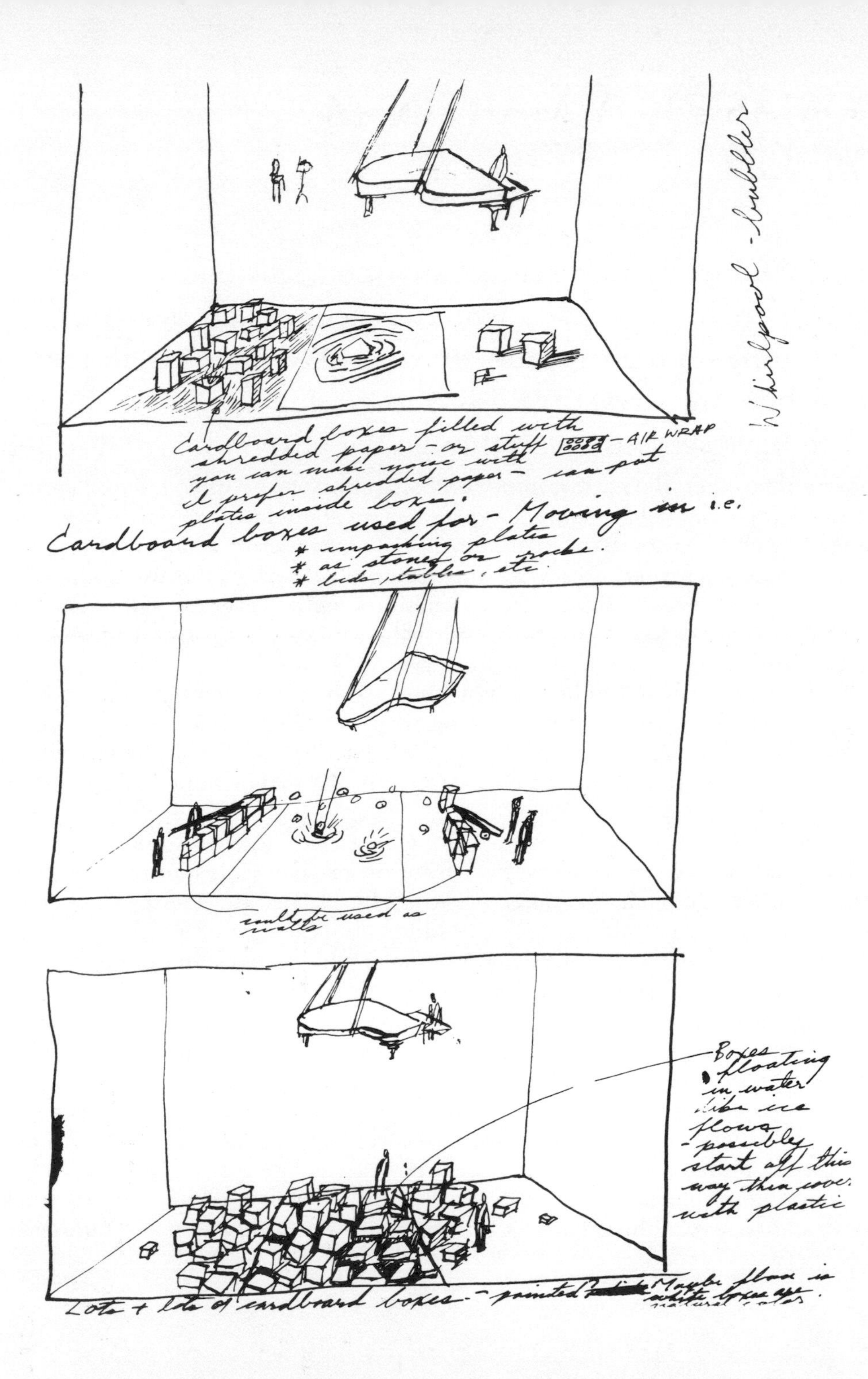
Whirlpool - bubbles
Cardboard boxes filled with shredded paper - or stuff you can make noise with
I prefer shredded paper - can put plates inside boxes.
Cardboard boxes used for - Moving in
* unpacking plates
* as stones or rocks.
* beds, tables, etc
Boxes floating in water like ice flows - possibly start off this way then cover with plastic
Lots + lots of cardboard boxes - painted

TOMÁS ELOY MARTÍNEZ
The End

In my country we never finish anything. The houses in which we live are only partially whitewashed, or still bear just the scaffolding on their façade, or are full of rooms built for no one where the drywall still has to go up.

We have seasons, even though we haven't learned to tell one from the other. Between summer and fall, or maybe between fall and spring, the crops rot in the fields. Cattle thrive, but roam about lost, and only a few cows wander by chance into the slaughterhouses. The flavour of what isn't there has always been our favourite flavour. The number of days in the week changes: sometimes it's five, sometimes three, sometimes eight. Never the same number, never the certainty that something – even the arbitrary measure of time – will reach its prime.

We have grown accustomed to not knowing in what country we are, even when returning home. Sometimes I think we've simply been left without a country, and that the vague horizon I call 'country' is, for my countrymen, the school playground or the neighbour's cat or the melancholic feeling of that which can't be achieved.

Nevertheless, from time to time, we are greeted with the news that there is an enemy ready to take the country away from us, or change its nature, or replace it for another. On such occasions, we are told, bullets are heard. They come from corners we can't quite place, and fade behind bodies to which we pay no attention. Who knows if they're really bullets. Objects, and the name of those objects, are eclipsed so fast that it doesn't really matter what we call them.

When these extraordinary events take place, often, by coincidence, a body also disappears. This doesn't astonish us. Logic teaches us that bodies have phases, like the moon. If they were there once, they will always be there. The bodies that don't return, don't return because they never were bodies; either that or because there's not a single person who can say, *I once actually saw them, I remember them.*

We are born incomplete or with a superfluity of senses. When we get stuck in the pelvis, the midwives forget us and move on to other births. Suddenly, without our mothers knowing how, we are there, lacking a beginning, because if we had a beginning we'd also have an end, and that would not be possible. What would be the purpose of our end?

Our women have never reached orgasm. The men, at least, have wet dreams. But there is no purpose to that, no end. We dream that there are creatures from other countries who ejaculate for us, and, to assure reproduction, we usually sleep with the penis lying inside the vagina of our mates, in uncomfortable positions.

I'm the odd one out in the family. As I indulge in the extravagant habit of embracing with both arms and kissing with both lips, I believe I inspire a certain repulsion. My older brother, who possesses two senses of gravity, is loved by many women. My mother, born with a single lip, has shared it with every one of the men living around her, except with me. If there is someone who loves me, I don't know it. I know what it is that I give, but that which I always long to receive drifts away without touching me. I've lived with my mate as a couple for so long now, that I can't remember when the relationship began or if my mate is still the same person. What does it matter? I'm faithful: not to another being but to a single kind of feeling.

And even so, I'm not myself – I'm only half myself. My body has grown like that of a circus freak: normally. The other half, that which lies inside, will never be finished.

Everyone in my family is transient. In spite of never having moved from here, they feel they don't belong, that their place is anywhere else except here. They live at odds with what they have become or that which they possess, and they imagine that, maybe, if they moved away, they'd see better things, or they'd see themselves in a better light. I, instead, have travelled a lot, or am still travelling, and haven't succeeded in making my own nature fit any other landscape except this one of what isn't there, of what I haven't got, of what I can't become.

The one who suffers most staying here is my father. He has a vast collection of bills of exchange, and feels such fondness towards it that if he hasn't left it's because he can't bear to leave it behind. He was born with two or three tactile senses, and believes that perhaps in another country he would have been born with more. It's true that he does need the tactile senses to oversee the collection, which grows at the slightest distraction, and which, the more it grows, the less it's worth. My father believes that the bills of exchange are linked by an umbilical cord to all that happens to us, and never stops fondling them. If his touch were to lose them, or if they were to stop feeling his touch, the things that happen to us would augment to the point of becoming infinite, and who knows what fate we'd come across then.

I, who only have the five basic senses, try to make up for the missing ones, or the extra ones, through thought and imagination. *Filling your head with illusions*, says my mother, who never even wanted to glance at an illusion. Her fears are understandable. There are days on which the bullets fly along strange curves and fall or are eclipsed by people with illusions. *There's no smoke without fire*, my mother explains. And even though she could try and poke around inside the smoke, she has never bothered. Little by little the smoke has settled amongst us, and by now it has become familiar, so invisible even, that everything that happens to us, even the most terrible thing, finds its justification in that smoke.

Occasionally I chance upon my parents, or rather, chance drops us off at the same place. I then tell them about my fear of being transfixed by a bullet. My father always asks, *A bullet?* And I tell him, it's not only the bullet but also the bodies by which the bullets are eclipsed, eclipsed so intensely they disappear. To which he answers, *A bullet?* and we never break the routine.

My mother, on the other hand, is usually more explicit. *How are you, son, how are you?* she greets me. So as not to change her habits I answer that I'm fine, but that I'm afraid a bullet will reach me. *If you're afraid, there must be a reason. No smoke without fire*, she says, and we never break the routine.

Once, out of curiosity, I wondered if breaking the routine would make a noise, create a disturbance. Just to find out, I answered, *Mother, I'm in a bad shape. I need your help*. You know what she did? She drew away. She said, *If you're in bad shape, there must be a reason. No smoke without fire. And if there's a fire, no one can help you.*

We have been told that if the number of bullets grows we'll end up in some sort of war, and if we enter the war we will never come out of it. There are those who insist that we must arm ourselves further in order to protect our country to the very end. But how, if we don't know where the country ends, where to look for its limits? Some say they've seen them, and with this argument they become generals. As soon as they arrive at the end, they keep on going. And every time they keep on going, the end is a little less close.

At some point, a bullet hit me. It chanced upon my stomach, or my illusions attracted it; I don't know. It's still inside me: at intervals I feel it stir. I went to the hospital to have it seen to. My father was there and I asked him to touch it. *A bullet?* he asked. And this time he said, like my mother, *No one can help you.*

Someone opened up my stomach, and when he found the bullet he stared at it. Then he stitched up the wound but, as always happens, didn't quite finish the job. And now that the pain is there, beating, it won't ever stop. The only end of pain is its beginning – only that.

Little by little, I have been told, this unfinished pain will lead me from one illusion to another. If I am to remain in one, it will be in an illusion I will find halfway there, or in an illusion already lost.

And with time, I will no longer be different. I will grow accustomed to the pain and I will make it part of my nature, until another, warmer pain, will supercede it, a pain even closer to the halfway mark.

Only then, I've been told, my words will become tuned until they turn to silence; I'll drift from substance to similar substance without ever being able to rest in mine; I will put an end to nothing in this endless country, to nothing ever again; I'll simply go to the ends of my own body and find there the beginning, and I myself will then enter

Translated by Alberto Manguel

EASY FISH
REMOVE CARD

CELEBRITY
PAVEMENT

MARQ DE VILLIERS
A White Tribe's Dream

We lay in the dust and dreamed. We pulled five-inch silver spines from thorn trees and made tiny stockades. The 'cattle' were dung beetles; but they didn't make good cows; they would climb the stockade and hang on the thorn tips, legs waving feebly, until we took them down. We made huts from more thorns and the nests of weaver birds, huts for the whole clan, a circle for dancing, a *boma* for the cattle, a *kraal* that filled the world. This was in a small hollow behind the hill beyond the town; all I remember of it is dust and devil-thorns and scrub *kareebosse*, the silence as the wildlife listened, the summer heat that filled the skin; we lay in the dust and dreamed. My skin was 'white', though brown from the sun; his was 'black' – dusty, the leathery brown of the south-east. His hands were pink and his blood red. But that came later.

Our stories were all of heroic times. His grandfather remembered (or the old liar said he remembered) the Zulu impis under Mzilikazi coming north-west, fleeing Shaka's pogroms, killing as they came, living off the land. His people fled into the hills, those who survived, and their herds wandered the plains untended. Later travellers only caught glimpses of them, his grandfather said, staring down from the rocks, fearful, vanishing at the slightest noise higher into the hills, skittish as baboons. Starving, desperate, they turned to cannibalism. His grandfather told these stories with relish, because they told of the fall that came before the pride. That was before Moshoeshoe the Great, whom we called Moshesh, came and settled in at Thaba Bosego, a wily old king dead then for only sixty years but barely remembered, legend substituted for truth. Moshesh had been his grandfather's great-grandfather on his mother's side. He told this with confidence, as if he truly believed it. His hair was sparse, his feet bulb-heeled and overly bony; his nostrils were wide, and snot accumulated on one side, but he didn't care. Moshesh had foiled Shaka, beaten the Boers, bullied the Great Queen, fathered hundreds of children, taken sixty wives and pleased them all. This was a hero and he was a hero's son.

I had my own Boer heroes. Andries Pretorius had left a sea of Zulu dead at Blood River. Christiaan de Wet, the devilish Boer commando, was in his way as wily as Moshesh, since he was apparently invisible and materialised only to leave behind in British imaginations the 'small blue hole' of a Mauser's bullet. There were also the many family stories of the transport riders, the whipcord-tough travellers whose bones were African bones even if their skin was white. But, truth to tell, for sheer style only the Lady of the Lake could really compete with Moshesh. We both knew there was a sword buried deep in a rock somewhere in Thaba Bosego that Moshesh could have pulled out, had he needed a sword. We transformed the legend, giving it an African reality. I looked down at my own white skin and thought of Arthur, black-haired and black-skinned (or so we both believed), with muscles that could wrench a sword from Thaba Bosego . . . We bound a *kleilat* (a long, whippy willow branch) with ropes to a thorn tree and took turns trying to pull it free. Arthur was part of the magical West, Moshesh part of the heroic Africa, and years later when I read that the Afrikaner poet Van Wyk Louw had urged the Boers to 'build a bridge between the heroic West and the magical Africa', I knew at once he had got it all backwards; it seemed the *karma* of his people. After that Arthur merged with Moshesh, and the search for the Holy Grail segued in my mind to politics and I lost interest in legends.

For the last year I knew him he stopped telling stories. His silences became longer. He no longer looked in my eyes. (And Arthur's skin was getting whiter.) The last time I saw him I was only ten, and he was running away from me, shouting to his friends in Tswana, a language I didn't understand; the *kleilat* was still tied to the tree, but no one any longer attempted to draw it out. I moved to the city with my family. I never knew his name, nor he mine. For a while it hadn't seemed to matter. We had scratched our skin with a thorn from the thorn tree and mingled our blood, a ceremony we had learned from books – they did such things in magical America, we had learned. His blood was red, and it looked no different on my skin. I still have the small scar where it landed, forty years ago.

Why do I think of him now? Because the children were there first, then the poets (even if Van Wyk Louw had got it all backwards), then some of the people and finally the politicians.

Of course I can remember the violence. We all can.

I remember black violence, black against black. I remember for example (one of many examples) the Medicine Murders near the small village of Thaba 'Nchu – a group of Rolong teenagers ambushed and killed, their entrails spread on the ground and their hearts eaten. This was how 'they' were. My boyhood was filled with stories of atrocities, most of them true.

I remember white violence, white against black. I remember coming home from a circus in a working-class suburb of Johannesburg. Ringling Bros. were in town, but after the clowns had finished I walked on to the street and a staggering black man almost knocked me down. He was battered and bleeding; I had only time to see his nose, which was torn open and bloody, before two white thugs dragged him away, threw him in the gutter and kicked him savagely. The black crowd turned its back on him, only filing the event in their heads, there to jostle with the others, waiting their turn. The white crowd turned away, whether from shame or fear I couldn't say. No one was shocked, or surprised. We had all seen these things before.

I also remember a different kind of violence, the casual violence of institutions, whole communities uprooted from the homes of generations, families torn asunder by bureaucrats made callous by their zeal for racial order, 'neighbourhoods' created on the arid sands that were chilling in their sterility and lack of life. This was the violence implicit in the bland titles of the laws of apartheid: The Group Areas Act, the Population Registration Act, the Separate Amenities Act, the Job Reservation Act, and the cascade of other acts by which the whites sought to circumscribe the lives of others.

I hardly ever saw the final kind of violence, black against white. Black violence was always just a potential. It was what whites frightened each other with.

But I would lie if I were to say violence dominates my memories. I remember my Aunt Nel, a small pale woman whose presence filled the lives around her; she made everyone she met feel not the violence of apartheid but how stupid, petty, *ignorant* it was. Her presence was so strong she became friends with Robert Sobukwe, the visionary who was ultimately killed by the prisons Nelson Mandela at long last escaped. Nel was a Boer woman too, part of Africa. Just as powerful is the memory of Dr Moroko, a Rolong physician who tended my Boer grandfather on his deathbed, two old reprobates sitting quietly together while one of them died in dignity. I remember the gravity of Moroko, his courtliness, his slow good humour. His memory flooded up as I watched the first few steps that Nelson Mandela took to freedom; as the camera closed on his face I saw there the same gravity and steadiness that had infused Moroko, and I remembered writing a few years ago that I believed there were Afrikaners 'whose hearts are large enough to make the dramatic leap, Afrikaners who see in the Great Trek an adventure of the spirit and not a retreat from reality; when they think of the Trek they are reminded not of grievances left behind but only of the restless search for new horizons, for the endless blue horizons of the African interior. For them, the

Afrikaner *volkseie* is a large enough space to contain fresh spiritual horizons of its own, a place for the tribe to go, the safe haven ultimately found, finally a place for dreaming . . . ' Mandela/Moroko/Moshesh can talk to these people, can finally sit in the dust and the heat under the African sun to make new legends, and even if he/they are swept away by the evil residues of apartheid, even if there is no black-and-white Arthur to draw the *kleilet* from the thorn tree, even if his own legend dissipates, drifts away in the banal compromises of mere politics, there are others that will take his/their place. For the first time, it is safe to dream a little.

ANITA DESAI
A Reading Rat on the Moors

Any child who has grown up a bookworm – in my family known as a *Lese Ratte*, a reading rat – will have known the secret rapture of Jane Eyre who, on finding herself closeted with the hated Reed family on a rainy day when there was no possibility of a walk outdoors, slips into the breakfast room which 'contained a bookcase: I soon possessed myself of a volume, taking care that it should be one stored with pictures. I mounted into the windowseat: gathering up my feet, I sat cross-legged, like a Turk; and, having drawn the red moreen curtains nearly close, I was shrined in double retirement . . . I was then happy; happy at least in my own way. I feared nothing but interruption . . .'

The physical conditions I knew in my career as a *Lese Ratte* were very different: a shower of rain would have drawn me, and my brother and sisters, outdoors to leap and dance and sing, tearing off our clothes and splashing in the puddles: it was so rare and jubilant a thing. To retire behind a red moreen curtain (what *was* that? In my home curtains were of striped Orissa cotton) on a summer's day in Delhi would have meant suffocation from heat and dust. But to stretch out, stripped down to a cotton petticoat, on one's string cot under a slowly revolving fan that hung and swayed from the high ceiling and creaked somnolently through the long afternoon, propping up a book on one's stomach and gulping down its contents till one was stupefied and sank like a waterlogged corpse into a heavy afternoon slumber, or to take the book of the moment out into the garden and curl up on a cane chair for the few cool hours of evening, or to climb with the book up into the leafy branches of a fig tree and sit there with one's head concealed and one's legs dangling down till a row of ants decided to crawl up them as if they were branches, too – drastically different though these were from Jane Eyre's experience, they allowed one the identical sensation of shutting out the real and unsatisfactory world and stepping into the far more satisfying one created by the writer.

No, it was not *Jane Eyre* which opened that window to me; I read it and thought it a fairly conventional tale of the romance of a plain maiden and a handsome *roué*. I was nine years old when I found *Wuthering Heights* on my parents' glass-fronted bookshelves alongside a German Bible, Nehru's *Discovery of India*, Galsworthy's *Forsyte Saga* and the complete works of Heine and Schiller. In its brown Rexine covers and with its yellowed and brittle pages, it had none of the attractions of Jane Eyre's *History of British Birds* by Bewick, but that did not deter me in the least – by that age I was perfectly aware of the power of words over that of mere sensations. My instinct was right, for once I had read the opening words: '1801 – I have just returned from a visit to my landlord – the solitary neighbour that I shall be troubled with', I knew I had stepped through the magic casement into a land that would haunt me all my life, and I read on till I reached the last lines: ' . . . and wondered how anyone could ever imagine unquiet slumbers for the sleepers in that quiet earth.' My own world of an Old Delhi bungalow, its verandas and plastered walls and ceiling fans, its garden of papaya and guava trees full of shrieking parakeets, the gritty dust that settled on the pages of a book before one could turn them, all receded. What became real, dazzlingly real, through the power and magic of Emily Brontë's pen, were the Yorkshire moors, the storm-driven heath, the torments of its anguished inhabitants who roamed thereon in rain and sleet, crying out from the depths of their broken hearts and hearing only ghosts reply.

I read every word I could find about the author – by Mrs Gaskell, Winifred Gérin, et al. The strangeness of a woman so reclusive, so reticent, with so little knowledge of the outside world, creating this tale of great passions of heroic and anti-heroic characters in situations of such drama and melodrama certainly was a teasing one. I devoured all the information I could glean about that extraordinary family that lived in the icy parsonage beside the stony churchyard. Aunt Branwell, Tabitha, Keeper, became a part of my extended family. With them, I sat by the fire in the kitchen, helping to stir the pudding while I listened to the four siblings excitedly read their sagas of Gondal and Angria. Shyly and furtively I glanced into the face of my chosen heroine Emily – pale and gaunt, her black eyes smouldering with an inner fire. I pictured her in a grey habit, like a nun's, stretched upon her couch, one hand holding a book of poems, the other resting on her dog Keeper's head. I dreamed her dream with her – of the dark stranger emerging from the storm on the moors – and sighed to see her carried on her bier to the churchyard, so tragically young and heroic.

Even though years went by when I no longer gave the book another and another reading – D. H. Lawrence's *Sons and Lovers* drew away my attention, and then Forster's *Passage to India*, and then Dostoevsky and Chekhov – and I no longer remembered the sequence of events and became a little ashamed of my early ardour, seeing it as puerile and somewhat embarrassing, even resented its influence upon my early writing, something of that first impression remained like a scar acquired in infancy, early but ineradicable, a scar that one preferred to hide and rarely remembered oneself.

Then I was asked to write an introduction to a new edition of Anne Brontë's work, and in order to do so re-read some of the many biographies that exist. Once again I was drawn into the fold. Like the first whisper of a moorland storm, I felt the familiar stirrings of my youthful passion. Anne and Charlotte were all very well, yes, but it was in Emily Brontë's sole work of fiction that the passion was contained in its quintessential form. I had to turn to her again:

> Once more the tapping at the window on a windy night. It is soldered shut but, 'I must stop it nevertheless!' I muttered, knocking my knuckles through the glass, and stretching out an arm to seize the importunate branch: instead of which, my fingers closed on the fingers of a little ice-cold hand!
>
> The intense horror of nightmare came over me; I tried to draw back my arm, but the hand clung to it, and a most melancholy voice sobbed, 'Let me in – let me in!'
>
> Terror made me a coward, and, finding it useless to attempt shaking the creature off, I pulled its wrist on to the broken pane, and rubbed it to and fro till the blood ran down and soaked the bedclothes: still it wailed, 'Let me in!'

And all those memorable scenes came flooding back to me:

Catherine, sitting up in her sickbed and pulling feathers out of her pillows: '"That's a turkey's and this a wild duck's and this a pigeon's. Ah, they put pigeon's feathers in the pillow – no wonder I couldn't die! And here is a moorcock's; and this – I should know it among a thousand – it's a lapwing's. Bonny bird, wheeling over our heads in the middle of a moor. It wanted to get to its nest, for the clouds touched the swells, and it felt rain coming. This feather was picked up from the heath, the bird was not shot – we saw its nest on the moor, full of little skeletons . . ."'

Mr Linton bringing her 'a handful of golden crocuses': '"These are the earliest flowers at the Heights!" she exclaimed. "They remind me of soft thaw winds, and warm sunshine and nearly melted snow – Edgar, is there not a south wind, and is not the snow almost gone?"'

Old Joseph, muttering in the stables, '"Mim! mim! mim! Did iver Christian body hear owt like it? Minching un' munching! Hah can Aw tell what ye say?"'

Of course, the romance, the romance!: 'Heathcliff had knelt on one knee to embrace her; he attempted to rise, but she seized his hair, and kept him down. "I wish I could hold you," she continued, bitterly, "till we are both dead! I shouldn't care what you suffered. I care nothing for your sufferings. Why shouldn't you suffer? I do!"'

The pathos – Catherine's dream of having been to heaven once: '"Heaven did not seem to be my home; and I broke my heart with weeping to come back to earth; and the angels were so angry that they flung me out, into the middle of the heath on top of Wuthering Heights; where I woke sobbing for joy."'

After so much *Sturm und Drang* it was a relief to sink into the grass around the gravestones in the final scene: 'I lingered around them, under that benign sky; watched the moths fluttering among the heath, and hare-bells; listened to the soft wind breathing through the grass, and wondered how anyone could ever imagine unquiet slumbers for the sleepers in that earth.'

I found myself totally enveloped by that grey and diaphanous mist off the moors; was it composed of Emily Brontë's life or of her work? If one did not know of her family, her childhood in the parsonage, her fantasies of Gondal and Angria spun by the fire on winter evenings, her wanderings on the moor, her burial in the Haworth churchyard, would the legend be quite so potent? On leafing through *Wuthering Heights* once again, I can answer, Yes! The book has such power, such intensity, that the Brontë legend is merely its shadow, or nimbus, while it retains its central position as surely as the flame of a candle. If it is the young who respond to it so ardently, so unreservedly, it is not a reflection of their immaturity but of the intensity of the book which is the intensity of youth and can never quite be recovered once it is overlaid by the grey dust of age and experience.

LILIANA HEKER

Early Beginnings or Ars Poetica

In the beginning (but not in the beginning of the beginning) there is a horse going up in the lift. I know he is brown, but what I don't know is how he got there or what he is going to do when the lift comes to a stop. As far as that is concerned, the horse is quite different from the lion. And not only because the lion climbs the stairs in a reasonable manner, but also because, above all, the appearance of the lion has a logical explanation. I say to myself, There are lions in Africa. I ask myself, If they walk, why don't they ever leave Africa? I answer myself, Because lions don't have a particular destination in mind; sometimes they walk this way and sometimes that, and therefore, just going and coming, they never leave Africa. But that fact doesn't deceive me, of course: if they don't have a particular destination, it might happen that at least one of the lions, unintentionally, might walk always in the same direction. He might walk by day, sleep by night, and in the morning, not aware of what he's doing, he might walk again in the same direction, then sleep again by night, and in the morning, not aware of what he's doing . . . I say to myself, Africa ends somewhere, and a lion walking always in the same direction will one day walk straight out of Africa and into another country. I say to myself, Argentina is another country, therefore that lion might come to Argentina. If he comes at night, no one will see him because at night there are no people out in the streets. He will climb the stairs up to my apartment, break the door without making a sound (lions break doors without making a sound because their skin is so thick and smooth), cross the hallway and sit down behind the dining-room table. I'm in bed; I know he is there, waiting, and my blood throbs inside my head. It's very unsettling to know that there is a lion in the dining-room and that he hasn't stirred. I get up, I leave my room and cross the dining-room – on this side of the table, not on the side of the lion. Before going into the kitchen I stop for a moment, turning my back on him. The lion doesn't jump on me, but that doesn't mean anything: he might jump when I come back. I go into the kitchen and have a drink of water. I come out again, without stopping, and the lion doesn't jump this time either, but that doesn't mean anything. I go to bed and wait warily: the lion isn't moving, but I know he's also waiting. I get up and go again into the kitchen. It is almost morning. On my way back, I glance sideways at the door: it hasn't been broken. But therein lies the real danger. The lion is still on his way and will arrive tonight. As long as he isn't here, one lion will be like a thousand lions waiting for me, night after night, behind the dining-room table.

But in spite of all this, the lion isn't as bad as the horse. I know all about him: how he came, what he is thinking every time I go for a drink of water; I know that he knows why he doesn't jump every time he doesn't jump; that one night, when I decide to meet him face to face, all I'll have to do is walk into the dining-room on that other side of the table. About the horse, on the other hand, I know nothing. He also arrives at night, but I don't understand why he has gone into the lift, nor how he manages to operate the sliding doors, nor with what does he press the buttons. The horse has no history: all he does is go up in the lift. He counts the floors: first, second, third, fourth. The lift stops. My heart freezes as I wait. I know the end will be horrible but I don't know *how* it will happen. And this is the beginning. Horror of the unexplainable, or the cult of Descartes, is the beginning.

But it's not the beginning of the beginning. It is the end of the beginning. The time has come in which the little people inside the radio will soon die, and also God will die, with his long mane and a gaucho's poncho, sitting cross-legged on top of the Heavens. (Because throughout the whole beginning, the world is built in such a way that God and the dead can sit and walk *on top* of the Heavens; that is to say: the Universe is a hollow sphere cut by a horizontal plane; moving on that plane are we, the living, and this is called the Earth. From the Earth, looking upwards, you can see the inner surface of the upper hemisphere, and that is called the Heavens. Or the floor of the Heavens as seen from below. If you go through it, you can see the real floor of the Heavens, Heaven itself, on which the good dead walk and where God is sitting; to us, this seems difficult, because the floor of the Heavens is rounded, but He's God. Underneath our floor, inside the lower hemisphere, is the burning Hell, where little red devils float around together with the evil dead.) Now, before the end of the spherical universe, and before the lions and the horse, in the very heart of the beginning, are four cups of chocolate on a yellow plastic tablecloth. I'm four years old, and it's my birthday. But there are no guests, no cake with candles on it, no presents. The three of them are there, of course, sitting around the table; but in the beginning they don't count, because the three of them have always been there, and a birthday hasn't. I am alone in front of four cups of chocolate and a yellow plastic tablecloth. I'm moved to tears. This must be what it's like to be poor, and I'm supposed to feel terribly sad. The roof of the kitchen is made out of straw and the walls are of mud and my body is covered in rags; wind and snow seep through the cracks of my poor hut. I'm dying of cold and hunger while, in the palace, the little spoilt princess celebrates her fourth birthday with a ball: there are coaches at the door, and dolls with real hair, and a monkey that dances for the princess alone. I drink my chocolate. I weep into my cup. And this really *is* the beginning. The trick of stories, the trick of the power of the imagination, lies in the beginning.

But this isn't the beginning of the beginning either. It is an awareness of the beginning. It is the beginning of an awareness of the beginning. Beyond this awareness, rising from behind strange faces, like flashing images, are a straw chair on a tiled courtyard, a wrinkled great-grandmother with a black scarf around her head, a madman climbing into a streetcar with a stick, and in the true beginning, a white hood. The white hood is mine. Or it was mine, I don't know, I don't understand what's happening, she has it on her head now. She arrived this morning, and ever since she arrived everyone is fawning on her. I've been told she's my little cousin, but she doesn't look like my cousin because she's littler than me, and she doesn't call me her baby, and she doesn't lift me up in her arms. But they lift her up in their arms, all the time, because she hasn't yet learnt how to walk, like the little babies in the park. I hate her. It's night time already. They say she's going to leave and they say it's cold out there. I run through the rooms, I throw myself against the legs of the grown-ups, I roll around on a mattress. I don't care if they scream at me, I'm happy; she's leaving. I look at her and it's there. She has my hood on. They say it looks big on her, they say she looks like a little old lady; they laugh. I'll push her eyes in, like with a doll; I'll bite her nose off; I'll tear my hood away from her. Then it happens. Someone looks at me and says, 'Won't you lend your little cousin your hood?' I don't know what 'lend' means; I know I want to tear her up into small bits. I look up at them. All eyes are fixed on me. Then I understand: all I need is a gesture, one single gesture, and the kingdom will be mine once more. They are waiting. They are laughing. I smile at them.

'Yes,' I say.

They laugh louder. They pinch my cheek, and tell me I'm a darling. I've won. It's the beginning.

Further back there is nothing. I look carefully for a taste of clementine, for my father's voice, for a smell of lip ointment. Something clean that will change my beginning. I want a whitewashed beginning for my story. It is useless. Farther back there is nothing. That hood, my first infamy, is, for ever, the beginning of the beginning.

Translated by Alberto Manguel

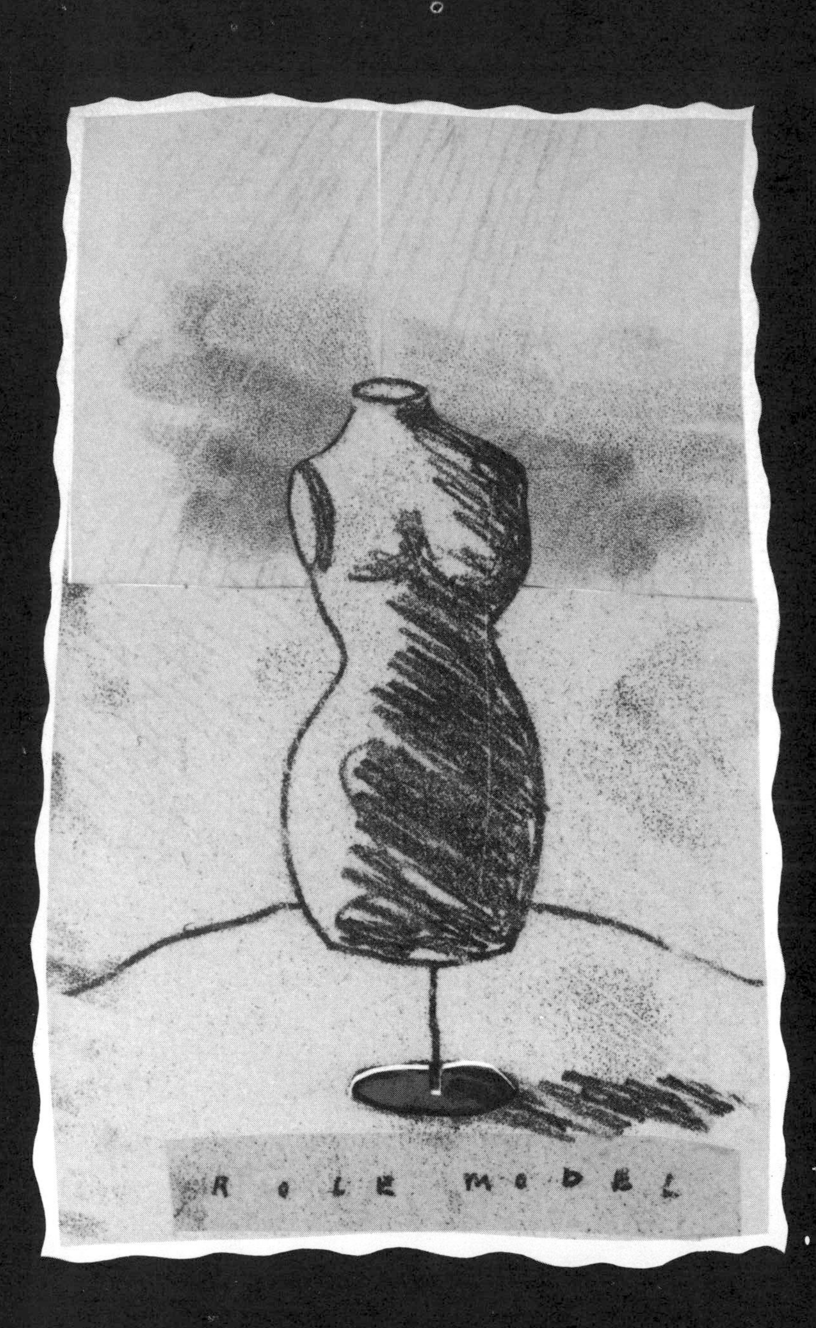
ROLE MODEL

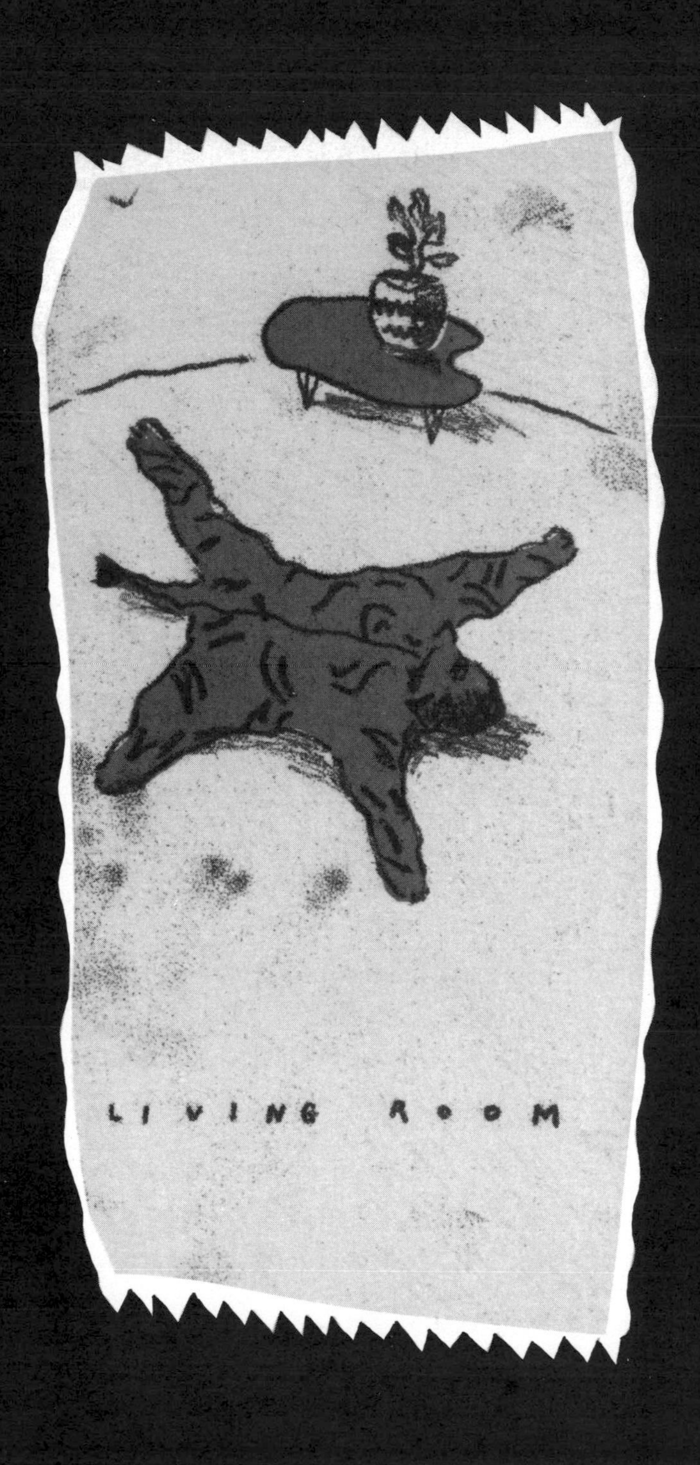
LIVING ROOM

FRIEDRICH DÜRRENMATT
Document

The story of my work as a writer is the story of my themes. Themes are actually transformed impressions. One writes as a complete man, not as a man of letters or as a grammarian. Everything hangs together because everything is brought together in a context. Everything can become so important, determinative, usually at a later date, unsuspected. Stars are concentrations of interstellar materials; writing is a concentration of impressions. There can be no excuse. As a result of one's environment, one is admittedly part of that environment. Nevertheless critical impressions leave their mark in one's youth. The horror stayed with me, the horror that seized hold of me when the vegetable man pushed the heads of lettuce apart in his little store under the theatre, with his handless arm. What comes later meets with what has already been formed, it will be worked over according to a predetermined scheme, incorporated into what is already in existence, and the tales we overheard as children are more decisive than the influences of literature. This becomes clear to us in retrospect. I am not a village writer, but a village produced me, and so, I am still a villager with a slow manner of speech, not an urban dweller, certainly not an inhabitant of a metropolis, and yet I am no longer able to live in a village.

The village itself stood where the Bern-Luzern and Burgdorf-Thun roads meet; on a high plateau, at the foot of a large cliff and not far from the gallows' hill, where once murderers and trouble-makers are said to have been taken in carts, from the local courthouse. Across the plateau flows a stream that the small rural villages and hamlets used as their focal point. The aristocrats in the surrounding area were poverty-stricken. Their residences had been changed into senior citizens' homes and convalescence clinics. At first, there was probably only an inn at the crossroads. Then a blacksmith's shop appeared across from it. Later, the two other fields in the remaining corners became a co-operative store and a theatre. The latter is not unimportant, as the village did produce a well-known dramatist, a teacher named Gribi, whose plays were put on by dramatic societies throughout the Emmental, and even a champion yodeller, named Schmalz. Along the Thun

Road, the printer's, the textile merchant's store, the butcher's shop, the bakery, and the school sprang up. The school was almost in the next village, whose lads beat me up on the way to school and whose dogs we feared, while the manse, the church, the cemetery and the savings bank were built on the small rise between the Thun and the Bern Roads. It was only when the large dairy, Stalden AG, was erected on the steep rise of Burgdorf Road that the village became a rural seat. Milk was brought here from all over the surrounding area, in heavy trucks that groups of us awaited on our way to the high school in Grosshoechstetten. We hung on to them so that our bikes were pulled up Burgdorf Road. We were gripped with fear, though we were not afraid of the police, for we all felt we were a match for the fat village policeman. Instead, we were rather afraid of the French and calligraphy teacher, whom we called Baggel, whose lessons caused us to tremble, because he was a wicked caner, pincher and hair-puller, who even forced us to shake each other's hands, saying, 'Greetings, learnèd European.' Hanging on behind the rattling trucks with the dancing, empty milk cans in the morning, we compared the teacher to a gigantic mountain that we had to climb over, with grotesque place-names and correspondingly difficult paths. That, however, was shortly before I moved to the city. The train station remains more important in my memory than the dairy with its high chimney, more the landmark of our village than the church tower. It was entitled to call itself a train station because the village was at a railway junction, and we villagers were proud of that fact: only a few trains had the courage not to stop, racing by on their way to far-off Luzern or nearby Bern. Sitting on a bench in front of the station, I looked after them with a mixture of longing and disgust, as they steamed back and forth on their way. But memory slides even farther, back through the underground passageway that let the railway tracks run across a bridge over the Burgdorf Road and that let us reach the station by some stairs. I felt it looked like a dark cave when I entered it, I, a thirteen-year-old boy, right in the middle of the street, having run away from home to the village. At the end of the hole was sunlight, out of which the dark shadows of the cars and vehicles grew. Not much more could be made out of where I actually wanted to go, because through the underground passage you could only get to the dairy and to the station. Even the better people had settled on the steep slope of the Ballenbuehl. This included my godmother who was the wife of the village physician, to whom I later had to bring for inspection my school report cards, which were never satisfactory. The president of the parish lived there, too, as did the dentist and the orthodontist. They both ran the Dental Institute which to this very day continues to mistreat a broad section of the country and make the place famous. Both owned automobiles and were thus privileged on that account, and in the evening they pooled together the money they had earned drilling, pulling teeth and making dentures, only to divide it up with their naked hands, without ever counting it more accurately. The dental mechanic was short and fat, preoccupied with questions concerning people's health. He used to make a kind of rough peasant loaf that would give you the shivers. The dentist was an imposing man, a French-speaking Swiss, probably from Neuchâtel. He was thought to be the richest man in the entire country; later this opinion turned out to be a tragic mistake. But he certainly was the most pious. As he drilled teeth, he spoke as a member of an extreme sect about Christ, and the only one to reach him in his religious fervour was a haggard-looking woman of indeterminate age, always dressed in black, to whom, according to her own statements, the angels would appear; a woman who read the Bible while milking the cows and to whom I had to bring pedlars and wandering academics from across the plain so that they could spend the night. My parents were a hospitable parson and his wife, and they never turned anyone away and let everyone eat with us, anyone who wanted to do so, including the children of a circus, which visited the village each year and which once included a black boy. He was very black, sat at the family table to my father's left, and ate rice with tomato sauce. He had been converted, but I was still afraid. There were quite a lot of conversions in the village. Revivalist camps were held, the Salvation Army appeared, sects formed, evangelists preached, but the place was best known in this respect for the Moslem Mission, which was located in a feudal chalet high above the village. It published a map of the world, on which only one place could be found in Europe, the village, a missionary conceit which gave rise to the crazy momentary feeling that we were living at the very centre of the world and not in an Emmentaler God-forsaken village. That expression is not exaggerated. The village was ugly, an accumulation of buildings in a *petit bourgeois* style that can be seen everywhere in the Mittelland, but the surrounding rural villages were beautiful, with large roofs and carefully layered manure piles, surrounded by secretive dark fir forests. The plain was full of adventure, with meadows of bitter clover and large wheat fields in which we crept about building our nests, while the farmers stood on the edges, swearing as they peered at us. Even more secretive were the dank pathways through the hay that the farmers had opened with their scythes. We crept about for hours in the warm, dusty darkness and peeked out into the stalls where the cows stood in long rows. For me, the strangest place was the upper windowless attic in my parents' house. It was full of old newspapers and books, which shimmered white in the darkness. Once I was frightened in the laundry room. A strange animal lay in it, a salamander, perhaps. The cemetery, however, was not frightening.

We often played hide-and-seek there. If a grave had been dug, I lay down cosily in it, until the approach of the funeral procession with its sound of bells drove me away. We were not just familiar with death, but also with killing. A village has no secrets, and a human being is an animal of prey that sometimes has human tendencies, which must make things difficult for butchers. We often watched as the butcher's apprentices did the slaughtering. We saw how the blood shot out of the large animals. We saw how they died and how they were carved up. We children watched, a quarter of an hour, half an hour, and then we went and played again on the path with our marbles.

That was not enough. A village is not the world. One could live out one's destiny in a village, with its tragedies and comedies. A village is determined by the world, left at peace, forgotten or destroyed, and not the other way round. A village is an optional point in the world, nothing more, a point that can be replaced by anything unimportant, coincidental. The world is larger than the village. Above the forests are the stars. I became acquainted with them at an early age, drew their constellations: the immobile pole star, the small and the great bear with the tiny dragon between them. I became acquainted with bright-shining Vega, twinkling Altair, nearby Sirius, distant Deneb, the gigantic sun Aldebaran, the even more powerful Betelgeuse and Antares. I knew that the village belonged to the earth and the earth to the solar system, that the sun with its planets moved around the centre of the Milky Way in the direction of Hercules. I perceived that the Andromeda Galaxy, which could still be made out with my naked eye, was a milky way like our own. I was never a Ptolemaic astronomer. Right there in the village, I was aware of my immediate surroundings, and, a little farther away, of the nearby city and a holiday spa in the mountains, beyond which I had travelled a few kilometres on school trips. That was all. However, up there, in Outer Space, a framework of monstrous distances developed. The same happened with the concept of time. That which was distant was more important than that which was immediate. The immediate could only be perceived as long as it was tangible as the real life in the village; even village politics were too abstract, and even more abstract were national politics, social crises, bank failures (in which my parents lost their fortune), the peace efforts, the appearance of the Nazis, too vague, all too unfathomable. But the Flood, which was comprehensible, was an artistic occurrence, God's wrath and the rains. He poured the entire ocean on to humanity, go forth and swim. And then brave David, the boastful Goliath, the adventures of Hercules, the strongest man that ever was, royal Theseus, the Trojan War, the sinister Nibelungen, the brilliant Dietrich von Bern, the courageous heroes of the Swiss Confederation thrashing the Austrians, and, at

St Jakob-an-der-Birs, slaying an immeasurably superior army, all held together in the mother's lap of the village, and the wild world out there, of history and the sagas, which were all one, but also the immeasurable figures of Space through the shadowy love of God, to Whom we prayed, having to ask for forgiveness, from Whom we also could expect goodness, the desired and the wished-for as from an incomprehensible super-uncle from behind the clouds. Good and evil were fixed. We were constantly writing an examination; for every deed, marks were given out immediately. This is why school was such an unpleasant experience: it continued the divine system on earth, and for the children the adults were half-divine. Horribly beautiful children's land: the world of experience was small, a silly village, nothing more; the world of the tradition was mighty, floating in a puzzling cosmos, run through with a wild flow of fables about heroic struggles, which could not be tested. We had to accept this world. We had been handed over to faith, we were vulnerable and naked.

Translated by Craig Thomas

FRIEDRICH DÜRRENMATT

The Sausage

A man murdered his wife and made her into a sausage. Gossip denounced him. The man was arrested. A second sausage was found. Indignation was great. The country's supreme judge was put in charge of the case.

The courtroom is well lit. The sun seeps through the windows. The walls are gleaming mirrors. The people are a seething mass. They fill the room. They sit on the windowsills. They hang from the chandeliers. To the right, the prosecutor's bald head burns brightly. It is red. The defence lawyer stands to the left. His glasses are blind man's glasses. The accused is sitting in the middle, between two policemen. He has large hands. The fingernails are rimmed with blue. Above them all the supreme judge sits enthroned. His robes are black. His beard is a white banner. His eyes are solemn. His forehead clear. His eyebrows angry. His face humane. In front of him is the sausage. It lies on a plate. Above the supreme judge Justice sits enthroned. Her eyes are blindfolded. She holds a sword in her right hand. A pair of scales in her left. She is carved in stone. The supreme judge raises his hand. The people stop talking. Their movement freezes. The room quietens down. Time is suspended. The prosecutor rises. His stomach is a globe. His lips a guillotine. His tongue a cleaver. The words pound the room. The accused falters. The judge listens carefully, a vertical frown between his two eyebrows. His eyes are like suns. Their rays hit the accused. Who caves in. His knees give way. His hands pray. His tongue hangs out. His ears prick up. The sausage in front of the supreme judge is red. It is speechless. It swells. Its tips are rounded. The string at one end is yellow. It lies there. The eyes of the supreme judge fall on the lowest of men. He is small. His skin is like leather. His mouth is a beak. His lips dried blood. His eyes pinheads. His forehead flat. His fingers thick. The sausage smells delicious. It comes nearer. Its skin is rough. The sausage is tender. It is firm. The fingernail leaves on it a half-moon shape. The sausage is warm. It is plump. The prosecutor stops talking. The accused lifts his head. His eyes are those of a tormented child. The supreme judge raises his hand. The defence lawyer springs up like a coil. His glasses dance up and down. The words bounce around the room. The sausage smokes. The vapours are warm. A penknife opens its blade. The sausage squirts. The defence lawyer stops talking. The supreme judge stares at the accused. He is far away below him. He is a flea. The supreme judge shakes his head. His look is full of contempt. The supreme judge begins to speak. His words are the swords of Justice. They roll like boulders over the accused. His sentences are ropes. They lash. They strangle. They kill. The flesh is tender. It is sweet. It melts on the tongue like butter. The skin is a little tougher. The partitions hum. The ceiling clenches its fists. The windows clench their teeth. The doors come off their hinges. The walls stamp their feet. The city turns livid. The forests wither. The waters evaporate. The earth trembles. The sun dies. The heavens fall. The accused is found guilty. Death opens its maw. The penknife lies down on the table. The fingers are sticky. They rub themselves against the black robes. The supreme judge stops talking. The room is dead. The air is muggy. The lungs are full of lead. The people tremble. The accused is glued to his seat. He is condemned. He has the right to one last wish. He is hunched over. The wish creeps out of his brain. It is tiny. It grows. Till it becomes a giant. He concentrates. It begins to take shape. It forces the lips to part. It bursts into the courtroom. It thunders. The perverted murderer wishes to eat the rest of his poor wife. The sausage. Horror is a single cry. The supreme judge raises his hand. The people are silent. The supreme judge is like God. His voice is the final trumpet. He grants the wish. The condemned man may eat the sausage. The supreme judge looks at the plate. The sausage is no longer there. He says nothing. The calm is heavy. The people stare at the supreme judge. The condemned man's eyes are wide open. They hold a question. The question is terrible. It spreads throughout the room. It clutches at the walls. It hangs all huddled up from the ceiling. It grabs hold of everyone. The room expands. The world becomes a monstrous question mark.

Translated by Alberto Manguel

Superior Quality

BEST QUAL

MARY MORRISSY
Rosa

From his palace in Rome the pope had ordered a holy year. Everyone in our small city was touched. Even Penbridges, the big department store where I work, had pushed Santa Claus to one side. Usually he holds the centre stage in the large foyer on the first floor, sitting beneath a great, needle-dropping tree, its branches laden down with silvered, snowy baubles. This year he was huddled in one corner while in the centre was a huge crib with life-size figures. The management had even considered having real animals, a donkey and an ox nuzzling close to the child, but they couldn't risk the possibility of steaming turds on the carpet and so they settled for plaster-cast models instead. But the *pièce-de-résistance* was the baby, a black baby. It was a stroke of genius. We rarely see a dark face in these parts and so it seemed Penbridges had absolved all our prejudices with one bold gesture.

It was Rosa who pointed this out to me. Rosa is my sister, younger than me by five years although it has never seemed that way. I live on the edges of her dark, livid world until it seems that without her I would barely exist, that I would be a mere spectre, passing in and out unseen through the sullen doorways of life. Even her name, Rosa, is a sort of concoction. At home we used to call her Rosie – a dark, freckled child squatting in patches of mud or clumps of grass, burrowing with her tiny, dimpled hands. When she came to the city she became Rosa, conjuring up an image of deep, sultry eyes and a small, fluid body. And in time she became that, as if, chameleon-like, her wish was enough to create.

In the last month of her confinement she visited Penbridge's crib daily. Then, I dismissed it as just another vagary of pregnancy like the early cravings for pineapple and raw meat. And I thought perhaps this, the ultimate picture of maternity, was actually taking hold of her. It was, at least, warm and safer there than the crowded, wet streets which she tramped constantly. She would come back to our rooms barefoot, soaked through, her hair wringing, her sodden shoes in her hand, their dye leaving faint red patches in the hollows beneath her ankle bones and in between her toes. But in Penbridges she made quite a pious picture, a heavily pregnant girl kneeling on the pew before the crib, tinselled angels hanging above her, little scrolls emanating from their trumpets with Gothic-red messages emblazoned on them. Oh, they had got everything right – the melting snow on the roof, the obsequious hunch of the shepherds, the stained wooden slats of the manger, even the acrid smell of the stable. But to me, all these things only added to the sense of it being an imitation. It seemed aimed at people – people like us, I suppose – who live fleetingly on the surface of things.

'Look,' Rosa said to me when we went there together. 'Look at Joseph and Mary, how pale they are. They don't seem a bit put out that the baby is a different colour.' She cackled. 'That's religion for you . . .'

He was like a cat fleeting in moonlight. I heard them thrashing in the night, then the sudden, shocked stillness of their union. Did I imagine a coldness in their pleasure? Perhaps. But, like the crib, it was a fine imitation. I watched them as one might trace with a finger the gentle lashing of fish against the glass of an aquarium. When he was gone she would sit with her back to me, her lips suppressed with a kind of excitement. I would stand behind her, one hand in hers, the other settled in the sad curve of her neck parting the tiny strands of her hair with my thumb until I had laid bare her forlorn nape and her bridled fervour had melted away into a sated melancholy. I knew, of course, that he would abandon her, and I simply waited. And, sure enough, one evening I heard him fleeing, his footsteps clattering down the stone flights that lead from our rooms into the hallways below, as if he had been hurled into the depths of a cold, echoing well.

We were left to count the days. The pale squares of the calendar seemed to grow hollow-eyed from our attention. Every morning I sought tell-tale signs on her white underwear but it yielded up only the indolent smell of sex which clung to her long after he was gone. Rosa grew strangely listless. When we went to the clinic she held my hand, placing herself trustingly in my care. We sat silent in the waiting room as a haggard woman with skin like suede and a soothered child on her lap addressed the room.

'Never had any trouble with the other three, but this one has my heart broke. Always sick, always cranky . . .'

The child sat, stoppered and somehow accusing. I winked and smiled at her, believing that such clownish behaviour was expected, but she stared back, unblinking, solemn.

As we went home, Rosa glanced at her newly confirmed shape in shop windows. Serpentine mannequins, their fingers arched mockingly like Balinese dancers, their heads tilted quizzically, smiled back at her. She stopped once, staring through them at her own reflection.

'It's not really there,' she said, flattening her stomach.

'Rosa, Rosa . . .'

'It's like a balloon . . . I could easily burst it.'

'Rosa, we are not murderers.'

And, even if we were, who would have helped us in a year when vigils were held at grottoes and rosaries were broadcast in railway stations?

'We must tell Father,' I said.

The thought of going home filled us both with dread, not for what we had to tell him, but for the mastery of his dismal existence over us. He has been alone for years, ever since Mother died in childbirth with our stillborn brother. Now he shuffles around our dark little cottage, swamped by moss-coloured clothes. Crumbs of cigarette ash settle on the sheeny crotch of his pants as he sits by the dim glow in the grate. He runs a crinkled hand through his thick, grey strands, which are as coarse as horse hair, and sighs. It is not great unhappiness. No, it is as if he expected this grim ebb-tide in his life and is mesmerised by its seething undertow.

It was I, in the end, who told him while Rosa sat in the overgrown garden, idly plaiting her hair. He shifted once in his chair but said nothing. I knew then that nothing *we* did or said could ripple the hypnotic stillness of his own gloom.

But as we were leaving, he caught me roughly by the arm and said with a sagging smile, 'She has won you over, our little Rosa.'

Was it then I crossed over into Rosa's world? No, even then, there were corners of it into which she retreated that I could only guess at. Once I found a half-empty bottle of gin in the bathroom and a rim of grime around the tub where she had lain for hours. Another time she tried to prick the surface of her belly with a safety pin as if to tear it open, until I prized the pin out of her hand.

I used to bring her gifts from the outside world – small, strawberry-filled chocolates, a pink velvet ribbon for her hair, a bright crimson dress. I brought her books, manuals of motherhood full of tranquil passages and soft photographs of swollen women, but she only pointed to the protective male hands on each of their bellies as if I were trying to taunt her. I remember the rolling gait of two, her arms encompassing the bump in a gesture of aborted protection.

When we passed blooming, bulbous girls on the the street she would point after them. 'Dromedaries, one-humped camels, beasts of burden, that's all we are . . .' And yet, she had never looked healthier. Abandonment had given her a luring, almost sexual glow.

But sometimes, late at night, I would hear her softly whimpering in her sleep. Once she woke in terror crying, 'How will it come out?' as mind overtook body in the nine-month race. The thumping being beat in her like a drum, she said, resenting its confinement, the distended part so ugly, displacing all her innards, leeching energy, dictating. I had no answers, but held her head in my lap until she went back to sleep. In time, her body answered for her, flexing its muscles, preparing regardless, tightening, clenching around its prize, her skin stretched to translucence. Full-blown, circumferenced, we awaited the eruption . . .

I could not be with her for the birth. The week before Christmas is Penbridges' busiest time and I had to report for work as usual. I was on Cold Cuts in the food hall, sawing through the flaky breasts of chickens or using the slicer on sweating joints of ham, the slices quivering for a moment before falling over drunkenly on to the greaseproof paper in my outstretched hand. While Rosa lay somewhere else on a cold slab, trussed like a turkey, the midwife in a butcher's apron, the nurses gathered around like spectators at a bullfight, their urgent cries mixing with hers of pain. As I passed cold, wet bags of giblets across the counter, there might be a great tearing of skin . . . the doctor would hold the balloon up, a small, shrivelled thing. It would hang there for a moment, then he would pass it to her. And Rosa would catch it up by its slim neck and put it to her lips. At first it might make no move – then it would leap salmon-like into life. But perhaps she wouldn't? Perhaps she would gently let it go, releasing her fingers from its slender neck, and watch it shudder and recede . . . I longed to be with her.

The store did not close until nine. I walked home through the soiled, littered streets thinking of her, of us. On my way I bought flowers for her – not roses because she said they reminded her of death, but speckled orange tiger lilies. She was standing on the doorstep when I arrived, the baby muffled in her arms.

'Rosa, what's happened?'

She put her finger to her lips and motioned for us to go in. We made our way up the stairways, slowly, because her stitches were still raw and broke her tread. Beneath her coat I could see a hospital shift. Her feet were in slippers, and her hair at the back was clotted with sweat. No one passed us. When we got to our rooms, we pulled out a drawer from the dresser, lined it with a soft blanket and placed the child in it. I lit a fire – for the room was icy – and made some broth. We sat for hours saying nothing, until I could bear the imposition of her silence no longer.

'You want to get rid of it, don't you?'

She nodded like a child being coaxed out of a sulk.

'But how? Where?'

'We'll leave it in the crib.'

We rose early on Christmas Eve. While Rosa fed the child, I gathered up what few belongings we needed to take with us and put them in a suitcase. I found a large plastic carrier bag to put the baby in. Then I had to leave and go to work. The day passed in a frenzy around me, while inside there was a stilled waiting. As usual, Penbridges gave each of us a small, wicker hamper packed with pieces of turkey, a bottle of wine, a pudding, and little jars of preserves, which I put to one side. The gesture, like all the others of the day, seemed at once endearing, and yet chilling, because this was a world I no longer inhabited. At five the store closed. We rushed to our lockers, changed out of our uniforms and then filed past the clock, which snapped our cards for a moment in its lips, registering our departure with a wheezing whir.

Rosa was sitting outside on the street, perched on the suitcase, the plastic bag sitting primly on her lap. I was suddenly very nervous. I took the bag from her and made my way back against the swell of the crowd. The store was in darkness but one of the managers was stretching up to shoot the last bolt on the door. I tapped on the glass. He peered out at me.

'What is it?' he cried.

'I've forgotten my hamper.'

He opened the door. I smiled at him, hoping he would not look down into the bag where I could hear faint movement.

'You girls are all the same.' He sighed. 'Go on, then.'

Although the store was dark I knew its alleyways by heart, and the light from the street cast a faint glow from which I could make out the outline of the escalator. I climbed up its frozen steps to the first floor. There was no one about. I made straight for the crib, pushing the pew aside so I could get closer. I lifted the shiny plastic baby out, and from the bag gathered up Rosa's frail child and placed it in the hollowed-out manger. It was sleeping and barely stirred as I settled it. Rosa was right – in the darkness no one would know the difference. The pale faces of Joseph and Mary looked down lovingly at the dark creature. I put the doll in the bag. I found its glassy eyes and puckered, rosebud smile unsettling, so I covered it up.

As I made my way down to the locker-room by a back stairway I thought for a moment about the child who would wake sometime in the night and wail, its cries echoing eerily around the empty store, which by then would be turning to coldness as the generators wound themselves down. I knew the pattern of the security men well. They would sit in their little box at the back entrance for the festive season, or go to a nearby pub and get quietly drunk. They would not hear the child, or if they did, would imagine it was some trick of the old building, releasing the daytime cries of hundreds of children slowly into the night. When they dismantled the crib in the new year they would find a creature as dead and as frozen as the one originally placed there. And Rosa and I would be far away. From the deserted locker-room, its metal cabinets closed firmly against me, I collected the hamper and put it in the bag. I passed out, unseen, by the staff entrance into a blind side-alley.

Rosa without her burden was almost gay. The Christmas lights strung across the scrawny neck of the street blinked dazedly. Hoarse-voiced hawkers thrust great bunches of balloons at us and frantic, whirring toys – furry creatures with metal hearts embedded deep within them, set off by the cold click of a key. We bought provisions – freshly baked bread, bottles of stout, eggs, a side of ham – because Father would have nothing in the house. From a stall I bought a pair of gold ear-rings for Rosa. She put them on there on the street, catching her thin lobes between her fingers as if each was a delicate scrap of gauze. We took the train home, crushed up against one another, rocking gently through the dark countryside, amid packages and boxes and bright peals of laughter.

For once, Father seemed pleased to see us. We swept through the house, cleaning and polishing. Rosa was energetic at first, scrubbing away at encrusted stains on the stove, but later she crumpled and I had to help her to the sagging double bed we shared in the back room. For the first time in years Father lit the Christmas candle and left it burning in the dark hollow of the window while we went to midnight mass together.

The village church was crowded. I was back once more in familiar territory, among women with soft, sloping shoulders cowled in downy coats. From the back it seemed they wore scarves of children's arms, while other small hands clawed excitedly at the crooks of their elbows. Behind us there was the scuffing of men and boys gathered at the back of the church, and as always that smell of candle grease, which as a child I thought was the smell of hair singeing in hell.

On Christmas morning Rosa and I moved the kitchen table into the arms of the bay window and threw a white cloth over it. The room was filled with bubbling smells as the ham and pudding spluttered on the stove. Father sat in his usual place by the fire, smiling moistly at us, as if sensing that it would be our last time together. He never asked about the child, although when we sat down to eat there were stains on Rosa's blouse – her milk was coming in and her swollen breasts were sore and tender.

After dinner he grew garrulous on the stout we had brought, and, as we cleared up, he began to sing in a voice entangled with phlegm:

There was an old woman and she lived in the woods
Weile, weile, wáile,
There was an old woman and she lived in the woods
Down by the river Sáile.

She had a baby three months old
Weile, weile, wáile,
She had a baby three months old
Down by the river Sáile.

She had a penknife long and sharp
Weile, weile, wáile,
She had a penknife long and sharp
Down by the river Sáile.

She stuck the penknife in the baby's heart
Weile, weile, wáile,
She stuck the penknife in the baby's heart
Down by the river Sáile . . .

From the scullery we joined in on the chorus, eyeing one another as we carried him through verse after verse. It made me wonder, as our voices rose and fell in ragged unison, if we all don't have murder in our hearts.

BONNIE BURNARD
Deer Heart

She wouldn't have gone on her own; two hundred miles across the prairie, it wasn't worth it. She'd read the embossed invitation immediately as a chance to be with her daughter, not the Queen, to be off with her on a long drive in the car, contained, remote, private.

The invitation hadn't come as a big surprise. She found herself, at forty-one, on some protocol list in Ottawa, the result of serving on a provincial board or two, the result of middle age. When she'd asked her daughter to join her at the luncheon the girl had said, 'What Queen?'

She was aware of orchestrating these spaces in time with each of the kids, she'd been doing it religiously since their father's departure. She would have named it instinct rather than wisdom. And they were good, the kids were fine; there was no bed-wetting, no nail-chewing, there were no nightmares, at least none severe enough to throw them from their beds and send them to her own in a cold sweat. If they did have nightmares, the quiet kind, they were still able to stand up in the morning with a smile, forgetful.

Her own acceptance, after nearly two years, took an unexpected form. She'd started files. One file contained the actual separation agreement, which listed all five of their names in full capitals, in bold type, the format generic and formal, applicable to any family; with the agreement she kept her list of the assets, the things that had to be valued against the day of final division. Another file held the information supplied by her government, little booklets on this aspect of family breakdown, supportive statistics on that. And the notification that she would be taxed differently, now that she was alone. In the third file she kept the letters. It was by far the thickest of the three, though growing more slowly now.

When the mailman began to leave these letters, casually tucked in with the usual bills and junk, she'd been dumbfounded. She'd sat on the couch with her morning coffee after the kids had gone to school unsealing, unfolding, reading one word after another, recognising the intent of the words as they arranged themselves into paragraphs of affection. A few of the letters contained almost honourable confessions of steamy fantasies, which apparently had been alive in the world for years, right under her nose. The words 'fond of' and 'hesitate' appeared more than once.

These men were in her circle, there was no reason to expect they would ever leave it. And they were, to a man, firmly and comfortably attached to women they would be wise to choose all over again, in spite of waists and enthusiasms as thick and diminished as her own. She disallowed all but one of the fantasies with laughter and common sense and a profound appreciation for the nerve behind the confessions.

Her defence, the time she gave in, had been what she called her net-gain theory, wherein she was able to explain that any increased contentment for her would mean an equal loss for some other woman, a broadside, with the result that nothing new had been created. Her admirer had stood with his hands on her hips and told her it wasn't her job to measure and distribute; he'd told her to relax. And she did relax, for about an hour.

She kept the letters. If she was hit by a truck on the way to the Tom Boy she would simply have to count on whoever went through her things to take care of them. The fireplace was just a few feet from her desk.

Her husband, her ex-husband, had found companionship more readily, young companionship, young smooth-skinned fertile companionship. A different marketplace altogether.

They began the drive to the small prairie city as she'd hoped, like an excursion. They stopped for gas and ju-jubes and two cans of Five Alive. They talked about school and the broad wheatland through which they were moving. She pointed out how bone-dry it all was, told the girl how rain would change the colour of the landscape and how this in turn would change the economy of the province. And she told her that when she was twelve she'd kept several scrapbooks with Queen Elizabeth II emblazoned on the cover, had filled them with this woman's life, her marriage and coronation, the magnificent christening gowns worn by her children, her scrappy younger sister, in love. She confessed all her young need for romance.

Then, without deliberation, she confessed how easily the romance had given way to tacky glamour, Ricky Nelson and James Dean, Brenda Lee. And how easily the glamour had been overtaken by Lightfoot, and Joni Mitchell, and Dylan. She tried to explain Dylan, what she took from him, without much success. The old intellectual distancing from all things usual sounded arrogant and smug, and predictable. She didn't confess the next phase, the disdain, though she'd been happy to discover it at the time. She'd used it, while it lasted, without restraint.

The girl took it all in and asked the right questions, to please her. And then they were silent, cosy in the car, and she set the cruise control and began to dream a little. She was interrupted by some of the questions she hoped might take their opportunity on this drive. There was a boy. Of course, there was a boy.

'Why can't he just talk to me normally? I haven't changed,' and, 'Why does he have to sneak looks at me all of a sudden?'

Old questions, easy to answer.

'Were you pretty?' Shared, intimate laughter, for the first time.

She told the truth as she knew it. She named the longing and the confusion and the hope of a crush and gave it a history common to all mankind.

When they arrived they had only to find the arena and it wasn't hard. The place was more or less deserted except for the parking lot and the streets leading into it. She guessed maybe a couple of thousand people would be involved in this little affair. She parked the car and they cut across the parched, leaf-covered ball-diamond to the arena. Inside they found the washroom and freshened up together, the girl imitating her mother's moves, though with her own style. At the entrance to the huge, high-beamed room which would in a month or perhaps even sooner be transformed into a hockey rink she found the invitation in her bag and handed it to a uniformed woman.

They waited only a few moments at their seats at the long table, and then the orchestra, from the area of the penalty box, began 'God Save the Queen'. They stood up and in she came – in a hot-pink wool coat and a trim little hot-pink hat, visible to all, waving and nodding with a fixed, flat smile.

She regretted not wearing what she'd wanted to wear, her cherry-red coat and her dead mother's fox stole, which she kept wrapped in tissue in her closet, an absurdity now with its cold glassy nose and the hooks sewn into the paws; she had no idea why she loved it and longed to wear it, somewhere, before she grew old. She had her mother's opal ring, which she sometimes wore, so it wasn't that. There was a prayer, for the Queen, for the country, for rain, and then the heavy noise of 2,000 chairs being scraped over the cold cement floor. Prairie people, in expensive suits and silk dresses and elegant felt hats sitting down to eat a roast-beef dinner for lunch.

She talked superficially and politely to the people around them at their table and her daughter listened and tried a couple of superficial lines of her own. 'Have you been looking forward to seeing the Queen?' she asked the woman across from her.

They didn't get to shake hands with the Royals, which was an obvious and unexpected disappointment for the girl, but they heard the Queen speak, crisply, about the settling of this land, about the native peoples, textbook talk. She was followed by government officials, unable to resist a go at the captive audience. And then the programme began, children in coy little dance groups, and choirs and a youth orchestra, and she could feel her daughter wanting to be up there on the stage, performing, taking the only chance she'd likely ever have to curtsey to someone. She wanted to tell her about Barbara Fromm saying there was no one she felt the need to curtsey to. She often caught herself wanting to hand over fully developed attitudes, to save the girl time, and trouble.

A couple of hours later, when it was over, they both gladly left the arena and drove to the outskirts of the city, where they found a new shopping mall. They wandered around together in the midst of sale signs and racks of last year's fashions and temporary counters filled with junk jewellery. The girl bought two pairs of ear-rings and did not ask why she never saw tiaras in jewellery stores, which was something she had wondered herself, when she was young. The prom queen, not her, not even a friend, had worn a tiara, so they must have been available then, somewhere. They were neither of them hungry, they'd eaten everything served to them, including pumpkin tarts, but they sat down to a diet Coke and watched everyone else who'd been at the luncheon wander around the mall. Then it was nearly five o'clock and she said they should get on the road. The girl had school in the morning, and the sitter might be getting tired.

'She looks so fat on TV,' she said. 'She's really not all that fat.' The girl laughed in complicity.

In the car, on a whim, she dug out the road map and found the big dam. They would have to take smaller, older roads to see it and she asked the girl if she was interested, told her it might take a little longer going home than coming, if they decided to venture off. 'Sure,' she said. 'Why not?'

She was glad the girl was game, capable of handling all this distance between their position here in the east-central part of this huge province and home.

She knew next to nothing about the dam, but she'd seen lots of others and she could improvise if she had to. They could get some books on it when they got home. There might even be a school project on it some day.

It would take about an hour and a half to get near it, and then some determining which little side roads to choose to get right up to the thing. She drove easily, there was no traffic left for the old highway, not with the new dead-straight four-lane fifty miles to the west. She felt confident, anticipating the curves, and, relaxed, she set the cruise control again. They cut through farmland and then into bush, far more bush than she'd seen in this province. The prairie ceased to be open and she began to wonder if this side trip was wise. The sun that remained was behind the trees, blocked, and dusk, she knew, would be brief. She put the headlights on. There had been a time when she loved being in the car in the dark, like a space traveller, someone chosen, the blue-white dash lights crucial, reliable, contributing precise information, the darkness around her body a release. Some of her best moments had been in dark cars.

The girl was quiet beside her, thinking. About the Queen? About her new ear-rings, which pair she would allow her sister to borrow if she promised not to leave them somewhere, or trade with a friend? About the boy who could no longer talk to her normally?

The deer appeared in the corner of her eye. It had every chance. It was thirty yards ahead of them, in the other lane. All it had to do was freeze. Or dive straight ahead, or veer left, lots of choices. She threw her arm across her daughter's chest, forgetting that she was belted in, and she kept her steering as steady as she could with just one firm hand. She braked deliberately, repeatedly. She did not slam the pedal to the floor. She locked her jaw. Just hold tight, she told the deer. Just close your eyes and hold tight. When it dived for the headlights she yelled, 'Shit,' and brought her arm away from the girl's chest back to the wheel. And then it was over. She'd hit it.

Before she could say don't look, the girl did. 'I think you took its leg off,' she said. 'Why didn't you stop? Why did you have to hit it?'

She saw again the right headlight coming into sudden, irrevocable contact with the tawny hindquarter, all in silence. The thump belonged to something else, seemed to come neither from the car nor from the deer.

'You killed a deer,' the girl said.

She pulled the car over to the side of the dark road and they sat there, waiting for her to do something. She put her hand on the door handle and unbuckled, but she made no further move. Wherever it was, it was beyond her help. Her daughter looked back again.

'He's in the ditch. I think he's trying to climb out of the ditch.'

'I'm sorry,' she said. 'I couldn't go off the road to save him. We'd be the ones in the ditch if I'd tried. I'm really sorry.'

She pulled slowly back on to the road and, remembering her seat belt, buckled up. She took note of the reading on the odometer.

'Are we just going to go?' the girl asked.

'I'll have to find someone to kill it,' she said. 'We'll stop in the next town. That's all there is to do. I don't feel really good about this either.'

The girl sat in silence, pushed down into her seat.

Ten minutes later there was a town, a small group of houses clustered around one long main street, the only sign of life the Sands Hotel. She pulled in and parked beside a blue half-ton.

'I'll just go in and talk to someone,' she said. 'You might as well wait here. I won't be long.'

She got out and walked to the front of the car. The fog lamp was bent like a wall-eye and the glass on the headlight was broken but there was no blood. She'd broken bones, not skin. She noticed for the first time a symbol on the Volvo's grille, the Greek symbol for the male, the circle with the arrow pointing off north-east. She remembered the first time she'd seen it, when she was a girl, wholeheartedly in love with Ben Casey, with his dark face and his big arms, a precursor to the men she would really love, later. And now it was later than later and here she was in a bleak prairie town with grey hair growing out of her head, with an angry adolescent in her car and a mangled deer twelve kilometres behind her on the road.

Inside the hotel she went directly to the young blond bartender to explain what she'd done, but she'd known the instant she was in the bar which of them would be the one to go back and find the deer and finish it off. They were sitting in a large group around a table, watching her, eight or ten of them in green and brown and plaid, drinking beer and coffee. She knew she looked ridiculous to them in her boots and her long dark trench coat with the oversized shoulders, like something out of a bad war movie. Still, they waited in well-mannered silence for her to speak.

'Talk to him,' the kid at the bar said, pointing. She approached the table and a couple of them, the older ones, tipped their hats. One of these hat-tippers leaned back in his chair and said, 'Pussycat, pussycat, where have you been?' and it took her a few stalled seconds to reply, 'I've been to London to visit the Queen.' He chuckled and saluted her with his coffee.

'I've hit a deer,' she said. 'About twelve kilometres back. I was wondering if someone could maybe take care of it.' She looked at the one she'd chosen.

'North?' he asked.

'Yes,' she said. 'On number 10.'

'How bad?' he asked.

'I think I pretty well ruined his hindquarters,' she said.

'Your car,' he said. 'I meant your car.' There was no laughter.

'The car's all right,' she said. 'I think my insurance will cover it.'

'You have to report it,' he said. 'You should phone the wildlife people. Unless you want to pay the two hundred deductible. You call and report it now, it's the deer's fault.'

'Is there a phone, then?' she asked.

He led her out of the bar into a cold back room. The light was amber, muted, dusty. There was a stained sink in the corner and a battered leather couch along one wall. The rest of the room was filled with liquor cases, stacked four feet high. There was a pay phone, and beside it, taped to the door frame, a list of phone numbers. He put his own quarter in and dialled the number for her.

She took the phone and talked to a woman who put her through to a man, and she gave him all the information she could, the time and location, her registration and licence numbers, her apologies. She couldn't tell him how old the deer might have been.

While she stood there, reporting the incident, the man stayed on the arm of the couch, watching her. She became aware of her perfume and her long, wild hair.

When she was finished he got up and stood beside her. 'Someone hits a deer here about once a week,' he said. He reached behind her head and turned down the collar of her trench coat, slowly. She would not have been surprised if his mouth had grazed her forehead. 'I can check your car.'

'The car's OK,' she said. 'The engine didn't take any damage.'

'Whatever,' he said.

'My daughter's out there,' she said. 'She's pretty upset.'

'Yeah,' he said. 'This kind of thing is hard on kids.'

Outside, he hunched down in the light from the hotel sign and ran his hand over the shattered glass. 'Looks like it was a young deer,' he said, standing up, stretching. He opened the car door for her and she climbed in behind the wheel. 'I'll go back for it,' he said. 'I've got my gun in the truck.'

'Thank you,' she said.

He tucked her coat around her legs and closed the door.

On the highway again, the girl listened to the explanation of the procedure. She sat in silence for a long time, her legs under her on the seat, trying, in spite of the seat belt, to curl up. When her mother turned on the radio, to some easy-listening music, she began.

'I don't see why she has to be there every weekend we go to Dad's,' she said. 'I don't see why we have to see her lying in bed in the morning. I think it's rude.'

'Where did this come from?' she asked. But she knew where it came from. It came from a very very young woman riding in a dark car through the bush with her mother.

'You could tell your dad if it bothers you, her being there when you are. Or I could, if you want me to.'

'I already have,' the girl said. 'He just tells her. They don't care.'

'Your dad cares,' she said. 'He's not himself. He misses you, he's told me.'

'She bought that nightshirt I wanted, the mauve one,' she said. 'She bought it for herself. And she doesn't get dressed till lunchtime.' She reached for the radio and punched in a rock station. 'She's everywhere you look.'

'That's why you changed your mind about the nightshirt?' she asked.

There was no answer.

The young lady in question had not shown any particular skill at the unenviable task of winning the affections of a middle-aged man's half-grown kids. Though she'd tried. One weekend she'd even done their wash, an effort to appease the mother who bitched about sending them off clean and getting them back, always, in disorder. When they got home they'd stood in the kitchen emptying their weekend bags, showing off their clean clothes. In her pile, the girl discovered pink bikini panties not her own. She tossed them across the room to her sister, who screeched and pitched them like a live hand-grenade to her defenceless brother, who cringed at the sight of panties of any kind.

'She loves your dad,' she said.

'Because you won't,' the girl said.

'I'll talk to him,' she offered.

'Don't bother,' the girl said. 'I'll just get a lecture about how everyone's got a right to be happy and all that crap.'

'It's not crap,' she said.

She wanted to be his wife again, just for a little while. She wanted to talk to him about what people, very young people, had a right to. She'd heard more than once, from her friends, from the inarticulate counsellor, from a home-makers' magazine, the theory that kids could withstand a lot. All you had to do was look around you, all these kids, carrying right on. She bought into it herself, sometimes, taking pride in their hard-won stability, their distracted smiles. Good little pluggers.

The girl stared out her window, watching the bush. 'Don't ever expect me to say good morning to some boyfriend of yours.'

'No,' she said. 'I won't be expecting that.'

They drove on. She could think of nothing light and harmless to say, nothing would come.

'I saw this TV show,' she said, hesitating.

The girl waited.

'There was a woman standing in front of a mirror, she was very unhappy. It was just a dumb mini-series. Anyway, she was standing talking into this mirror, to someone behind her, and she said when she was a kid she'd been driving with her father in a car, at night, like we are, and it was winter, there was a lot of snow, and they saw a deer draped over a fence. It was dead. She said she began to cry and her father told her it was all right. He told her that deer have a trick. When they're trapped like that they don't have to wait to die. They can make their hearts explode.'

'A trick,' the girl said.

'I think it would be fright,' she said. 'I think it would be a heart attack brought on by fright. That would be the real explanation. But it means that our deer could be out of its misery before the man gets to it, maybe could have been even before we left it in the ditch.'

Even as she recited this she knew it was unlikely. She assumed the deer was back there dying, not far from the ditch, the hard way. It would likely see him approach, hear the soft, 'Easy now. Easy.'

And she knew that one of them would hold the deer in her mind for a long time, the deer not dying, but fully alive in the bright shock of the headlights. And that the other would hold it just as long cold, wide-eyed, after the hunter.

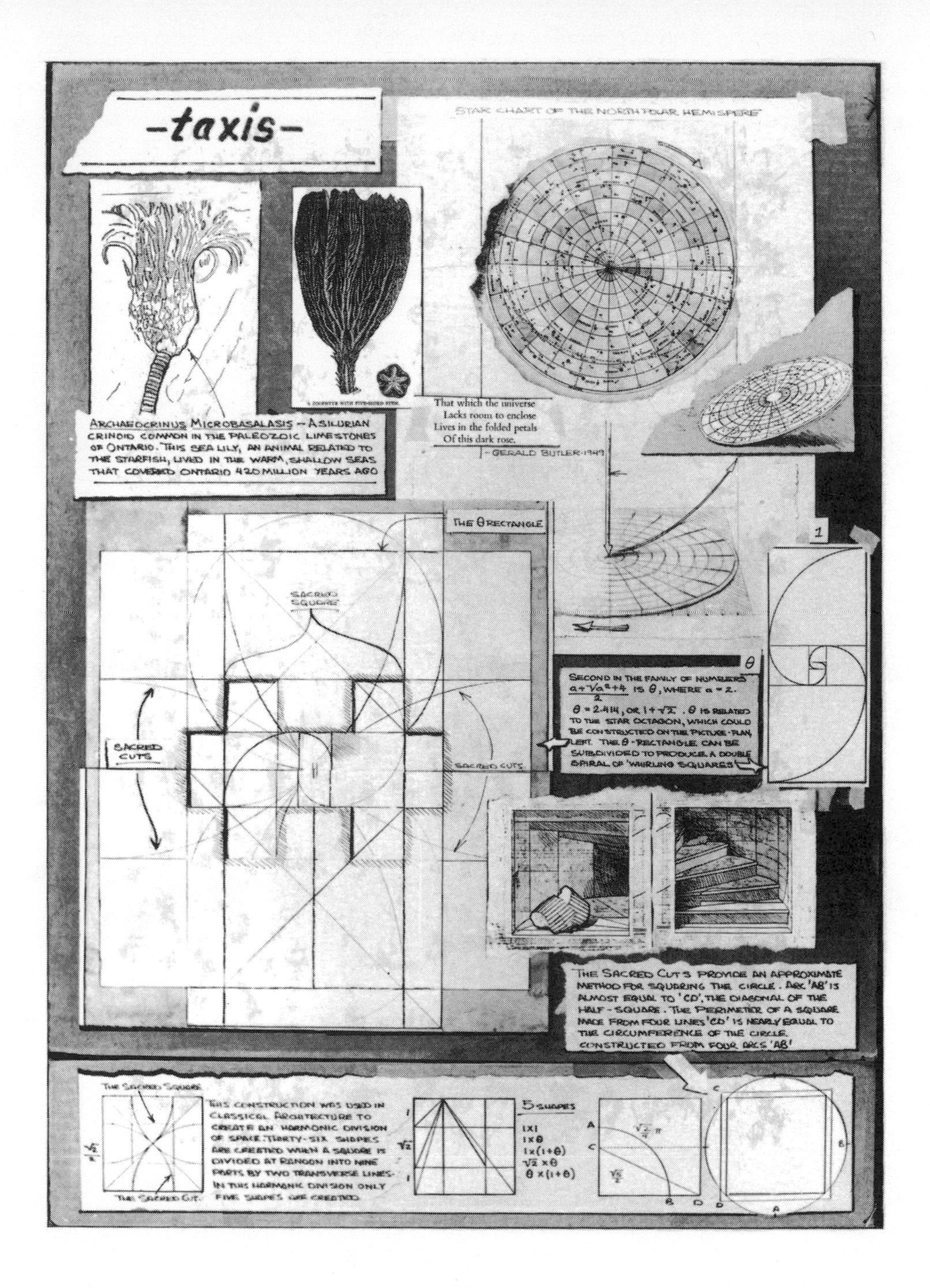

-taxis-
STAR CHART OF THE NORTH POLAR HEMISPERE
ARCHAEOCRINUS MICROBASALASIS – A SILURIAN CRINOID COMMON IN THE PALEOZOIC LIMESTONES OF ONTARIO. THIS SEA LILY, AN ANIMAL RELATED TO THE STARFISH, LIVED IN THE WARM, SHALLOW SEAS THAT COVERED ONTARIO 420 MILLION YEARS AGO
That which the universe
Lacks room to enclose
Lives in the folded petals
Of this dark rose.
– GERALD BUTLER 1949
THE θ RECTANGLE
1
SACRED SQUARE
SACRED CUTS
SACRED CUTS
θ
SECOND IN THE FAMILY OF NUMBERS $\frac{a+\sqrt{a^2+4}}{2}$ IS θ, WHERE a = 2. θ = 2.414, OR 1 + √2 . θ IS RELATED TO THE STAR OCTAGON, WHICH COULD BE CONSTRUCTED ON THE PICTURE-PLAN, LEFT. THE θ-RECTANGLE CAN BE SUBDIVIDED TO PRODUCE A DOUBLE SPIRAL OF 'WHIRLING SQUARES'
THE SACRED CUTS PROVIDE AN APPROXIMATE METHOD FOR SQUARING THE CIRCLE. ARC 'AB' IS ALMOST EQUAL TO 'CD', THE DIAGONAL OF THE HALF-SQUARE. THE PERIMETER OF A SQUARE MADE FROM FOUR LINES 'CD' IS NEARLY EQUAL TO THE CIRCUMFERENCE OF THE CIRCLE CONSTRUCTED FROM FOUR ARCS 'AB'
THE SACRED SQUARE
THE SACRED CUT
THIS CONSTRUCTION WAS USED IN CLASSICAL ARCHITECTURE TO CREATE AN HARMONIC DIVISION OF SPACE. THIRTY-SIX SHAPES ARE CREATED WHEN A SQUARE IS DIVIDED AT RANDOM INTO NINE PARTS BY TWO TRANSVERSE LINES. IN THIS HARMONIC DIVISION ONLY FIVE SHAPES ARE CREATED.
5 SHAPES
1×1
1×θ
1×(1+θ)
√2 × θ
θ × (1+θ)
A
C
B
D

ALEJANDRA PIZARNIK

Four Poems

Being There

You stand guard in this room
where the fierce shadow is your own.

No silence except the words
you refuse to hear.

Signs on the walls
tell of a lovely absence.

(Let me not die
without seeing you again.)

Ransom

to Octavio Paz

And it is always the lilac garden on the other bank of the river. If the soul asks: is it still far? one should answer: on the other bank of the river, not this one, but that.

Lines Written in Escorial

I call out to you,
As long ago friend to friend,
in diminutive songs
fearful of dawn.

On Your Birthday

Receive this face of mine, beggarly, dumb.
Receive this love I have asked you for.
Receive what is in me which is you.

Translated by Alberto Manguel

living
on a river

URSULA K. LE GUIN

Texts

Messages came, Johanna thought, usually years too late, or years before one could crack their code or had even learned the language they were in. Yet they came increasingly often and were so urgent, so compelling in their demand that she read them, that she do something, as to force her at last to take refuge from them. She rented, for the month of January, a little house with no telephone in a seaside town that had no mail delivery. She had stayed there several times in summer; winter, as she had hoped, was even quieter than summer. A whole day would go by without her hearing or speaking a word. She did not buy the paper or turn on the television, and the one morning she thought she ought to find some news on the radio she got a programme in Finnish from Astoria. But the messages still came. Words were everywhere.

Literate clothing was no real problem. She remembered the first print dress she had ever seen, years ago, a genuine *print* dress with typography involved in the design – green on white, suitcases and hibiscus and the names *Riviera* and *Capri* and *Paris* occurring rather blobbily from shoulderseam to hem, sometimes right side up, sometimes upside down. Then it had been, as the saleswoman said, very unusual. Now it was hard to find a T-shirt that did not urge political action, or quote lengthily from a dead physicist, or at least mention the town it was for sale in. All this she had coped with, she had even worn. But too many things were becoming legible.

She had noticed in earlier years that the lines of foam left by waves on the sand after stormy weather lay sometimes in curves that looked like handwriting, cursive lines broken by spaces, as if in words; but it was not until she had been alone for over a fortnight and had walked many times down to Wreck Point and back that she found she could read the writing. It was a mild day, nearly windless, so that she did not have to march briskly but could mosey along between the foam-lines and the water's edge where the sand reflected the sky. Every now and then a quiet winter breaker driving up and up the beach would drive her and a few gulls ahead of it on to the drier sand; then as the wave receded she and the gulls would follow it back. There was not another soul on the long beach. The sand lay as firm and even as a pad of pale-brown paper, and on it a recent wave at its high mark had left a complicated series of curves and bits of foam. The ribbons and loops and lengths of white looked so much like handwriting in chalk that she stopped, the way she would stop, half willingly, to read what people scratched in the sand in summer. Usually it was 'Jason and Karen' or paired initials in a heart; once, mysteriously and memorably, three initials and the dates 1973–1984, the only such inscription that spoke of a promise not made but broken. Whatever those eleven years had been – the length of a marriage? a child's life? – they were gone, and the letters and numbers also were gone when she came back by where they had been, with the tide rising. She had wondered then if the person who wrote them had written them to be erased. But these foam words lying on the brown sand now had been written by the erasing sea itself. If she could read them they might tell her a wisdom a good deal deeper and bitterer than she could possibly swallow.

Do I want to know what the sea writes? she thought, but at the same time she was already reading the foam, which, though in vaguely cuneiform blobs rather than letters of any alphabet, was perfectly legible as she walked along beside it. 'Yes,' it read, 'esse hes hetu tokye to' ossusess ekyes. Seham hute' u.' (When she wrote it down later she used the apostrophe to represent a kind of stop or click like the last sound in 'Yep!'.) As she read it over, backing up some yards to do so, it continued to say the same thing, so she walked up and down it several times and memorised it. Presently, as bubbles burst and the blobs began to shrink, it changed here and there to read: 'Yes, e hes etu kye to' ossusess kye. ham te u.' She felt that this was not significant change but mere loss, and kept the original text in mind. The water of the foam sank into the sand and the bubbles dried away till the marks and lines lessened into a faint lacework of dots and scraps, half legible. It looked enough like delicate bits of fancywork that she wondered if one could also read lace or crochet.

When she got home she wrote down the foam words so that she would not have to keep repeating them to remember them, and then she looked at the machine-made Quaker lace tablecloth on the little round dining table. It was not hard to read but was, as one might expect, rather dull. She made out the first line inside the border as 'pith wot pith wot pith wot' – interminably, with a 'dub' every thirty stitches where the border pattern interrupted.

But the lace collar she had picked up at a second-hand clothes store in Portland was a different matter entirely. It was handmade, hand-written. The script was small and very even. Like the Spenserian hand she had been taught fifty years ago in the first grade, it was ornate but surprisingly easy to read. 'My soul must go,' was the border, repeated many times. 'My soul must go, my soul must go,' and the fragile webs leading inward read: 'Sister, sister, sister, light the light.' And she did not know what she was to do, or how she was to do it.

122.75 PP VIIL CII @R40.

Keteymöwskimoneisky.*
(Sbronitkeisky)

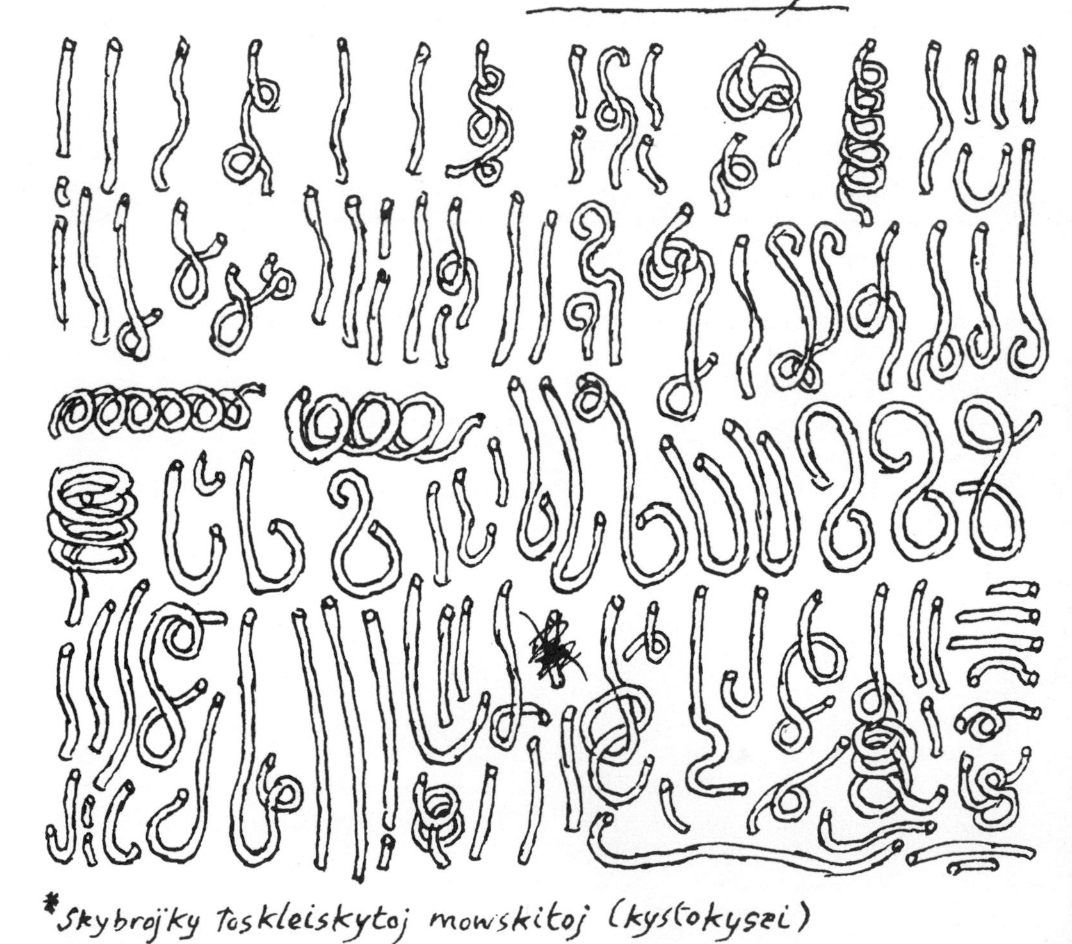

*Skybrojky Toskleiskytoj mowskitoj (kystokyszi)

IZAAK MANSK

Genesis According to Leon Hartman

*(from **Emil Brut**)*

They say He laboured for six days and on the seventh rested – to which some irreverent wit has added: and doubtless has been resting since.

But surely this cannot be true, if we accept the pronouncements of physicists and mathematicians. Moreover, I don't believe, nor have I ever believed, that He is an individual. It's inconceivable!

It may have been conceivable, perhaps, in that far-off day when everything was more one-dimensional, and that people, that ridiculous people, thought of Him so, as One. But even then, or even long before, He must have realised it couldn't remain a solo-deity performance. It had to expand – mathematically that was essential. And with expansion – as in government and commerce – there would have come delegation, co-ordination.

Yet where could He seek for those who would answer to His will, to His ineffable conceptions? Why, in *Himself*, since there was none other. He had to re-evolve Himself for other spheres of creation – sensible, inevitable – and so He became a corporation.

But a corporation, no matter how immaculately conceived, becomes corrupt by its very organisation: leads to favouritism, contention between the parties. And this too He was obliged to suffer: from Himself, or rather His selves, His surrogate selves.

We can imagine them, prancing arrogantly through the empyrean, these hubris-crazed siblings, feverishly planning this and that. Not the planets, or stars, or galaxies, or outward-pouring space, for that was *his* dominion, and Man, too – glorious, insubordinate Man – for want of any other model adumbrated in his image. And the more reasonable animals – those with four legs and two eyes – and the normal fishes and birds.

But the others! Those which fester yet in the bark of trees, or lurk under slimy stones. And the protein-devouring monstrosities – vipers of the viral world. Then the unspeakable proliferations with hairy microscopic appendages, which sliver in crevices or through the sludge of the ocean floor – perpetuated anachronisms of *creatio dementiae.* And the world of the bacterium and parasite. And those too which did not survive – those aborted miscreations which nibbled the tops of trees, or rent at each other's mountains of flesh.

Daily they came, gaily shrieking, into his presence, 'This have *I* made – and I, *this* – and *I* – and *I* – ' and He was appalled.

'But they will have no sustenance! You have been overborne by your mad enthusiasm.'

'Let them eat meat,' urged they. 'Let them devour each other, or those inferior in strength.'

'Ah, opinionated, wilful. You have undone my planning.'

'Like your precious Man,' persisted they, 'who already consumes his fellow.

'Listen! Listen well! You can hear them! The countless jaws cracking and scrunching. From the mountain peaks of Earth to its plains. From its plains and woods to its inhabited seas. Masticating, swallowing, belching, evacuating. The feast of the living, your species and ours.'

'I gave you a mandate for lesser creation, and asked for consultation.'

'Yea!' cried they. 'But you were vague, and not always ready to receive us, being abstracted with your mighty spatial problems. Nor were we sorry, for since we were restricted we sought to multiplicate in variety and quantity what we were denied in quality.

'We, who are you, and yet not you, were carried away, yea, it is true. But we regret nothing. It was fun!'

And He, whose words are always few, was silent. He, the physicist absolute, the mathematician absolute, progenitor of worlds in space, infinite theoretician of micro- and macro-cosmos, Lord of the Universe – discomfited by the demonocracy of His benighted progeny – withdrew from the pleroma . . .

Have you heard of the *tsimtsum*? It's an impossible concept propounded by certain kabbalists of the Middle Ages: they who wrestled day and night with the problem of evil in an ordainedly just world.

How could He, they asked, whose mercy and compassion embraced all living, allow His people to wander in exile: to suffer, to bleed, to endure nameless torments and death – and all this within His sight?

They were astute, those kabbalists, and only too aware of the metaphysical inconstancy. And out of their pain and horror they removed him to a point far in space: so far that even those infinite eyes and ears would not see, could not hear. They decreed for Him His own exile, where He could retreat within Himself, and eliminate from His pure Being those excrescences of evil which had attached themselves to Him.

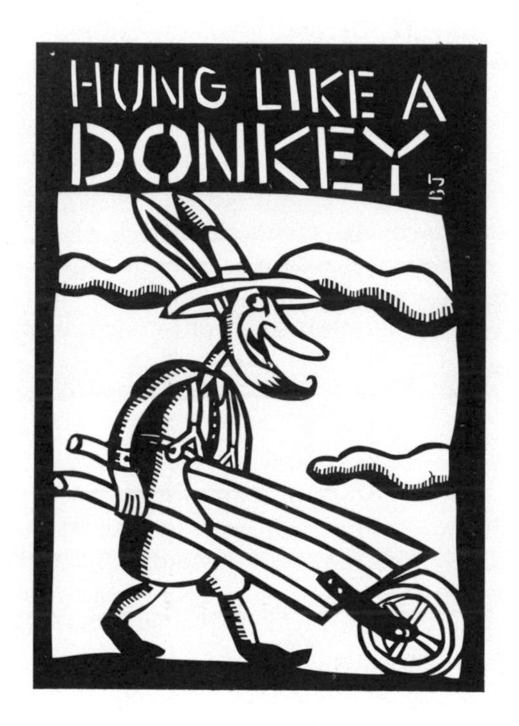
HUNG LIKE A
DONKEY
BJ

LAISSER
LE
PISSER
MERINOS
BJ
Than a
FULL
OF
MONKEYS
BJ
BJ
I COULD EAT A HORSE
MENAGER
BJ
LA CHEVRE ET LE CHOU

ROHINTON MISTRY
The Scream

The first time I heard the scream outside my window, I had just fallen asleep. It was many nights ago. The sound pierced the darkness like a needle. Behind it, it drew an invisible thread of pain.

The night was suffocating. There was no sign of rain. The terrible cry disturbed the dry, dusty air, then died in silence. Bullies, torturers, executioners, prefer silence. Exceptions are made: for their instruments' sounds, their own grunts of effort, their victims' agony. The rest is silence. No wisdom like silence. Silence is golden. I associated silence with virtuous people. Or at least harmless, inoffensive people. I was thinking of Trappist monks, of gurus and babas who take vows of silence. I was wrong. Even at my great age, there are things to learn.

The scream disturbed no one inside the flat. None in the building opened a window and poked out a head. The buildings across the road were also hushed. The light of the street lamp grew dimmer by far. No witnesses?

Could I have dreamt it? But the scream was followed by shrieks: 'Bachaav, bachaav!' Save me! yelled the man, help me, save me! I opened my eyes, there were more screams. Frightened, I shut my eyes. It was utterly horripilating. He appealed to his tormentor, or possibly tormentors. I was afraid to rise from my mattress and look out the window. He begged them to stop hitting, to please forgive. 'Mut maaro, maaf karo!'

That was many nights ago. But as soon as it gets dark and the light is switched off, I think of nothing else. If I do think of something else, sooner or later the scream returns. It comes like a disembodied hand to clutch my throat and choke my windpipe. Then it becomes difficult to fall asleep, especially at my age, with my many worries. Signs of trouble are everywhere. The seagulls screech. The seedlings are wilting and ready to die. The fishermen's glistening nets emerge from the sea, emptier than yesterday. All day long, there is shouting and fighting. Buses and lorries thunder past. Politicians make loud speeches, fanatics shriek bloodcurdling threats. And even at night there is no peace.

I sleep on a mattress on the floor, in the front room. In the front room the light is better. The dust lies thick on the furniture. The others use the back room. My place used to be there, too, among them. All night I could hear their orchestra of wind instruments, their philharmonia of dyspepsia, when, with the switching off of the lights, it was as if a conductor had raised his baton and given the downbeat, for it started immediately, the breathing, snoring, wheezing, sighing, coughing, belching, farting. Not that I was entirely silent myself. But at least my age gives me the right; pipes grown old cannot remain soundless. In that caliginous room, verging on the hypogean, with its dark nooks and corners, often the air would be inspissated before half the night was through. And yet, it was so much better than being alone, so much more comforting to lie amidst warm, albeit noisy, bodies when one's own grew less and less warm day by day.

Horripilating, caliginous, hypogean, inspissated. It pleases me that these words are not lost on you. But you wonder why I use them when gooseflesh, gloomy, hot, steamy, would work just as well. Patience. I am no show-off. Though I will readily admit that if words like these sit inside me unused for too long, they make me costive. A periodic purge is essential for an old man's well-being. At my age, well-being is a relative concept. So I repeat, I am no exhibitionist, this is not a manifestation of logorrhoea or wanton sesquipedalianism. At my age, there is no future in showing off. There are good reasons. Patience. Soon you will know.

All my life I have feared mice, starvation, and loneliness. Now that loneliness has arrived, it's not so bad. But I knew the others did not want me among them. For some reason I was a nuisance. Now I sleep in the front room on a mattress on the floor, wedged between the sofa and the baby grand. I am in a tight spot. One wrong turn and I could bruise a knee or crack my forehead. The others were only too glad to see me go. They even lay out my stained and lumpy mattress for me each night. Once, I pointed to the servant and said, 'Let him carry it.' 'He is not a servant, he is our son,' they said. 'Don't you recognise your own grandchild?'

Such liars. Always, such lies they tell me, always, to make me think I am losing my mind. And they carry my mattress, wearing their supererogatory airs, as if concerned about an old man's welfare. But I know the truth hiding in their hearts. They are poor actors. They think at my age I can no longer separate the genuine from the spurious, the real from the acted, so why make elaborate efforts to dissimulate. But they will know, when they are old like me, that untangling the enemy's skein of deceit becomes easier with the passing of time.

With your permission, I will give you an example. Sometimes I find it difficult to rise from my chair. So I call the servant, 'Chhokra, give me a hand.' If his masters are not watching, he comes at once. If they are, he ignores me, naturally, not wanting to cross them. Taking a leaf from their book, he even mocks me. I wonder why they spoil him so much. Servants are hard to find, yes. But to let him eat with them at table? Sleep in the same room, on a bed? And for me a mattress on the floor. What days have come. Whole world turning upside down.

My excuse for moving to the front room was to read till late. In the back room they used to say my old eyes were too weak to read past midnight, I must rest, I must not go blind, I must see my grandson grow and marry and have children. But my eyes were quickly forgotten as they carried out my torn, stained, lumpy mattress. 'Whatever pleases you,' they said. 'We are here on earth only to serve our elders.'

In the front room, sometimes I read, but more often, after switching off the light, I go to the window. There is a deep cement ledge on the inside, the window is recessed. Imagine a bay window that has retreated indoors. I sit on the ledge. Never for more than a few minutes, though. The cement is hard on my bones, on my shrivelled old-man arse of wrinkled skin-bags. But once it was firm, smooth, and bouncy. Once it was a bum that both men and women enjoyed gazing after. Not as deep as a well, nor as wide as a church door, thank God, but just the right size. Without blackheads or pimples, without any blemishes or irregularities whatsoever. Firm and smooth and bouncy are the precisely operative words. Not bouncy like a woman's, just enough so that if you were to slap or squeeze it in a friendly manner both of us would feel good.

The window ledge feels cool to the touch. You might think that a blessing in this hot climate. I don't. Not when I am craving warmth. Would you believe me if I told you the ones in the back room chill the ledge with slabs of ice, just to harass me?

The window is convenient for making water at night. The water closet is through the back room, and if I stumble past after the others are asleep, cursing and screaming follow me all the way. There are some bushes outside the window. The neighbourhood dogs use them. They do not mind me. An old man's water is pure H_2O, no smell, no colour. Nothing much left inside me, neither impurities nor substance.

I used to keep a large old milk bottle. I had labelled it Nocturnal Micturition Bottle, just to avoid mistakes, so no one might use it for something incompatible with piss. The ones in the back room said I had spelt it wrong, that it should be *a-t-i-o-n*, not *i-t-i-o-n*. Their audacity is immedicable. When I was young (and they were little), they used to ask me for meanings, spellings, explanations. I inculcated the dictionary habit in them. Now they question my spelling.

Like you. Yes yes, don't deny it. I see you reaching for the *OED*. No need to be so sneaky, do it openly and proudly, it is one of the finest acts. To know a word, its spelling, the very bowels of its meaning, the womb which gave it birth, is one of the few things left in life still worth doing.

Something strange happened after I began keeping the bottle. The volume of water I passed increased night by night. The one bottle was no longer enough. It would not surprise me if the others were slipping a diuretic into my food or medicine. Soon there were six milk bottles standing in a row at the foot of my mattress each night, all duly labelled. They were always full before the sun rose. At the crack of dawn I emptied them down the toilet bowl. I felt a pang of loss. Was there no better use for it? If India and China, and all the nations of the Third World, were to piss in unison, the land mass of the First World would disappear under a sea of urine. We could all take diuretics for a successful flood. Events thenceforth would be classified as ante-urinal or post-urinal. A new chapter in history could begin.

One night, a bottle slipped through my fingers while micturating. Piss and shards glinted on the floor. The others went on for days about it. My hands keep shaking because of this disease I have. They tell me there is no cure. Should I believe them? The doctor said the same thing, granted. But how long does it take to bribe a doctor, slip him a few rupees?

The first night of the scream, I was not reading or sitting on the ledge or micturating. I was asleep. Then the scream rose in the street, the man begged for mercy. There was no mercy. He pleaded with them to be careful with his arm, it would break. It goaded them to more cruelty. He screamed again. Still no one awoke. Or they pretended not to.

Why do I have to listen to this, I asked myself. If only I could fall asleep again. So difficult, at my age. Oh so cruel, finding sleep after long searching, only to have it slip away. And afterwards? Only this, my scourge of worries and troubles. Sadhus agitating for a trade union. Cows spurning grass from strangers' hands. The snake charmer's flute enraging the cobra. Stubborn funeral pyres defying the kindling torch.

Afraid to rise from my mattress on the floor between the sofa and the baby grand to look out the window, I shivered and sweated. An upright would have made more sense than a baby grand, I thought. Lying in the darkness on the mattress, I could reach the pedals with my feet, or lift my arms to raise the lid and tickle the ivories, joining distantly in the back-room orchestra.

Once I took piano lessons, practising on the baby grand. After the second lesson my right-hand fingers were caught in a lift. Its doors, made from a mighty oak, closed on my hand. I did not scream. When I removed my hand the fingers were a good bit flattened. I smiled embarrassedly at my fellow passengers. There was no pain. My first thought was to restore the proper shape. I squeezed and kneaded the crushed fingers, comparing them to the undamaged left hand to make sure I was achieving the correct contours. I could hear faint crunches. Then I fainted.

If I listen hard, I can still hear those crunches of my bone fragments when I flex my fingers. Flexed in time and rhythm, they resemble dim castanets. I can do Spanish Gypsy Dance and Malagueña. Nowadays, the only person who plays the piano is the servant boy. Makes no sense to me. A piano for a servant, denying my mattress the floor space.

The other night a mouse ran over my ankles on the mattress. That was not unusual. Almost every night a mouse brushes my hands or feet. What was unusual was my feeling comforted by its touch. Happily, disgust and revulsion followed the pleasant sensation. Unusual responses can be disconcerting in old age. Never know what might happen next. I hated mice as a young man. I prefer to keep hating them as an old one. This way the world stays a safer place.

Mice nibble human toes without causing pain or waking the sleeper. The saliva of mice induces local anaesthesia, promotes coagulation, and curbs excessive bleeding. Their exhaled breath, blown with expert gentleness on the digits in question, is quite soothing till the morning comes.

I tell the ones in the back room about the mice, about my fears. They don't care. No doubt they would be pleased if one morning I woke up missing a few fingers or toes. They laugh at me. Whatever I say is for them a laughing matter, worthless rubbish. I am worthless, my thoughts are worthless, my words are worthless.

'Floccinaucinihilipilificators!' I screamed at them once, having lost my patience. Not comprehending, they laughed again, assuming I had lapsed into the galimatias of senescence.

You seem like a sensible person, not laughing. Thank you, I appreciate it. Doubtless you have also run into a mouse or two. If my knowledge of zoology, particularly the feeding habits of *Mus musculus*, impresses and interests you, I could tell you more. It does? Say no more. We shall return to it presently.

The screams on the street gave way to groaning. There were muffled thuds, blows landing on unprotected parts. Diaphragm, kidneys, stomach. Groaning again, then violent retching. I was sweating, I trembled, I wished it would end. The air was parched, if only there were thunder and rain. If there were screaming, and also thunder and rain, it might be bearable.

The mice leave the piano alone. They never run over the keys or romp among the wires and hammers. I keep hoping to hear plinks, plonks, and musical sounds in the night not of my making. Expectations created long, long ago by children's stories, I suspect. They have turned out to be lies, like so much else.

Flying cockroaches are as terrifying as mice. The secret is to keep a cool head when the whirring comes close to the face, switch on the light, take a slipper, stand absolutely still instead of flailing wildly, and then, when its flight pattern becomes predictable, to kill it on the wing. It's not as difficult as it sounds. I am proud to do it so well at my age. The family Blattidae, flying or non-flying, holds no fear for me. No, it is the insidious mouse with its anaesthetic saliva and soothing suspirations that I dread when darkness falls.

One night – another one, not the night of the scream or the soft and pleasing mouse – when I looked through the window, around midnight, unable to sleep as usual, a *chanawalla* came from the direction of Chaupatty, from the beach, his basket hanging from a sling round his neck. I smelled quantities of unsold gram and peanuts. A tin can with its mixture of chopped onions, coriander, chilli powder, pepper, and salt, along with a slice of lemon, added its aroma to the dry, rainless air. The tin-can mixture was optional: for those who wanted *masaala* gram or peanuts.

The ones in the back room have forbidden me all *masaala*. They say it causes a bad throat, tonsilitis, diarrhoea; and the burden of these sicknesses will fall on their heads. So they give me food insipid as saliva. And it always has too much salt or no salt. Deliberately, believe me. In the beginning it made me a little cross; I would yell and scream and throw the food about. Then I realised this was exactly what they wanted to see, to starve me to death. I abruptly changed my tactics. Now the worse the food tastes, the more I praise it. Their disappointed faces, deprived of the daily spectacle, are a sight. Of course they pretend to be glad that I am enjoying the food.

And their tricks do not stop at food. Even my medicine they deprive me of, disregarding the schedule prescribed by the doctor. Then, when my hands and feet shake more than ever, they point to them and say, 'See how sick you are? Let us take care of you. Be good, listen to what we say.' Such wickedness. Such tyranny. But I will get the better of them. One of these days they will forget to hide my cupboard key. Then I will be dressed and gone to my lawyer before they can say floccinaucinihilipilification.

The silhouette of the *chanawalla* and his neck-slung basket made me yearn for something. I could not identify the object of my yearning. He had a little wire-handled brazier to roast the gram and peanuts. A bit of charcoal glowed in the brazier. I wished I could reach through the window and feel the heat of that ember.

The *chanawalla* was accosted by three men. They jostled him viciously, though at first they seemed like friends. They grabbed handfuls – of gram or peanuts, I could not tell – and brazenly sauntered off. When the *chanawalla* walked under one of our dim Third-World street lamps, I saw tears on his face. It might have been sweat. He lifted a hand and wiped his face. Once my eyes were stronger than today. Strong and piercing was my gaze, powerful and intense my vision. Never a chance of confusing tears with sweat.

The men who sleep outside the building across the road were still awake. But they did not intercede on the *chanawalla*'s behalf. Most of them are very muscular fellows. They went about preparing for sleep as if nothing was happening. They might have been right. It is hard, at my age, to know if anything is happening.

Watching the muscular fellows is my favourite pastime at this hour. There is always laughing and joking as they unroll their beddings, strip down to their underpants, and take turns to use the tap in the alley beside the building. Pinching and slapping, pushing and shoving, they prepare for bed. Some share a bedding roll with a friend, cuddled under a threadbare cloth, hugging and comforting. I know what it is like, the yearning for comfort. Sometimes a woman appears. She spends a little time, then departs.

Unlike the one I live in, this building across the road includes a private nursing home, an accountant's office, residential flats, a twenty-four-hour horoscope and astrology service, a furniture store, a restaurant, an auto shop, and a huge godown in the basement whose windows look out at street level. Periodically, lorries with various gods and slogans painted on their sides arrive at the building. The muscular men load or unload the lorries during the day. They work at a flat, per-lorry rate, always in high spirits.

Sometimes the Prime Minister visits from the capital to consult the astrologer about a favourable time for introducing new legislation, or an auspicious month for holding general elections. Police cordon off the area, no one can pass in or out of the building. There are long traffic jams. People who want to obtain their rations, take children to school, give birth, or go to hospital, have to wait till the Prime Minister has finished with the nation's business.

The men who own the lorries also ask the astrologer's advice for a propitious time. The muscular men do not quibble about this. On the contrary, they are grateful: when the business was owned by unbelievers who did not take necessary precautions, a crate slipped and killed one of the muscular men.

On days when the stars forbid the loading of lorries, the men watch the traffic. Once, on just such an idle day, a beggar took a bun from the restaurant. The waiters gave chase to impress their manager. They caught him and thrashed him soundly before he could bite the bun. A policeman ran up to deliver the obligatory law-enforcement blows. The sun was very bright and hot. I was not squeamish about watching. I am not frightened of physical pain inflicted on others. Especially if it is in moderation. There was nothing excessive about the action. Not like the policemen in that very backward north-eastern state, poking rusty bicycle spokes in suspected criminals' eyes, then pouring in sulphuric acid.

The waiters took back the mangled bun. The muscular men produced a coin. They insisted that the beggar return to the restaurant and purchase the comestible with dignity. They stood around him, satisfied, and watched him eat it.

But the muscular men do not go to the rescue of the screamer. I cannot understand it. Nor can I understand, given my unsqueamish nature, why I cannot endure the screaming any more, the heart-rending cries which occur at intervals every night, after midnight. I am shivering, my sweat is cold, the night is dark, my knees are aching, my brow is feverish, I am running out of things like mice, cockroaches, *chanawallas*, to fill my mind: the scream and pain keep displacing them. The neighbour's dog begins to bark.

Brownie begins to bark. Brownie is the brother of another dog, Lucky, who died of rabies. The others in the back room like dogs, but blame me for their not keeping one. I would trip over the dog, they say, I would trip and fall and break my bones, and the burden of my broken bones would land squarely on their unprotected heads, they say.

Sometimes they bring Brownie in from next door to play with him, feed him the bones they save at mealtimes. Nowadays, they won't let me suck the marrowbones. They snatch them from my plate for Brownie. Even my marrow-spoon has been hidden away. The reason? A tiny bone splinter might choke me, they say. Always they have an excuse ready for the eyes and ears of the world. They try to teach Brownie to shake hands. The crotch-sniffing cur is not interested. He sticks his snout in my groin and knocks my onions around, like a performing seal. They, my onions, that is, hang lower and lower each day. What I would not give to have again my scrotum tight as a fig. Great care must be taken every time I sit. The indignities of old age. Shrinking cucumber, and enlarging onions. What fate. But that's the way the ball bounces.

What destiny. Everything is my fault, according to the ones in the back room. They are so brave when it comes to mistreating and subjugating an old man. They want to hear no more about the scream, they threaten me, it is all my imagination. Every day they tell me I am mad, crazy, insane. That I have lost my mind, my memory, my sense of reality.

But you be the judge. You form your own opinion. Weigh the evidence. Listen to my words, regard the concinnity of my phrases. Observe the elegant coherence of my narrative. Consider the precise depiction of my pathetic state. Does this sound like a crazy man's story?

Of course not. Take a minute, later on, I beseech you, to plead my case with the ones in the back room. It is no more and no less than your duty. Apathy is a sin. This old age did not come upon me without teaching me virtue and vice. I keep my promises. I am kind to the young and helpless. The young are seldom helpless.

Apathy is a sin. And yet, not one of them goes to help the screamer. How they can bear to sleep through it, night after night, I don't know. What heroes they were, though, that morning, when we found a drunkard under the stairs. He was asleep, clutching a khaki cloth bag containing three hubcaps. Stolen, everyone said at once. They shook him awake. Neighbours came to look. They asked him questions. He did not wish to answer. They kicked the desire into him. When he answered, they could not understand his thick-tongued mumbles. They have seen too many films, so of course they kicked him again. Blubbering, he took out a screwdriver from his pocket. 'Murderer!' they shouted, poking him over and over with the screwdriver. Somebody suggested he was dangerous, should be tied up. One of the heroes got some string. It was the flat kind, like a thin ribbon, with print on it: Asoomal Sweets. They tied him with it, trussed him like a stuffed bird.

What heroes. Not one dares to go out and look. The screams keep coming. I weep, I pray, but the screams do not stop. I sleep with two pillows. One under my aching head, the other between my withered thighs. Some mornings I have woken up to find the back-room heroes standing around my mattress on the floor. Standing around and laughing, pointing at the pillow between my thighs. I am silent then. I know the day will come when they too seek comfort in ways that seem laughable to others.

When the screams drive me over the edge of despair, when I am tired of weeping and praying, then I remove the pillow between my thighs and press it over my ears. Now the screaming stops.

In the morning I am neglected as usual while the back room comes to life. I open the curtain and look out. I scratch my low-slung onions. Men go about their business. The sun is hot already. There is shame and fatigue on their faces. Since the night of the first scream, I have begun to see this shame and fatigue everywhere. The ones in the back room also wear it.

The dust is thicker today on the furniture. I look in the cold, pitiless mirror. The reflection surprises me. Now I know with certainty: if the others have not already heard the screaming, the time is not far off. Soon it will pierce their beings and rob them of their rest. Their day will come. Their night will come. Poor creatures. My anger towards them is melting. All is forgiven.

The air is still dry, we wait for rain. The beggars have gone on strike. The fields are sere, the fishnets empty. The blackmarketeers have begun to hoard. People are filling the temples. The flies are dropping like men.

tiger

BUKKITINGGI
tiger

JANE URQUHART

The Inner Landscape of Saint Kathleen

1. The Miracle of the Locked Gate

After she had been seduced, betrayed and abandoned, Kate knew exactly what to do. 'I must,' she said to herself, 'drown myself in the Liffey as many a poor girl has before me. I must go down to the very bottom, to the mud of it. And then, if God has any mercy, I will drift out to sea before the next low tide and perhaps there become a mermaid with a drowned sailor for a lover.' But God himself had other plans for Kathleen and there were no sailors in them.

She stood sadly on Aston Quay near a wrought-iron gate which surmounted the ramp that led to the river. 'This is the gate,' Kathleen said to herself, running her hand along its spiked top, 'that opens into the other world, and this is the gate that shuts worldly life away for ever.'

And as she whispered these thoughts she opened the gate and closed it again, absently, ignoring the creaking of its rusted hinges and looking at the bottom of the Liffey which was exposed – it being low tide in an unusually dry season. Rubber tyres flourished there, and iron bedsteads, and refrigerators, and toilet bowls, and empty tin cans, and smashed bicycles. My life is like a smashed bicycle, thought Kathleen. I can ride it no longer so might just as well throw it in the Liffey. But not, she added mentally, till high tide.

Hours she spent, then, waiting for high tide, and finally, at dawn the following day, after she had finished quietly singing a song concerning seduction and betrayal, she perceived that deep water flowed beneath her. 'The Liffey has come home to Dublin,' she said aloud, 'and now I must make myself at home in the Liffey.' She crossed herself and pushed on the cold iron of the gate, finding, to her surprise, that it held fast. God, she suddenly knew, had locked the gate to the Liffey. She turned in wonder towards the rising sun and saw, instead, a shining disk with the number '4' emblazoned on it. She understood immediately. God wanted her to walk aimlessly all over the city for four hours. Then there would be a sign.

2. The Miracle of the Inner Landscape

Kathleen walked aimlessly up Grafton Street. She walked aimlessly down Dawson Street. She circumnavigated St Stephen's Green four times. She walked along Cuffe Street, Kevin Street, and turned right at Patrick Street. She took four turns around the inside of the great cathedral and during the fourth she received a meaningful look from the interior of an empty confessional. It was a black look, a vacant look, a look that said, *Search elsewhere – there is no light here and no one is home.* In later times, Saint Kathleen would refer to this look in her writings as *the black glance of furniture* and suggest that it was responsible for her belief that one should (as she did) turn away altogether from furniture – whether religious or secular – in one's quest for spiritual enlightenment.

Leaving the cathedral Kate consulted the gold watch she had cleverly removed from her lover's pocket minutes before his departure. It told her that she had exactly forty more minutes of aimless wandering to accomplish; and in order that it should be, in fact, aimless, and partly because of the message that had been given to her by the furniture of the world, Kathleen began to construct an inner landscape as she ambled along in a westerly direction.

It was a vague, as yet an unformed inner landscape. It was shaky, delicate, and had a tendency to list to the left – it being in the very early stages of creation. Various undecipherable organic shapes shimmered, grew, and shrank on its surface. It resembled, to some extent, a bouquet made of earth and string. Occasionally little rubber tyres appeared along its edges and then it resembled the low-tide Liffey. But not for long. As it was at this time merely the embryo of her inner landscape, it was, like all embryos, in a state of flux, growth and change. Soon it began to simplify itself and, as it became warmer, it began to cast off its garments – even the four tree-like growths that had attempted to form a grove near its centre. There is heat around this landscape in my mind, mused Kathleen, and there is simplicity.

She put the beginnings of her landscape aside for the moment and consulted her pocket watch. It was exactly four hours since she had begun the aimless wandering. She examined her surroundings and recognised by the smell, the crowds, and a cacophony of bird and animal sounds, the Dublin Zoological Gardens.

3. The Miracle of the Sleeping Camel

She was standing in front of a circular iron-mesh cage: a cage that, like the confessional, exuded a message. *There is light passing through me, there is light in me, this is* not *furniture and someone is home*, the cage seemed to say. But who is at home, Kathleen wondered, searching the cage's interior. And then she saw him. At first, until he twitched, she had mistaken him for a yellow-ochre rock – so sound asleep had he been – but now she had to admit to herself that he was, indeed, a camel. And what a camel! So old, so thin he was that his beautiful bones were evident all over his body. Kathleen understood at once. Her inner landscape was to be a desert, she was to fast, to become as old and thin as the camel, and the camel himself was to be her companion.

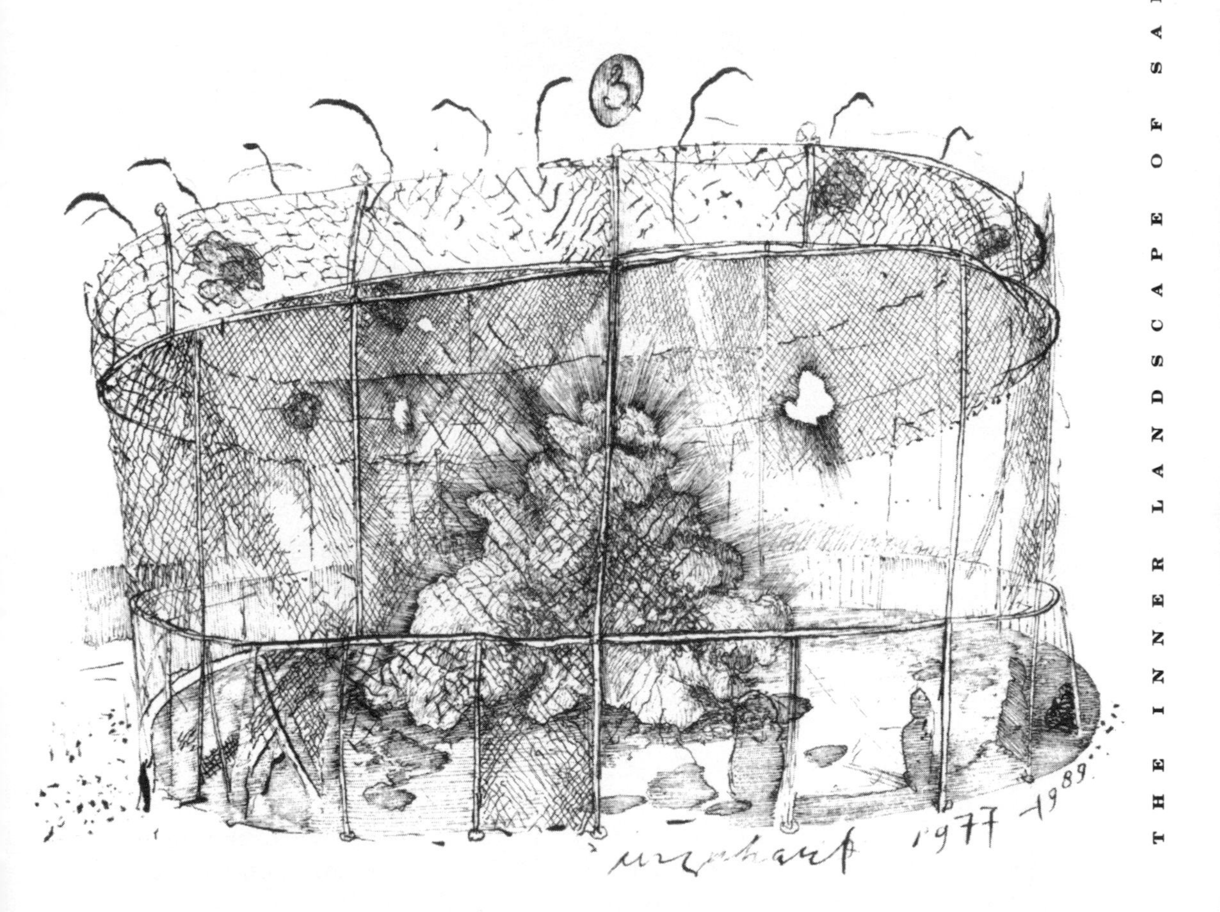

The camel suddenly awoke, looked at her, showed his yellow teeth and long eyelashes. Kathleen sank happily to the ground beside the cage. She spent the next week or so in that spot, busily refining her inner desert, experiencing mirages and entertaining the camel with songs of seduction and betrayal. She sustained herself by drinking one cup of water from the fountain each day and by eating four pieces of discarded, slightly soiled popcorn four times daily.

And had not saints before her withdrawn to the desert? Yes, they had. Had they not forsaken the world's furniture in order to more easily converse with God? Yes, they had. And had they not taken a beast as a companion? Indeed, they had!

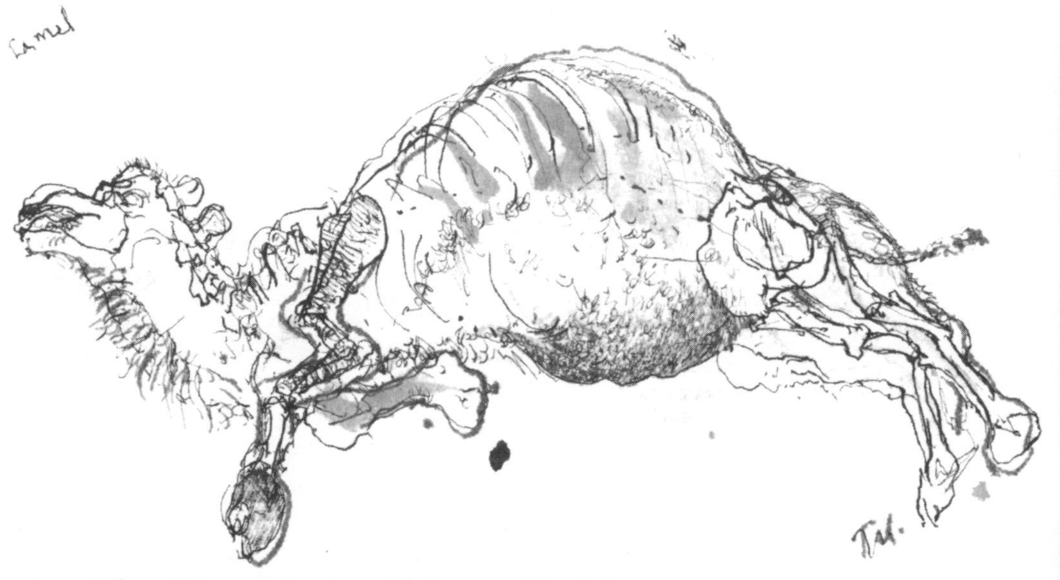

4. The Temptation of Saint Kathleen or the Miracle of the Potato Lobbing Machine

The inner desert is a suitable landscape for a saint to inhabit. Harsh, hot and hallucinatory, it is guaranteed to turn one's thoughts, most of the time, towards the *Great Omnipotent One*. But even saints with highly polished, perfected inner landscapes are subject to temptations from the outer world.

Ten days, forty swallows of water and 160 pieces of popcorn later, Kathleen encountered *The Potato*. Old, uncooked and sprouting, it fell at her feet from a basket that was carried past her by a fishwife with a gaggle of noisy children. There it lay, leering up at her, all eyes and hair and teeth. Suddenly its mouth burst open at the bottom. 'Eat me!' it demanded.

Although the camel had looked at the vegetable only once and had then walked disdainfully away, Kathleen knew that this was not a potato to ignore.

'Eat me!' the potato said again.

At this point four Nubian slaves carried a small construction into Kathleen's inner landscape. 'This,' they said in Egyptian, 'is a potato-lobbing machine. This can be used to send the potato far, far away from you. It can also be used as spiritual weaponry with which to conquer doubt.'

One of the most miraculous aspects of this miracle was that Kathleen was able to understand Egyptian.

The next day the potato had completely disappeared.

5. Her Death and Relics

Without the furniture of the world, and with only wire mesh between them, Kathleen and her camel lived happily, side by side, for many years. Even though popcorn fell like manna, daily, the saint soon became as old, as thin, as wrinkled, and as yellow as her four-footed friend. The skies of her inner landscape were bright turquoise in the daytime and royal-blue with stars at night. Her sunsets were spectacular. Certain groups of Bedouins occasionally arrived, unfurled their colourful tents, and gathered them up again, busy with aimless wandering.

'I was once an aimless wanderer,' Kathleen told the camel. 'I was even once seduced, betrayed, and abandoned.'

The camel and the saint died on the same day – both at the age of forty.

It is said that Saint Kathleen's Reliquary sometimes appears in the low-tide riverbed near the locked gate of the Liffey. It has been described as being constructed of wrought-iron, camel hair, camel hide and the empty case of a gold pocket watch. In the centre of the case there is a small whitish lump that has been identified, variously, as a camel's tooth, a fragment of bone, or a piece of popcorn.

There is light in it and around it – the clear light of a desert landscape. It does not resemble the furniture of the world.

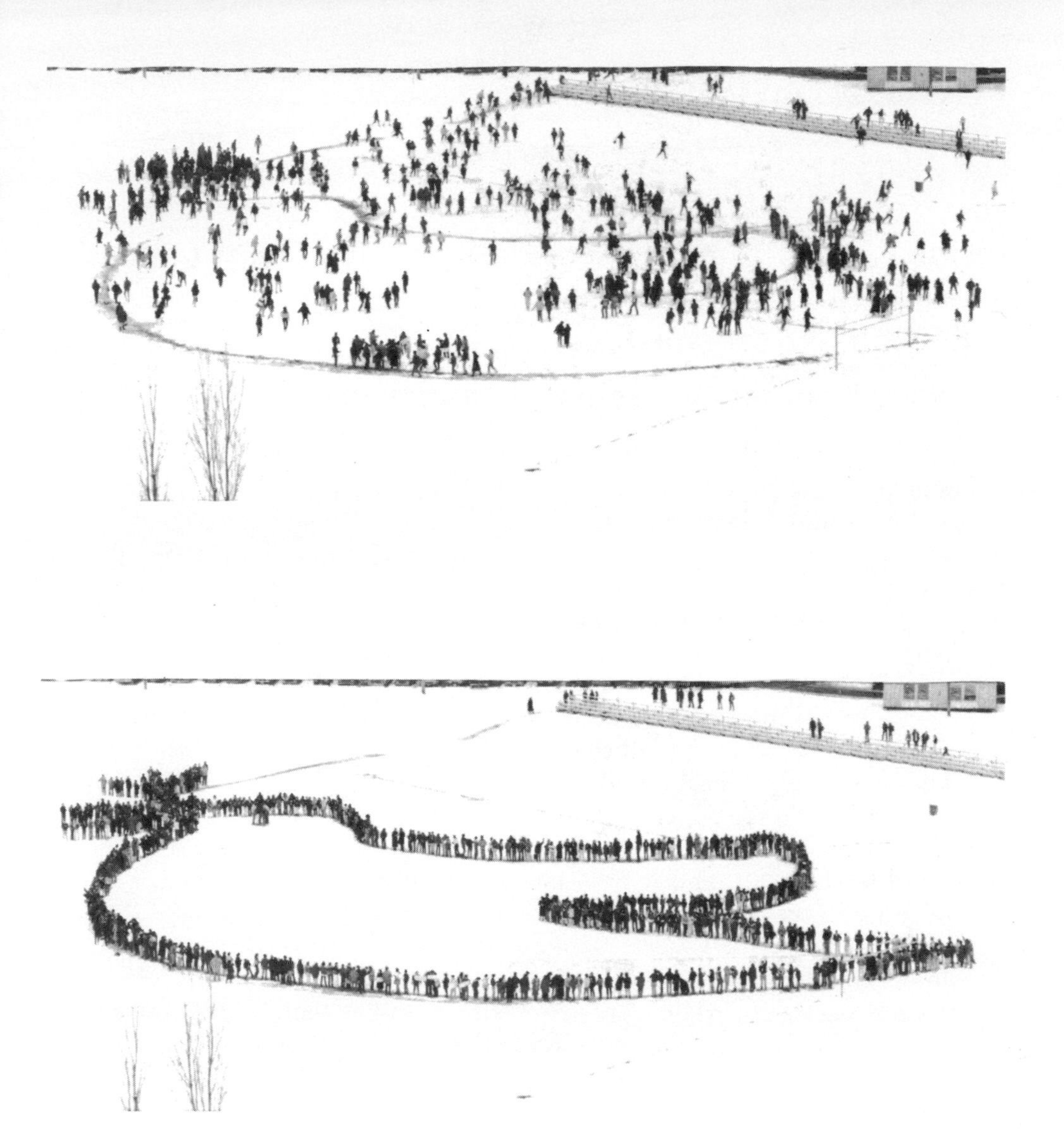

HARUKI MURAKAMI
A Perfect Day for Kangaroos

Inside the pen were four kangaroos: one male, two females, and finally a new-born baby.

In front of the kangaroos' pen were just the two of us. The zoo wasn't popular to begin with, and it was Monday morning to boot. The animals far outnumbered the visitors.

The object of our visit was, of course, the baby kangaroo. To my mind, it was the zoo's one and only attraction.

The baby kangaroo's birth had been announced in the 'local news' page of our daily paper. Since then, we had been waiting for just the right sort of morning to go see it. Yet that perfect morning never seemed to arrive. The first morning it was raining. The following morning it rained again. The morning after the ground was all muddy, and then there were two days of nasty wind. The next morning a rotten tooth was bothering her, and the morning after that I had to pay a visit to our local ward office.

A whole month passed in this fashion.

A month can do that, too, can't it, just fly past before you know it. And, for the life of me, I can't recall a single thing I did during that whole time. It feels like I did a whole lot, and it feels like I did nothing at all. Indeed, I had no idea a month had gone by until someone came on the last day to collect the newspaper money.

At any rate, the morning for viewing kangaroos finally arrived. We woke up at six, drew back the curtains, and ascertained at once that, beyond the shadow of a doubt, this was indeed perfect weather for kangaroos. We washed our faces, finished breakfast, did the laundry, put on hats to ward off the sun, and headed out.

'Honey,' she said on the train, 'the baby kangaroo – do you think it's still alive?'

'Yes, I guess so. There's been nothing about its death in the papers.'

'Well, maybe it's sick and in hospital somewhere.'

'They'd still report it.'

'Maybe it's turned neurotic and gone into seclusion.'

'Who, the baby?'

'Don't be silly. The mother, of course. Maybe she's holed up with the baby in that dark room they have at the back.'

Girls sure can dream up all kinds of possibilities, I thought admiringly.

'I can't help feeling this is our last chance to see a baby kangaroo,' she continued.

'Why do you say that?'

'Well, have you ever seen a baby kangaroo up to now?'

'No, I guess not.'

'And can you be confident you'll get another chance?'

'I don't know.'

'That's exactly why I'm worried.'

'Look,' I said. 'Even if you're right, I've never seen a whale swim either, or a giraffe give birth. So why make such a big deal about a baby kangaroo?'

'Because it's a baby kangaroo,' she said. 'That's why.'

I gave up and went back to reading my newspaper. I have yet to argue with a girl and win.

The baby kangaroo was, of course, still alive. He (or she) was much bigger than the newspaper photo had shown, and was energetically hopping about on the ground. It was not really a baby but a miniature kangaroo. She was a bit disappointed.

'It doesn't look like a baby any more.'

'It could still be called a baby,' I consoled her.

'We should have come here sooner.'

I went to the concession stand and bought two chocolate ice-creams. When I returned, she was still pressed against the fence gazing intently at the kangaroos.

'It's not a baby any more,' she repeated.

'Really?' I replied, passing her the ice-cream.

'A baby would still be in its mother's pouch.'

I nodded and licked my ice-cream.

'And this one's not.'

At any rate, we looked around for the mother. The father was easy to pick out. He was the biggest and most serene of the bunch. He was perusing the green leaves in his feed box with the air of a composer whose creativity had long since dried up. The other two were both females, identical in build, colour, and expression. Either could plausibly be the mother.

'Still,' I said, 'one is the mother and the other isn't.'

'Uh-huh.'

'So where does the one that isn't fit in?'

She said she didn't know.

Untouched by such concerns, the baby kangaroo hopped about, pausing here and there to dig meaningless holes in the ground with its front paws. It seemed to be a creature who didn't know what boredom was. It hopped around and around its father, stopped to nibble some grass, pawed at the earth, teased the two female kangaroos, sprawled out on the ground, and then got up and started racing around again.

'Why do kangaroos hop so fast?' she asked.

'To escape from their enemies.'

'Enemies? What enemies?'

'Human beings,' I said. 'Human beings kill them with boomerangs and eat their meat.'

'Why do the babies go in the pouch?'

'So that they can escape together. Babies can't run very fast.'

'So that means they're being protected, right?'

'Yes,' I said. 'Every child is well looked after.'

'Up until what age?'

I kicked myself for not having checked my illustrated encyclopaedia of animals beforehand. I should have known this was bound to happen.

'Until one or two months, I guess.'

'Well, this one's a month old,' she said, pointing at the baby kangaroo, 'which means it should still ride in the pouch.'

'Uh-huh,' I said. 'I guess so.'

'Boy, don't you think it would be great to curl up in a pouch like that?'

'Yes, I suppose so.'

'I wonder about Doraemon's pocket,' she said, mentioning the cartoon cat whose pocket held an endless supply of marvellous inventions. 'Do you suppose it's a kind of return to the womb?'

'I don't know.'

'I bet it is.'

The sun was really up now. Children's excited voices came drifting across from a nearby swimming pool. Summer clouds, with their distinct shapes, floated through the sky.

'Feel like something to eat?' I asked her.

'A hot-dog,' she said. 'And a Coke.'

The hot-dog stand was shaped like a wagon, and the young student running it had brought his big radio-cassette player. So while I waited for my hot-dogs, I was treated to songs by Stevie Wonder and Billy Joel.

When I returned to the kangaroos' pen, she shouted and pointed to one of the female kangaroos.

'Look! The baby's in the pouch!'

Sure enough, the baby had slipped into its mother's pouch, which was now immensely swollen. All that was poking out were two pointed ears and the tip of a tail.

'Wouldn't it be awfully heavy?'

'Kangaroos are very strong.'

'Really?'

'That's how they've survived up to now.'

Although she was standing in the blazing sun, the mother showed no trace of sweat. She looked as if she were taking a break in one of Aoyama Boulevard's fancy coffee-shops after finishing her midday shopping.

'So the baby is still being looked after, isn't it?'

'Uh-huh.'

'Do you suppose it's sleeping?'

'Probably.'

We ate our hot-dogs, drank our Cokes, and bade farewell to the kangaroos' pen.

When we left, the father kangaroo was still searching in his feed box for his lost score. Fused together, the baby kangaroo and its mother were being borne along by the flow of time, while the mysterious female was hopping about as if running a test on her tail.

It promised to be the first real scorcher in a long while.

'Honey,' she said. 'Wouldn't a beer be nice?'

'Sure would,' I said.

Translated by Ted Goosen

JOHN HAWKES
Sire

Note: the following excerpt is from a novel in progress narrated, in the first person, by a twenty-two-year-old former race horse who is attempting to understand his life at its end. The work is tentatively titled ***The Last Talking Horse****.*

In retrospect I have no idea how I managed to preserve my innocence for as long as I did. How, the very brink of maturation, I was able to remain oblivious to the fact that I, like every other horse, had been sired as well as carried and dropped. How it was that I gave not a thought to the stallion to whom I owed my life. Was I merely gulled by blissful arrogance into false security? Blinded by vanity to that other male horse in whose shadow, like it or not, I lived? Was fear the cause of it all or self-absorption? Weakness or peculiar strength? Whatever the case, such as my condition: to be more susceptible than most to the vulnerability of innocence. So much for my resolve to live by my wits and willed restraint. So much for my faith in consciousness. At least my loss of self-control was short-lived.

A shiny day. A grey day. A misty day. A grey misty day in spring with the morning light refracted through a prism of cool wet air. A day of disappearing wintry colours both subdued and bright. A day on which the death of an entire season occurs. A day of change when merely to be out of doors was to experience the exhilaration born of one time of year giving way to the next. Snow was two months past yet its scent was strong; dead leaves were turning green. The dampness was laden invisibly with melted snow and sunlight, wind and calm, and lay on everything it touched with the crystalline sheen of clear ice on still water. The surfaces of even the most dejected-looking tree or barn, animal or empty field, were rippling with life that was over, life to come.

On this grey day, when memories of the previous spring and the particularities of this day itself combined to swell my feelings of well-being, on this very day the contentment that had been mine in privacy was, all at once, no more. Innocuous moment. Half an hour of rude awakening.

I heard footsteps. I paused and, with a few strands of hay still hanging from between my lips, I turned my head, peered into the dimness, waited. It was the new girl, I recognised the smell of her and the sounds of the lazy way she walked, and suddenly I was certain that the new girl was coming down the aisleway for me. I was suspicious. I was on my guard. What business had such a girl with me? What business did she have at Millbank? She was large, she was big-chested, she smoked cigarettes and smoked them, as yet undetected by any person, here in the barn where as everyone knew and large signs clearly said, flames or sparks of any kind were forbidden. But this girl's voice was falsely cheerful, she was too familiar with horses and humans alike, mysteriously she spent a few days among us and then just as mysteriously and none too soon was gone, this nameless girl, this casual yet, I am still convinced, deliberate destroyer of my innocence.

'Hi there,' she said in her offensive voice, and without the slightest hesitation entered my stall, dared intrude into the comfortable space that was mine alone. Behind her the stall door stood ajar – had she no fear at all that I might bolt through that open door? My rope and halter dangled from her left hand.

'New shoes, big boy,' she said, and calmly, infuriatingly, reached up, grinning the while, and plucked the last wisps of hay from between my lips. The gesture so surprised me that I did not recoil, though in the next moment I stepped aside and stared down at her with eyes that should have frightened her but did not. She began to whistle – back went my ears – and still she did not respect me as a horse that might not tolerate such trifling. I tensed myself and yet submitted to the halter when she raised it and hooked her arm around my head and, in her clumsy indifferent fashion, managed to buckle my leather halter in place. I could have bared my teeth, given her a quick nip, threatened her with all my weight, made one swift movement as if to kick, but I did not. Never had I been approached and touched by such a girl, and now I was both repelled and fascinated by her self-centredness. Distaste was one thing, threats another, and harm or challenge this simple-minded full-bodied girl I would not. And yet and despite the strength of my forbearance, little did that big girl know how much she risked when, in the next moment, she drew down my head, puckered her lips and gave me a playful kiss on my broad nose. It was a kiss not kindly meant, a shocking liberty, and years later the second of her sort paid dearly for teasing me in just this way. Nonetheless I controlled myself, stayed docile, though I could not help but wonder how anyone could be as insensitive, as imperceptive, as was this girl in her tight grey sweatshirt and tight jeans.

She led me out of my stall, again she whistled; meekly enough I accompanied her down the wide road between the main barn towards the building set aside for the farrier's visits. We heard the steady ringing sounds of his work, already the girl's black hair was bright from the mist, I felt my own dark coat growing damp. All around us lay a sparkling wet world freshening moment by moment in the morning light. All was quiet, except for the girl's tuneless whistling and the rhythm of my footfalls that matched the rhythm of the farrier's hammer. Then suddenly we heard a burst of disruptive sounds that reached us from the round barn-like enclosure of the covering yard. Men's voices, silence. A burst of squealing, more silence. An angry clamour, a muffled shout, a horse's trumpeting. I had heard such sounds before, and now, as then, they aroused in me instantaneous dislike. So I changed my ambling walk to a jogging pace, the quicker to reach the farrier, who was a kindly man, and the quicker to put the covering yard behind me.

'Hey,' said the girl, 'not so fast!' and gave a yank on my lead rope, stopped me, turned me, started us off briskly in the direction of the very place I knew we should avoid. It loomed in the distance, that building with its circular and windowless walls and domed roof, and again from its interior came the sounds I feared. I hung back, the impatient girl gave a short encouraging laugh and pulled me on. By now we were thoroughly dampened, the girl and I, and in passing I noted that the wetter the girl became the livelier she grew, and the fleshier, the more spirited. She glanced up at me, she winked, she gave another little tug on my rope. What, I wondered, was wrong with her? How could she be this curious?

Unnoticed we stood just outside the open doorway; unnoticed we watched.

'Wow,' whispered the girl. 'Look at that!'

Well might she have so exclaimed, this mindless girl, though of all her disagreeable qualities it was her vulgar speech I deplored the most. However, for now I was as much the helpless witness as was she, and like her I stared with fixed attention at the scene in progress inside the covering yard and under its cluster of bright lights. But mine was a guilty attention while the girl's was not. This, after all, was the second time I had spied on the activities of one to whom I owed my life, and now my spying was unjustified beyond a doubt, a travesty I felt but could not understand. So with guilty absorption I stood in perfect stillness beside the excited girl and watched what no horse should ever be allowed to see.

In the centre of the yard's soft deep carpeting of dark earth stood none other than Winsome Kate, the bay matron I did not know well but had always admired. She was a trim pretty brood mare of uncommon sweetness. Now the lovely creature could not move, stood unnaturally out of her usual context of fields and foals, the pathetic object of what to me was a frenzy of senseless activity.

She was hobbled. Her left front leg was raised and sharply bent, and from it long leather straps extended to her hind legs where they were fastened to huge leather cuffs around each ankle. One attempted step and she would fall. She could not move, she could not kick or in any way defend herself. Spread atop her withers was an ungainly oft-stained leather shield, the ugly thing strapped to her withers like some monstrous parody of a saddle. It was a protective device, so that at least in the midst of this unwholesome business she could not be bitten. Finally there was the twitch, the small loop of rope twisted about her nose and affixed to a wooden handle held, this day, by the traitorous Jane, as I thought of her. No horse can bear pain applied to her nose and Jane had only to give the wooden handle the slightest turn in order to inflict on her sweating charge the worst kind of pain. Kate's passivity was thus ensured. Stand she must and stand she would – with raised tail and dimmed and daunted eyes.

'See him?' whispered the oddly eager girl whom by now I had quite forgotten. 'He's your dad!'

See him? How could I not see him? Great jet-black frantic stallion whose very urgency thwarted his own desire. Uncooperative to the two men, Jim and Bob, who wanted only to assist him to accomplish the conclusion of what for me was his inexplicable beastliness. There he was, struggling and straining against Bob and Jim, lunging backwards and attempting just as suddenly to rear, as the two men, more agile and wary, more serious and taxed than I had ever seen them, applied their energies to hold and manoeuvre him, Bob with his chain-and-leather lead rein, Jim darting in to push the black stallion this way and that. So of course I saw him – the wet black coat, the thin lightning flash of whiteness down his nose, the wide eyes bloodshot in lust and terror. But 'dad'? 'Dad'? How dare the girl, I thought – what did she mean? Though naturally from the first I had understood conceptually that this very stallion was my sire. Throughout my days at Millbank I had seen him occasionally, briefly, from far off. I knew him, I could recognise him, I knew that his name was Harod after one of the greatest of all racing horses from the distant past. Yes, I was one of his progeny, but over some vast number of years he had sired as many as twenty foals a year on twenty mares, so that Harod's progeny were like chaff in the wind. Such was I, only a slight and worthless speck in the cloud of life that Harod had loosed on the world. Now he stood before me, immense, intolerable, and I before him, unseen, unknown, unacknowledged. And no word could have been less appropriate to the stallion I now secretly confronted than 'dad'. Sire he was, and in this instant the emotional shock of that truth went through me. Sire, handsome ugly sire.

'Come on, old guy,' I heard her whispering. 'You can do it!'

Desperation filled the covering yard, the captive yet receptive mare turning her head and eyes in mute appeal to the stallion, Jane's forehead as slick with sweat as were the men's, whose task, of course, was dangerous. Most desperate of them all was the stallion who, it became apparent, had taken an unreasonable dislike to Kate and now wanted to rush the mare, to kick her as well as to somehow vent that larger longing which I perceived but still denied to my consciousness.

'He's ready!' cried Jim.

And now the stallion gave fresh and terrifying voice to his demented instincts, as I thought of them, tossing his great head to the left, the right. His jaws were wide, his eyes were white. The sounds he made might have been coming from my own silent and constricted throat, so keenly did I feel the pain of his lonely trumpeting. Yes, from my own torn and silent throat, and I listened in fear and watched in horror as the stallion, finally positioned to the rear of the mare, suddenly rose up like some greater-than-life-sized horse statue come to life, and, kicking and grappling with his front legs and flashing hooves, propped himself for an instant on Kate's haunches. Then he slipped, fell back to all fours, and Bob leapt out of his way, Jim cursed. Then up again went the stallion, hunching himself grotesquely atop the mare. His eyes rolled, his tongue hung foolishly from between his brutal jaws; aghast I saw poor Kate bracing her hindquarters beneath the weight of Harod. But down he fell a second time, lathered in rage and ignominy, then up again, Bob and Jim both pushing against his shoulders, then down, then up, and this time found his footing and kept his balance and stayed aloft on Winsome Kate like a ship on a rock.

'Hurray!' whispered the girl, and still she continued to stroke my neck – in the midst of this ordeal I had become aware of her palm and fingers circling distractedly on me – and still Jim and Bob applied themselves to the task at hand, and still the destructive scene was incomplete, brought to a near standstill in the centre of the soft, dark, brightly illumined earth. Harod clung to his post half buckled over the stalwart Kate; the eyes of the men were as fierce as those of the stallion; Jane's slight chest was heaving; at my side the dampened girl was stroking now my neck, now my flank, with increasingly insistent tenderness. How I detested the sight of my sire lolling clownishly above the patient mare; how I suffered the plight of the mare.

'Hold him!' I heard Jim say to Bob.

'Come on,' urged the girl under her breath. 'Give him a hand!'

And oddly enough, Jim, who could not possibly have heard that girl, none the less complied. He stooped, he reached down, swiftly and steadily he moved. I saw the sureness of Jim's grip, for an instant saw the flashing of his wedding band beneath my sire. Then Jim, suddenly quite calm, stepped away, and the mare shuddered and the stallion heaved.

'In situ!' Jim said, laughing and rubbing his hand on the seat of his breeches.

'Good boy!' whispered the girl.

Bob grinned, Jane smiled, I watched, and still the coupled mare and stallion struggled. A tiny bird flew past us into the covering yard and alighted, immediately took to the air again and fled the scene. Jane wiped her face on her arm, glanced casually at Kate. I watched, I waited.

Then, 'Done!' cried the girl in a triumphant whisper, and off slid Harod, more like some gigantic barnyard dog than a horse, and Kate slumped; quickly Jane removed the hobbles. Bob turned my now completely docile sire and, as if nothing of any consequence had taken place, prepared to lead him off.

There was little else. Except that in the midst of the now falling rain, midway between the covering yard and the outbuilding where the farrier waited, suddenly the girl tugged me once more to a halt and laughed, looked up at me. 'You're cute,' she said, giving a little yank on my mane. 'Just like your dad!'

aHaH
BOUM
1999

On s'évade profitant du grand Cacafouillage
305
221
74
88

DAVID BROOKS
The Wood

The line – is it a row of pines, doubled and redoubled acre after acre, channelled by property, the shape of fences, winter fields? – progresses relentlessly. I write 'a circle' but can you follow it? Accomplished – attempted – by repetition or a strategic reversal, an ostentatious coup de typographie, *you may feel, when you again reach 'circle', that you have been there, have come about, but have you? This trail laid, this long concatenation of footholds over snow, these stepping-stones over invisible water, these pines, may they not also be tit-bits, morsels, leading to a trap? And what is it, hunger, curiosity, desire, that drives you? Even as I turn you in foment, have you not really gone forward?*

I walk, when I enter the wood, alone. This is not only because, when I am walking there – when that is what I have chosen to do – it is the wood that I am walking in, and the presence of another can only be a distraction, but also because there is a sense in which you can never be alone there in the first place, and to be *not* alone – to take someone with you – is to distract you from the one that you are with already. Not only must you always follow or transgress paths that some other, in planting these rows, has laid, but there is always the feeling of a more immediate presence, a sense that you are somehow walking, if not at another's bidding, then within the wishes of another, and the almost certain knowledge that there are also others like yourself not walking with you, but walking none the less, pursuing a goal that may or may not be your own.

'I wanted to say how it was, you see, but the difficulties were insurmountable. It wasn't as if I could just open my mouth and let it issue forth (whatever the It was at the time: let's say the wood, the bed). I had to put it into words, to start with, and then explain why it was there at all. There were, you see, the problems of language *and* story. Wood, *I could have said, or* bed, *but anyone who might have heard me would have thought a different wood, a different bed, and to try to tie it down I would have to go into particulars, such as "snowy" or "trees" or "woman", and whenever this happened there was the question of order, of priorities: would "fence" come before "dark", "hair" before "scent" or "knife", and then what next?'*

In the wood I do not know whether to walk or to stand still. The trees look so much the same that, walking, I cannot tell whether I am making progress or simply retracing paths already taken. If this wood is like the others I have explored, the rows will be straight, and when one eventually reaches the end one will have the choice of striking out across the open field or looking for a road which might lead back to the lodge or, if one still has the energy, of turning back, having moved a little to one's left or right, and following another row to its end. And always, of course, there is the possibility that the wood one has chosen for this walk, today's walk, will be set out differently from those walked in before – the possibility that, instead of following straight lines, the rows will gently curve or meander, that one might be led in a great circle, or that – more peculiar, more frightening still – one has been lured into a maze that one might not escape before nightfall.

Can direction be abandoned? Something like lust, perhaps, or loving, intervenes. First clues must find a second; a pattern, an order must underlie the whole. Slowly, carefully, they – Franz? Margit? – are moving over the snow towards each other, or is it some third place, some goal, of which neither as yet knows, but which they both will recognise? Will they be reconciled there? Will they satisfy desire? Will they meet at all, or will one find only the trace of the other? And what is it that they, the traced, expect?

The tit-bits form a path, yes, but has another path disappeared among the trees? Forewarned, I have found one morsel, then another, and so have discovered a trail. But have I chosen correctly? Is the clue I have found the one that was placed out for me? Had I chosen another thing entirely, is it not just possible that then, too, I would have found a second, a third, and so determined quite a different direction? Even supposing that the path I have found or thus assembled is indeed the one that has been laid, what is its relation to that other – for I am sure there must have been a firmer, truer, *summer* path, closer to the contours of the land, respectful of obstacles, diversions on the way – beneath the snow? Indeed, now that I think of it, the message at the lodge spoke only of a trail, a wood, but a trail of what, and of this season or another? How long ago was the message left? Was it this wood? Was the snow here then?

The rules, the inveterate habits, the manifold stratagems of love, are in the snow, invest the air about them like the lack of temperature, the absence of humidity. Again and again one will come here, will revisit them with motive. And it will always be as one expected; it will always be as one thought; it will always be as thought.

The landscape in this region, if one could strip it bare of trees, would be found to be of gently rolling hills, of frequent easy inclines and declivities, so that one can never see sufficiently far ahead or behind to make sure that the path is straight. True, one might leave the row entirely – might pass at any time between the trees to the left or right into one of the other rows which flicker in a kind of Doppler effect on one's peripheral vision – or, ignoring the rows completely, break out into transverses, zig-zags or diagonals, but the choice of such defiance is laborious in the extreme, and one is quickly exhausted. Alternatively, of course, one might stand still – there is the exhilaration of silence, the joy of the stark winter lines, even the chance, perhaps, of a communion, a rare meeting – but in so doing one loses the benefit of the exercise one came for (if it was only that), and besides, it being midwinter, the cold, which one escapes while moving, all too soon catches up with one.

Truly there is path, but there is also desire for path.

Truly there is Margit, but there is also desire for Margit.

Sometimes as I am walking here I encounter someone sitting just as I am now, the wind moaning in the bare trees, the snow creaking whenever I move my feet, the blueness leaning out of everything. Sure, almost that they are not the person I have come to meet, I do not approach them very closely, never actually break through the row of trees, but from what I can see they are wearing a dark-blue coat much like my own, with the collar raised much as I want to raise it. Their hat – again, almost identical to mine – is too tightly drawn down for me to make out their features. All I can see, or think I see, between collar and brim, is the suggestion of a further darkness: a beard, perhaps, somewhat like this.

'. . . *and already, anyway, what might have begun in my head as* whole *wood,* whole *bed, was becoming a thing of highlights, selections strung out like a row of washing. Of course, it didn't* have *to be selections – at least, not* severe *selections – since I could probably have put a lot more in, but it would have been hours, days, pages, books, listing every twig, every detail of snow or sky, every hair or wrinkle in the sheet. And who would have read it? It wasn't* wood or bed *they cared about, or not much. It was* why *wood,* why *bed? And in trying to answer that you helped make the selection, the what of before determining the what of now and so forth. Besides, I didn't* remember *every twig, each strand of hair. It was as if, in seeing it in the first place, my eyes had already generalised, already made a selection before they told my mind the story. And all of this was only part of it: the selections, the priorities, weren't entirely up to me. Even when I got as close as I could to telling the story just as my eyes had told it there were rules, directions, in the language itself: whether* black *came before or after* trunk, *for example, and where that could go in a sentence.*'

One fantasises, of course. Perhaps, were I to approach in the belief that this person seated or leaning against a tree were in fact the person I have been summoned here to meet, there would be a sudden glint of steel, a blade from within the deep folds of the coat, or a glimpse of alluring nakedness – a white breast, a bone-pale thigh – before she moved off into the trees. Is it an old lover who has summoned me? Is it someone who wishes to kill me? Is it me at all? My collar drawn high and tightly about my face, my hat pulled low, it may be that even my own identity remains a mystery to those I almost encounter, and that I shall become heir to a signal, a fate that was never intended to be my own.

Can one abandon them? Can one return, like one who has outguessed them, or whose curiosity has now been satisfied, to whatever it is that one returns to over the white fields: a lodge, a waiting sleigh? In the pineforest it is very cold. Can you wait until the sun goes? Or are there perhaps too many things already urging you forward, locks without keys, rings without fingers, indecipherable whispers with the shape, the pattern, the undulation of words, names you think you have heard before?

It is only when I do not look too closely that the path seems clear. Head up, staring at a point some thirty or forty yards before me, the row is evident and I can move swiftly, almost unimpeded. Let me look at my feet, however, or some point just before them, and I slow down, I stumble, become easily distracted. When one has one row, one direction, in view, the trees seem all the same, like so many calibrations on a ruler. Look to the right or left, however, and one becomes the hub of a wheel, the rows extending out from oneself in all directions. But can this be? Is it possible that the whole forest has been so carefully planted that from any point within it rows extend to all points of the compass? Or is it merely an affliction of the percipient, the rows proliferating only to the extent that one allows them to, so that stillness, the stationary, becomes the position of greatest confusion, greatest possibility?

'That, the sentence was one of the hardest parts. It wasn't as if the story of the wood, the bed, could even be a seamless story. There had to be this grid, this fracture, like a fly's-eye view, and one sentence chosen that could go before another so that there would be an order of sentences just as, within them, there was an order of words, a hierarchy of things. And that wasn't all. Every sentence had to have a verb – that was part of the law – and, even in the simplest, one thing had to be on one side and another on the other. Wood *could never be just* wood, *or* bed *just* bed. *One had always to be doing something to the other. Even if you just said,* The wood was, *for example, it could never be that simple.* Time *and* doing *had already happened. You could say,* The wood was, *sure enough, but there would always be the question,* What*: the wood was* what*? And if the answer was just* wood, *The wood was* wood, *you had it being itself, doing something* to *itself, as if there could never be, in language, wood alone, but only wood* being *wood, wood that was never quite there as such, but always a little behind or apart or different from itself,* acting *itself as if it had alternatives.'*

When one stops, when one examines a tree or some fallen branches, the idea of the path begins to crumble. Is it a row of trees themselves that one should follow, or is it perhaps a trail of something *within* or *about* them? Should one be following not trees as such, but only those with a particular configuration of limbs, a certain gnarl, a distinctive scar in their bark? The very branches, once one looks at them, seem to point directions, sometimes with the form, the very texture of a human arm. And if one follows, if one casts one's eye as indicated, one is sure to find something which takes up the hint of a trail and so lures one further. When, sooner or later, one does slow down, examines more closely the things about one, allows oneself to be drawn along the trails that only then become apparent, it is less in the expectation that they will lead somewhere, although this is always a tantalising possibility, than to find out more about one's being led: whether, for example, it is something in the trees or in the self – whether signs, morsels, trails, or the appetite for them.

So many paths, so many stories of the wood. Which one is true? There is only one truth, and that is the relativity of truth. Even that is only a truth about truth.

How much do they know? It is not clear, for example, whether I am to meet or to be met, to approach or be approached. Are the others any better informed? Or do they wander with the same questions, the same speculations? It is not certain, for example, that the message was message at all, and not an answer, a quotation, a fragment of something quite different. Neither is it certain that there are others here at all and not phantasms, projections of myself, or that I have been brought here for anything other than to know, to see what is here.

'Can it be that the language cannot notice things that have not broken in two? Whether the brokenness is there already or something that the language makes can not be known, but clearly, once language happens, once it enters words, there is this little bit of time, of action, a fragment of story in everything.'

Staring up I see not branches only but the cones. The wood is ancient but these are something different. Falling to the ground, seeding, in the summer they are starved of light, but in this season, stark against the snow, the doomed saplings seem to form a counter-wood, a trace.

Franz's need for Margit, Margit's for Franz; what each gives unwittingly to the other to make them the other that they have. 'Truly there is Margit, but there is also desire for Margit.'

Dead branches, more twisted than the living trunks become, taking the shape of an arm or leg. This one, for instance, fallen into the barbed wire of a leafless blackberry, the clear outline of the letter *M*, its last stroke descending from a withered knee, the final serif the suggestion of a foot. Is there direction, trailness, or only the desire for direction? On its own, perhaps – one tree, one cone, one fallen branch – there is nothing but the thing itself. But if another is found, and then another?

The woods surround the lodge and intersect in such a manner that if one so desires one might continue walking there indefinitely, rarely if ever having to break into the open. There is also the possibility that this circle, this ring of plantations, might at some point intersect another, or that it meets one of those forests which stretch up into and over the mountains and extend toward the south. Those times, for example, when one finds the straight rows bending, breaking up, the parallel arrangement of the trees becoming erratic, or another beckons, or the trails multiply: is one then at the edge of something else? Something not planted, not cultivated, wild?

There is only one truth, and that is the relativity of truth. Even that is only a truth about truth.

But the wood?

ROBERT BRINGHURST

All the Desanctified Places

What is is what has happened, Hegel says,
and what has happened is what is
spread out through time.

Farmers and shopkeepers, labourers, coopers
and Quakers, they came like sprung prisoners,
beating the tongues of their women
out into wagon sprags, axeheads and spades,
beating their own ears into ploughshares.
It is written that history
is the saviour of nature, time
the saviour of space. What is there,
in that case, to sing of?
What is there to hear?

Fleeing Copernicus, fleeing from Galileo, they came,
refusing the news that what is
is bigger than history, that time
is the earth and the sky turning imperfect circles,
not God on his tall parade to the end of the line.

At Cuzco, Tenochtitlan, Acoma, Kitwancool,
the churches squat on the ruins.
At Pisaq and Tikal, Chaco Canyon, Tanu,
visitors gnaw at the moth-eaten light
with mechanical eyes. At Frijoles and Gila,
whole towns are trussed up in the webs
of our fences and service roads,
guardrails, turnstiles, interpretive signs:
the truth predigested in place, like a caught
moth, through the alchemical weight of our hands.

In Denver, Toronto, Los Angeles, Boston, Vancouver,

the motorised spirochetes move on their cancerous business,
the tumours of asphalt and neon enlarge,
and their beauty is visible from the aircraft,
like that of bacilli seen through the microscope in the lab.

The distance that brings what we do into focus
shrinks and increases; our legs
stay the same length. And the path from the kiva
is empty. Black trails unroll through the hills,
and sheetmetal thoroughbreds gleam at the kerbside.
This is the dance, now, and these are the masks,
worn at all seasons. Four-wheeled kachinas
live, year round, in the town. Therefore
the deer remain dead, and the pronghorn
are spooked by the fences.

Up the Xingu and Uraricoera:
the ashes still warm and the blood still fresh
in the logging slash. And the featureless mud
of the goldfields, pulped with a high-pressure hose.
The pitmines at Kimberley, Bingham and Cerro de Pasco.
At Alamogordo the acres of radioactive glass.
This is not history. This is the whipped
earth already ceasing to whimper,
closing her mask. In our presence
the real is frequently speechless.

What is is an idea recurrent in time,
and there is no end to it: not
your apocalypse, not your jihad
nor your sweetly machined Armageddon.
That is the wet dream of impotent men
and of overdosed children,
starved for the sight of the bright knife of the world,
looking for birth, touching death
and unsure of the difference, shouting *kapow*

and greening their knees on the manicured lawn.

At Gods' Narrows the children
play tag in the ditches, dodging the corpses
of dogs and the used plastic diapers
and Kleenex and Kotex and broken machines.
Their food has come 2,000 miles in bottles and cans.
Their bread, the colour and odour of old snow,
has come 500 miles in cellophane. Their songs
come to them weekly on tape from Tennessee.
What stories they have have been brought in a book
from a place without caribou, moose, wolf, lynx,
whiskeyjack, black spruce, tamarack, beaver or bear.
They are taught to call it the holy land.

Weaned from the earth, they are fed
on the eggwhite and sugar of visions
of life after death in a different world,
not on the meat of the knowledge that this
is that different world. I do not know how many
worlds, past, present, and future, exist.
I know there are many. I know,
nevertheless, there is no other world
than this, with its different faces, its trees
full of voices, its eyes like trap doors. What is
is not what we have built; it is what
we have not yet found time to destroy.

The hunger for life everlasting
will kill us. We know this. We ought not to care
for ourselves, but it is hard not to think
of the others: the trout, the mountain hemlock,
deermice, deer. Something will be here.
Being will be here. Beauty will be here.
But this beauty that visits us now will be gone.

The deer are as violent with trees

as wolves with the deer, and the number of beings
is many. The number of ideas of being
is many, though not beyond counting.
The size of the heart is the number of creatures.
The size of the mind is the number of species
of creatures. And I do not know how to measure
the depth of what is in the world, but I think
that when counting the gods, zero and one
are two answers equally useless.

What is is an idea recurrent in time,
but what is is right here. There are no blueprints
or duplicates elsewhere. Descriptions
and photographs will not do for rebuilding the world.

The stories are maps; the songs are not maps,
they are trails, like the hoofprints of elk
or the pawprints of bears. The waves of their shoulders
and hips are transcribed into particles.
All of it dances, and all of it falls
as it rises. The music is wordless: a sign
in the silence. No lyric, no hymn,
and no set of instructions descends from the spheres.

Song is edible thought but not seedgrain.
The singers bring in the hands of their voices
thought like dried meat
and thought like the light it is given
by water and oil.

I return to the earth's lap all that remains
of all she has given me: meals
for the eye, the belly, the hand – and what held them:
the mind like a mildewed jewel, ruined meat,
the crazy panpipes of the bones
that sang when certain women touched me
and when I touched the world.

The children of those who cross over
the water must wander. Their children's
children must swim through the ground.

But these aren't the words I set out to listen for.
There is a song I thought you should hear,
and a story that tells where to find it.
Year after year the song sinks deeper
under the sea cliffs. Year after year
it sings itself farther back into the hills.

JOSEPH SKVORECKY
from **The Miracle Game**

Vojtech's hands trembled with emotion as he took the rare and precious hand-written copy of Kopula's poem out of its velvet folder and, in his most sepulchral voice, began to read how the poet, who was already behind bars at the time of the miracle, imagined it to have been.

It was the first time he had read the work. Later, 'Litany to Joseph's Wife' made it as far as the Prague 'Hyde Park', where Novotny recited it to a crowd of 10,000 young men and women so wrapped up in their enormous and fantastical dreams that they were open to anything. But that first evening, he read it at what amounted to a private seance for a narrow circle of friends.

The devotions were held at the Novotnys' apartment, which consisted of a kitchen, a tiny bathroom, and a sitting-room that doubled as a bedroom for the parents and the two children. The room was lit with candles, and a large dish of small, round poppyseed cakes sat on a table, a culinary homage, perhaps, to the poet's Moravian roots. Under an enormous Candlemas candle with a cross of black wax on it sat Juzl, Vojtech's *intimus* – an expert on ecclesiastical art and an editor with the Catholic daily *Lidova Demokracie*. The son of a famous Catholic novelist, also deceased, sat on the threadbare couch with a rosary peering out of his pocket. On one side of him sat Vojtech's epigone, Sadovec, and on the other side the only person who didn't really belong there. She was not in Vojtech's circle at all; she was a colleague of Vixi's from the gynaecological clinic where Vixi had gone to work when the children were old enough. I had a strong suspicion that she was also Vixi's confidante in matters having nothing to do with Catholicism. She had dropped in unannounced, but when she saw the candles and the food she ignored the poet's pointed remarks about the lateness of the hour. Vojtech finally gave up and decided to let her stay for the privilege of the First Reading. He no doubt reasoned that, since the other Novotny – the dangerous president – had abdicated by then, there was no longer any risk.

In the end – and here again an incomprehensible Providence seemed to be at work – it was the uninvited guest who set the mad merry-go-round of Juzl's crime story spinning.

Vojtech gave a passionate reading of the work. Against all my expectations, it radiated a darkly poetic beauty, thus refuting the idealistic belief that truth alone gives greatness to literature.

All during the reading the unknown acquaintance noisily sampled the poppyseed cakes, and as soon as the poet had finished, she broke the sacred silence. She had a voice that grated with its innocent ignorance, like a film *ingénue's*. 'So what's this miracle all about?'

The woman's question hung in the silence like a blasphemy.

Vixi made a face at me behind her husband's back. Her part in the miracle, as well as the fact that I had once taught her social studies in the lilac-bowered town, had remained a secret between us. I saw Vixi's husband stiffen as a wave of righteous ire seemed to rise in him, and I was expecting a replay of the scene in that little Renaissance house beneath Prague Castle so long ago – only this time the fiery sword would be wielded by the one who had himself been driven out of paradise. But at the last moment, Juzl intervened.

'We're talking, of course, about the miracle that took place in the Chapel of the Virgin Mary under Mare's Head, in the spring of 1949,' he said drily. 'During a sermon delivered by Father Josef Doufal, an early baroque folk statue of Saint Joseph moved in a way that could only be explained as a *suspensio legis naturae* – a way that defied all natural law. Eyewitnesses claimed that the statue appeared to be giving a sign to the faithful.'

'Is this true?' asked the friend. With an apologetic grin at Vixi, she helped herself to another cake.

The novelist's son now joined the conversation. 'You mean to say you've never heard of it?' he asked tartly.

The *ingénue* shook her head, not realising that in the corpse-washer's household such ignorance amounted to complicity, *post factum*, in the regime's version of the event.

'Where in the world were you?' asked the novelist's son. 'The newspapers were full of it at the time! Of course, they went to great lengths to prove that it was no miracle at all,' he added sarcastically, more to the others than to her. 'In those days they could prove whatever they wanted.'

The woman quickly realised that frankness was out of place here and she began to backtrack. 'I mean . . . well, now that you mention it, I may have actually heard . . .'

I felt sorry for her and wanted to divert the conversation to the poem we'd just heard. But Vojtech had brought his anger under control, and when he spoke it was with the voice of Christian charity. 'We mustn't be too surprised that some people weren't aware of it. Don't forget, the whole affair was quickly hushed up, despite the fact that they'd sounded the trumpets so loudly at first. It was all very suspicious. The priest was never brought to trial, and that was the end of it.'

'Why wasn't he?' asked the *ingénue*.

The assembled company exchanged sad, knowing glances.

'Because to the best of our knowledge, miss,' said Vojtech, 'they tortured him to death before they could put him on trial. We don't have any concrete proof. But the priest wasn't the only one who vanished without a trace at that time. He had no next of kin, and people like that were easy to liquidate because who was there to take an interest in their fate?' He looked around with a bitter expression, then went on, 'I don't think there can be any doubt about it. Like Jan Kopula, Father Doufal died a martyr's death.'

The faithful nodded their heads, and the wick on the Candlemas candle above Juzl sputtered in the silence. Then the woman spoke again, but now she no longer sounded like the voice of blasphemy.

'What did you say the priest's name was?'

'Father Josef Doufal,' said Vojtech.

She thought for a moment, the cake suspended halfway to her mouth, while little wrinkles appeared at the base of her fleshy nose. I suddenly had an odd feeling, as though the group was sensing, collectively, that what she was about to say would have a bearing on the case – and that, once again, I was being touched by something predetermined. Of course, that could be said of any coincidence. If coincidences exist.

'Listen, I don't know if I should say this or not,' said the unknown acquaintance, 'but I guess it's all right to talk about it now. I mean, the papers are writing about all sorts of rotten stuff that went on, even the business about Jan Masaryk dying like that –' She still hesitated. The inhibitions of twenty years in a people's democracy were too powerful. Embarrassed, she looked at Vixi's husband.

With a kindly severity he said, 'What were you going to say, miss?'

'It was something strange that happened . . . I've never told anyone about it, because Dr Dvorak told me to keep my mouth shut, but –' She stopped, that habitual fear still struggling inside her. But the Prague Spring was building up a full head of steam now; the first madmen were revealing the truth about the various ignoble acts that together had constituted the noble class struggle; people were starting to feel the intoxication of non-dialectical freedom. The cake-eater too plucked up her courage. 'Still, it was practically twenty years ago,' she said, 'and even Nazi collaborators aren't punished any more –' She hesitated again.

The poet wanted to say something, but Juzl beat him to it. 'Of course. There's nothing to be afraid of, miss. Anything you say will be in strictest confidence, even though nowadays we all have a responsibility to – otherwise, how will we ensure that such things never happen again?'

He fixed her with an eager stare, and the woman began to spill the beans.

'I really don't remember anything about that miracle. But when you said his name – the thing is, I remember Dr Dvorak made a silly joke –'

'Joke?'

'I remember him saying to one of the nurses in reception, "So his name is Do-fall? Well, that was some fall he took. I don't give him much hope." That was when he was washing his hands after the operation. Doctors can get pretty cynical sometimes, as you probably know. But this Doufal was a lieutenant of some kind – that's what the policeman who brought him in said.'

The faithful exchanged meaningful glances.

'He was the first patient who ever ex'd out on me,' she went on. 'I'd just started working at the Military Hospital, that's how I remember the date.'

'And what was the date?'

'The summer of 1949.'

'What did he die of?'

'Well, the operation was for a perforated ulcer, at least that's what Dr Dvorak put down on the death certificate. But what it really was, I couldn't say. He was a real mess, though, I can tell you that.'

Once again the faithful exchanged glances, and I looked over at Vixi, who was staring at her friend with an expression that was not in her usual repertoire.

'What do you mean, "a real mess"?' Juzl probed gently.

'The cop said it was a car crash. Said they'd flipped their car. But I'd seen a few accident victims by that time. And the cop who brought him in didn't have a wrinkle or a tear in his uniform, let alone an injury – nothing – but he talked about "our car". The patient had a broken leg – fine, that fits. But then he had these strange bruises all over his body, and that doesn't make sense – at least, not that many. And the main thing was –' and again, as though astonished at herself for having said so much already, she stopped and looked around the room. 'I don't know. Should I say it?'

Juzl leaned over until he was close to her. His eyes were ablaze in the light of the Candlemas candle. I realised that I had seen just such a flame in the eyes of some Party members, back in the days before the flame had petered out. 'Miss,' he said, 'perhaps God has chosen you to testify to things that others can no longer testify to!'

Under the weight of such a trust, the woman nervously swallowed the rest of her cake and blurted, ‘Two things –’ Her voice faltered. ‘On his right hand, the patient’s fingernails were – missing,’ and she stopped, although this time what stopped her seemed to be the ugliness of her own memories. I glanced at Vixi; her eyes were closed and her jaw was clenched tight. Juzl had turned noticeably pale.

‘It must have been a strange car crash, is all I can say,’ said the woman. The room was silent. No one said a word.

‘What was the second thing?’ asked Juzl after a pause.

‘When they were taking him out of the operating room, I noticed his hair. It was thick and grey and it was cut short, but right here on his crown,’ and she reached up and touched her bun, ‘there was this small bald spot, like priests have done to them. I mean, it seemed strange, but they said he was a lieutenant and who was I to –’

She stopped. And then the assembly was given a sign, for suddenly, without warning, the Candlemas candle sputtered and went out. Vojtech looked up in alarm and stared at the candle. He reached for it weakly, took it out of the candle-holder, and raised it towards the ceiling. He stood there for a moment, then quickly knelt. The novelist’s diminutive son slipped off the couch; as he thumped his knees loudly on the hardwood floor, his rosary tumbled out of his pocket. Juzl slowly sank to the floor, and Vojtech’s epigone followed suit. Only the two women remained sitting on the couch. I stood up.

In his most funereal voice, Vojtech Novotny began to pray. ‘Our Father, who art in heaven . . .’

Translated by Paul Wilson

14

☉ Восх. 8.53
Зах. 16.25
Долгота дня 7.32

☾ Посл. четв. 12 января
Восх. 3.46
Зах. 11.34

—14 +352

ЯНВАРЬ ЧЕТВЕРГ

ШАХМАТНАЯ ЗАДАЧА

Мат в пять ходов

ISABEL HUGGAN
End of the Empire

Long ago, when I was young, I was in love with King George VI. It was, as you might imagine, a lopsided relationship, but within its limitations so real that his death, in 1952, diminished for some time my expectations of happiness in this world. Even now, all these years later, I sometimes suffer from an aching sadness wandering through the hallways of my mind, as if unsure of where to settle, until I realise that, ah, it is for the King of England I still pine. In him I recognised such a thin and bewildered dignity my heart was quite pierced through with arrows of devotion. Neither his daughter's anxious stiffness nor his grandson's self-deprecating wit can duplicate the winsome charm of his stammer, his long-faced sincerity and sweetness. Nothing, nothing can bring him back.

The day he died I was so stricken with grief I had to be kept home from school that afternoon. We received the news of his death on the CBC at noon, from the small brown radio on top of the refrigerator. My father was on evening shift that week so he was home and we were all sitting at the kitchen table eating our lunch, the usual Campbell's chicken noodle soup, soda crackers, carrot sticks, as the announcer's deep rolling voice and the tolling British bells brought the truth home to us and the rest of Canada. I fell from my chair as in a swoon, with a terrible gasp of, 'Oh no, my King!' and toppled to the floor at my mother's feet. My father told me to straighten round immediately if I didn't want the belt, and my mother said, 'Now, now, there's no need for that,' but it was unclear whether it was to me or to my father that she spoke. I gathered myself up with sobs and ran from the kitchen to the bedroom I shared with my older sister, whose laughter I still heard as I slammed the door, cold, older-sister laughter. I flung myself across the white chenille bedspread, felt the fuzzy ridges of its pattern pressing against my cheek as I wept out my despair. My hope for rescue was gone, gone to the grave.

My love for King George had been, until that moment in the kitchen, a private thing, a rare passion that could not be shared with a family such as mine – I'd always known that, it was part of what made my secret royal life a necessity.

As a kind of balance, the King understood me absolutely; we were connected at some deep level that ran beneath our visible lives like an underground river. This became apparent the first time he saw me, the lids of his blue eyes fluttering momentarily and then opening with something like delight. He saw me for the first time many times, as I refined the pleasurable details of the scene. But always the heart of it was the same: we belonged together, the King and I. Because of his age, and mine, the way in which we would fit would be father and daughter – but that was merely a matter of convenience, and fate.

The events leading up to King George's happy discovery of me, Hannah Louise Clement, were always the same. I would have been found in a large green park by his younger daughter, Margaret Rose, and taken home to the Palace. Although I knew her to be a dozen years older than I, she always appeared nearer my age, looking rather as she did in the photograph of herself and her older sister that hung on the dining-room wall at my grandmother's house. She and Elizabeth were seated at a grand piano and they were wearing matching dresses of pink lace and tulle, tied round the waist with satin ribbon. They were smiling and there were two small brown Corgi dogs at their feet.

Even in the park where it was rainy and chilly, dusk coming, mist rising up from the lawns, Margaret Rose appeared to be dry and comfortable. The park in my mind's eye bore a rather strong resemblance to Victoria Park in London, Ontario, which was the only park I knew, but the boundaries of my imagination extended it far past Richmond Street and Wellington, and made of it something else, something enormous and green and full of pale roses and statues and round ponds, where the weather was always English. But Margaret Rose was never damp, for she was, after all, a princess who was meant never to feel distress. And it troubled her royal heart to see a wet cold creature like me, Hannah Louise, huddled on a park bench, fearful and alone. She would scrutinise me by bringing her dimpled face in its nest of curls quite close to mine, and then she would pronounce that she must take me home to her father.

Exactly how it became clear to me that King George would want to adopt me as soon as he set eyes on me I am not to this day sure. I saw him only infrequently – in black-and-white newsreels at the movie house on Saturdays, and in a few colour photographs at my grandmother's or in the corridors at school. But I knew, with the intuition of the truly blessed, that he and I were cut from the same cloth. That is not to say that I had delusions of grandeur or that I believed myself to be of royal blood, my lineage lost and muddled through the years, my heritage denied because of some Dickensian nursemaid's foible. Rather, it was the fine certainty that station in life meant nothing, a kind of childish notion of equality. I felt that King George was not any different from, and longed to be connected to, the real world of real people. I sensed that he was, like me, a little scared. And I knew that he knew that I knew.

I was a thin, unadventurous child, who preferred fantasy because less than a decade in the world had convinced me that reality was a punishing, difficult affair. Sometime shortly after kindergarten, perhaps as a result of a determined teacher insisting that I use my right instead of my left hand, I developed a slight stutter, which had a way of coming and going so that I never knew exactly when I was going to stumble and fall over a syllable. The very random nature of this thing meant no one could find a way to cure it, and the family doctor simply assured my mother that I would, eventually, grow out of it. Which, of course, I did, except for occasional lapses still, when I am very tired, or angry, or afraid.

As a child, I found a lot to be afraid of. My mother used to say she thought I looked for trouble and she was probably right. In those years after the war, it was hard for a child to differentiate between the horrors one saw in *Life* magazine and the newsreels, and the horrors one imagined. It was difficult to grasp the levels of hate and fear in the world, and translate it all properly so that none of it applied to you. There was, for example, in our end of the city, a number of families who were known as the DPs, and their children, who went to school, were always known as the 'Dumb DPs'. In my fearful heart, I knew how those kids must have felt, in their moth-eaten hand-me-down cardigans, with their funny accents and bad breath and knobby knees. I felt like that when I was teased for my stutter, or for being a beanpole, or for being a smartypants. It was all the same, and it was awful.

It did not make me open my heart to them, you understand. I befriended not one solitary DP child. I turned instead to the King of England for companionship and solace.

Margaret Rose, on the other hand, had a heart of gold, and I feel for her still a grateful fondness. She did not hesitate to share her father and her life with the wet little waif that I was. Elizabeth I always found a touch surly, a little sulky in a self-interested way, much like my older sister, that meant she wanted to remain the apple of her daddy's eye, unthreatened by any damp-eyed stranger. I always had the shaky feeling that, if she had her way, she'd whisk me out of Buckingham Palace in a wink.

Margaret Rose would lead me to the throne room, taking my hand in a bossy but kind way. Oddly, the Queen was never present but her absence was easily explainable. A Queen was *meant* to be out and about, hovering by a veteran's wheelchair, offering sticks of candy to children, cutting ribbons, pouring tea, the impersonal, dutiful charities of *noblesse oblige*, requiring little of her but large hats and powdery smiles. I was not cynical, but I knew the Queen did not matter. The King, however, liked sticking closer to home and that was as it should be, the King on his throne, ruling. He didn't wear a crown, but he usually had on a peacock-blue smoking jacket, made of shiny, patterned brocade. It must have been handed down by his brother, I think. It made a nice, if surprising change from the military gear one usually saw him in, and the informality of his costume made him appear relaxed, nearly jolly. He would be sitting with his hands folded in his lap, as if he'd been waiting for me to appear, and when I did, he would say to Margaret Rose, 'What's this, then?' I would walk, carefully, up the long purple carpet to where he sat, and make a deep curtsey, and he would rise from his throne and touch my hair with his hand and say, 'There, there, child. Enough.' And I would look up at his face – the long, sad cheeks, the remarkable expanse from nose to lip, the thin lip itself – and see in his eyes the perfect understanding of which I spoke earlier, the flicker of paternal joy.

Painfully, for neither of us were any good at conversation, we would talk to each other about our lives. This episode usually served as a kind of review of what I was doing in school at the time and I would tell King George everything I knew – the routes of the explorers, the toughest multiplication tables, all the verses of all the poems I had memorised by Walter de la Mare and Christina Rossetti, the bits and pieces of information that I had about the world – all this without hesitation or stutter. And he too spoke clearly and calmly, in a voice rich and warm and even, in the voice that a king should have. In the voice that I gave him. And he would say, in this voice, that he was amazed at the depth and breadth of my knowledge.

'Why, I think you know more than *either* of my girls do,' he would say. And then, 'What would you think about coming to live here at the Palace? You are *just* the sort of girl I like to talk to.'

It was the kind of swift decision-making one might expect from a king. For although the invitation was phrased as a question there was no doubt that it was a royal command, and that I would now live there, with him.

Conveniently, I was only recently orphaned, my insensitive family having perished in a car accident or tragic fire or from food poisoning at a picnic, and so there were no obstacles to surmount. I would nod my assent shyly, and the court stenographer would be called to draw up immediately the adoption papers. I'd sign my name, Hannah Louise, with a flourish, and King George would raise his eyebrows with astonishment and appreciation at my fine hand, and then apply himself to his own signature. This would be followed by a hot wax seal, red and dripping, as the parchment would be lifted up, and the announcement made. 'Hannah Louise Clement is now of the House of Windsor.'

Generally speaking, I never progressed beyond this point – the ceremony in itself was such a fine culmination of my hopes and dreams there was no need for denouement. And it was only his death that brought me back to the suburban street and the two-storey frame house in which I dwelled with a father and a mother and a sister who thought I was . . . well, weird.

Her name was Phyllis Anne, and in the weeks that followed my downfall in the kitchen, she needled and teased and made me miserable at every turn. Three years older than I, she was exactly the right age to take the Coronation seriously, and she began a scrapbook, starting with the newspaper clippings that told how the Princess had been given the news she'd be Queen at Treetops in faraway Africa. Then she added to her collection all the booklets about the Coronation itself, drawings, photographs, long explanations of the meaning of the event, the symbolism of the orb and crown and ermine-bordered robes. Phyllis Anne purposely left all this stuff out on the bureau, knowing I would see it, knowing it would make me suffer. Well, perhaps she didn't know – who but I could know the bitterness of dashed hope?

I had longed for that name-change with my whole being – I had heard in the King's last name the *win* and *wind* and *soar* of Windsor – and it made me feel strong and free, an eagle, a lark, lifted high above the ground where my unimaginative family congealed, dull and hard as cement. Clement, cement, stuck in my name for ever. I felt so weighted with sadness I could not bear to think of it, and with some self-preserving instinct went off to the public library, where I took books off shelves and flipped over pages until I found a paragraph that took me away. And so I entered the novels of Zane Grey, and turned to the West with a passion.

I began to ride in my dreams with the King of the Cowboys, Roy Rogers, and his Queen, Dale Evans, and I spent all my allowances on going to their movies, over and over again. I listened to their adventures on the radio, felt always calm and satisfied by the way the programmes ended: *Happy Trails to you, until we meet again . . . brought to you by Ovaltine.* Sometimes I found myself alongside Pat Brady in his jeep Nellybelle, more often I was galloping on my own palomino, just slightly behind Roy and Dale. In my own quiet way I became a rip-snorting cowgirl who never rode sidesaddle, who could blast the eyes out of a rattlesnake with her six-shooter, who was ever vigilant in her defence of justice out there on the wild American plains. My allegiance had been transferred, my mutable soul transformed and expanded by all that sunshine and fresh air.

As the hot dry winds of the desert swept away the chilly park at nightfall,

England itself receded into the fog just as Elizabeth ascended the throne. It had been easy to feel the world was all of a piece when King George was the centre of my universe – the differences were as nothing, England, Canada, Canada, England, one could connect in those days, we were all the same. But now I found no need to imagine the Palace and its power, I gave up the idea of adoption as a way out, and the entire Royal Family slipped out of my dreams into the cold Atlantic that separated their cold little island from my new American Life.

And with that, the Empire was over.

DON COLES

Three Poems

Princesse Lointaine

He taps the adjectives and verbs of love
On to his screen. They infiltrate the green
And faintly glowing ground, arriving not from above
Or either side or below
But as if they've been sown here long ago,
These tiny, dark-faced seeds of self,
And made to wait during quite a few years of
Not exactly being alone, but worse. Such
A small, pure sound
When they tip up out of the green,
He thinks they're bound
To be better than those noises between,
Aren't they? Meanwhile behind the verdurous screen
Something's impending. What can it be?
Far off, never to be seen
Hereabouts, but the cause of everything? It's she.

Girl Unexpectedly Come Upon When Issuing from an Elevator at 10 a.m. in a Hotel Lobby in Budapest

Farcically beautiful (to raze, only by
Standing here, all the boulevards and palaces
Of my well-considered tourist day),
She waits out tranced seconds in which I
Brood on vertiginous syllables of a
Meeting. Life ripples but does not
Open. So familiar processes take over:
In halting English she modestly avows
Half-a-dozen fated passions –
Poetry, an as yet unpeopled panorama of
Happiness, bedtime nakedness, others
Too snug a fit to say. I note
The desk clerk, a bellboy, and
A seated man with a slack newspaper
Drafting alternative scenarios.

Lapidary Voices from the Nursing Home

'Today I saw my daughter, Mitzi, my favourite,
With her baby, smiling and smiling,' she was tellin' us this morning –
She never had no daughter, pore old thing.

'This is not Paradise, I don't care
What you say,' that one over there was cryin' out, matter of fact
She just stopped when you come in, 'It is insipid
From dawn till dusk!'

This one over here now, many's the time
I've heard her greet visitors sayin'
With her teeth clackin' away,
'How're the Free French?'
She really is a caution . . .

Sure, mostly women here, they live longer –

– *In room after room*
Long-dead fathers counsel their troubled daughters, accidentally grown old,
With yearned-after, secret, caressing voices.

MARY FLANAGAN
Not Quite Arcadia

In the dark she hardly recognised him. He spoke to her and passed before she realised he was Stevie, the butcher's assistant. He had made her a cup of tea last week in Mr Agrippa's shop and brought her a stool to sit on until she stopped sweating and the room had ceased to rotate. He was a kind man, Mr Agrippa. He kept Stevie on and didn't mind that he was damaged. A birth defect? Myra didn't know. She had problems of her own and never thought much about Stevie.

She could not remember what he had said. His voice was thick, like a patient under morphine. It was difficult to understand Stevie. It was difficult to look at him – small and thin, his face too long and his eyes too large, favouring his left leg and speaking in a mumble. Myra descended the steps to the door of her basement flat and turned the key. The cat came to greet her, wanting Whiskas. The envelope on the mat contained an entry form for a £135,000 prize draw, the third such letter this week. She would enter, as she had the others, and with the money she would get a face-lift at one of those clinics that advertised in the back pages of *Vogue*. Clearly, the Very Emollient Nourishing Night Cream With Placenta wasn't working.

Myra changed into a dressing-gown; resolved not to glance in the bathroom mirror. But she couldn't help it, she turned and ended as she always did, searching in vain for her lost looks. What she found were puffy eyes, a crumpled mouth, and gaping pores surrounding her roseate nose with its smatter of remaining freckles. She switched off the overhead light and stood in the dark, panic rising. The cure was to lie down, play 'Casta Diva' and breathe deeply. This she did, assailed by the scent of hyacinths dying on the table.

'Happens to all women,' her GP had said. 'Not as if it was fatal, is it? You're not the only one.'

'Yes, I am. To myself I am.' She whispered to Lily who sat purring and grooming on her tense abdomen. Oh, to be as beautiful as her broad-faced cat whose green eyes looked only outward. What *had* Stevie said?

Returning from the library with her Friday stack of soiled novels, she again failed to see him approach. He was suddenly beside her, speaking in his damaged voice.

'Come in, Stevie,' she said.

He followed her down the stairs. Lily fled, the cat door going flap flap behind her.

'It's dark.'

Myra could understand him now. 'I don't like bright lights,' she answered as he handed her a white packet stained red and tied with butcher's twine.

'What's this, soup bones?' How could she be speaking to him this way, familiarly, without preliminaries?

'For you.' The sight of his teeth repelled her. 'For your problem.'

'Really?' She opened it. 'Ah. Organs.'

He nodded.

'Are they fish, fowl or mammal?' It was hard to tell.

'Mammal.'

'I love mammals.' She now returned his smile. 'They're all that interest me.'

For three days after cooking and eating the organs she aired the flat but could not get rid of the awful smell. The saucepan was put out with the rubbish.

She felt very well until the following Friday when she came home with her stack of new novels, changed into her dressing-gown and bravely faced the mirror. She saw with alarm that her face had begun to pucker and bubble like the white of an egg when it was fried too quickly. On Monday she called the office and feigned illness.

When she awoke at 4 a.m. her face was itching, not unpleasantly. She stumbled to the bathroom and watched her reflection scratching at the base of its neck. She pushed with her fingertips, carefully inserting them under the loose skin. Gently she pulled and lifted. The dead face peeled off in its entirety like a layer of warm wax. She dropped it into the toilet where it floated, a bloodless afterbirth. She pulled the chain and flushed away her face.

Myra gazed at herself with satisfaction. Her pores had tightened and the circles had gone from beneath her eyes. In eight weeks the marbled tracks of cellulite on her thighs and bottom had vanished and the flab on her upper arms had firmed. Within a year she acquired a waist and ankles.

Myra's boss, Mr MacKenzie, asked her out. Her GP asked her out. She dined with them, slept with them, did the same with a bricklayer she met in a pub. She began affairs with a handsome married man on the second floor and with her bank manager, also married. She left them all. They were too old for her.

She went to a gym. She swam. She needed release for the energy coursing through her nice new endocrine system. She wore dresses that exposed her apricot skin. Every few years she peeled off her old face and threw it away. She disappeared into London, changing her name and acquiring a new set of friends and lovers. She married a lawyer, divorced him, and bought a flat in South Kensington. She moved on before anyone noticed the change in her appearance.

Her memory began to fail. It was as if she had never known what Celsius was, or a 747, or a duvet. Everything was unfamiliar and fresh. (It was just as well she had money because she could not have held down a job.) She felt a compulsion to learn all the things she had forgotten and decided to begin at a butcher's shop in E8.

Mr Agrippa scratched his head and laughed. 'You do *look* familiar.' She wanted to ask which animal's death had been the price of her youthing. Instead she asked if he remembered a customer named Myra Dent.

He snapped his fingers. 'The daughter!' And Stevie? Stevie was gone.

She enrolled in an A-level college, but didn't like studying and failed her exams. She preferred to go skating, listen to the Everly Brothers or paint by numbers. Her periods stopped. She was hungry all the time and wanted to see her mother. Furtively she bought a doll. When one day she discovered she had been wearing her shoes on the wrong feet, she knew she could no longer look after herself.

A suitable woman was engaged, but Myra escaped her. She unlocked the gate to the communal gardens and squatted in the dawn light, watching the worms at work. She rejoiced in the taste of dirt she consumed by the fistful. The police found her wandering down the Fulham Road. She could not answer any of their questions, and they had no choice but to have her taken into care.

She was now a toddler, spilling her orange juice and building yellow and red cities out of plastic blocks. She was an infant, a small helpless mammal who screamed to no avail, suffocating in the heavy air that pressed her to her cot, panting for a liquid world.

An ambulance brought her to St Bartholomew's, the ancient hospital which stands opposite Smithfield Meat Market where men in stained white coats and huge rubber boots wheel beef carcasses to and fro like frocks on a rack. Myra was not aware of her surroundings. Her tiny fists seemed to the observing nurses to beat at nothing. In fact she was knocking, pounding, at wet red gates. She pounded soundlessly until they opened and swallowed her whole into the inner darkness.

LIMA

GRACE PALEY
Three Days and a Question

On the first day I joined a demonstration opposing the arrest in Israel of members of Yesh Gvul, Israeli soldiers who had refused to serve in the occupied territories. Yesh Gvul means: *There is a Limit.*

TV cameras and an anchorwoman arrived and *New York Times* stringers with their narrow journalism notebooks. What do you think? the anchorwoman asked. What do *you* think, she asked a woman passer-by – a woman about my age.

Anti-Semites, the woman said quietly.

The anchorwoman said, But they're Jewish.

Anti-Semites, the woman said, a little louder.

What? One of our demonstrators stepped up to her. Are you crazy? How can you . . . Listen what we're saying.

Rotten anti-Semites – all of you.

What? What! What! the man shouted. How you dare to say that – all of us Jews. Me, he said. He pulled up his shirtsleeve. Me? You call me? You look. He held out his arm. Look at this.

I'm not looking, she screamed.

You look at my number, what they did to me. My arm . . . you have no right.

Anti-Semite, she said between her teeth. Israel hater.

No, no, he said, you fool. My arm – you're afraid to look . . . my arm . . . my arm.

On the second day Vera and I listen at PEN to Eta Krisaeva read her stories that are not permitted publication in her own country, Czechoslovakia. Then we walk home in the New York walking night, about twenty blocks – shops and lights, other walkers talking past us. Late-night homeless men and women asleep in dark storefront doorways on cardboard pallets under coats and newspapers, scraps of blanket. Near home on Sixth Avenue a young man, a boy, passes – a boy the age a younger son could be – head down, bundles in his arms, on his back.

Wait, he says, turning to stop us. Please, please wait. I just got out of Bellevue. I was sick. They gave me something. I don't know . . . I need to sleep somewhere. The Y, maybe.

That's way uptown.

Yes, he says. He looks at us. Carefully he says, AIDS. He looks away. Oh. Separately, Vera and I think: A boy – only a boy. Mothers after all, our common trade for more than thirty years.

Then he says, I put out my hand. We think he means to tell us he tried to beg. I put out my hand. No one will help me. No one. Because they can see. Look at my arm. He pulls his coatsleeve back. Lesions, he says. Have you ever seen lesions? That's what people see.

No. No, we see a broad fair forehead, a pale countenance, fear. I just have to sleep, he says.

We shift in our pockets. We give him what we find – about eight dollars. We tell him, Son, they'll help you on 13th Street at the Center. Yes, I know about that place. I know about them all. He hoists the bundle of his things to his back to prepare for walking. Thank you, ladies. Goodbye.

On the third day I'm in a taxi. I'm leaving the city for a while and need to get to the airport. We talk – the driver and I. He's a black man, dark. He's not young. He has a French accent. Where are you from? Haiti, he answers. Ah, your country is in bad trouble. Very bad. You know that, Miss.

Well, yes. Sometimes it's in the paper.

They thieves there. You know that? Very rich, very poor. You believe me? Killing – it's nothing to them, killing. Hunger. Starving people. Everything bad. And you don't let us come. Starving. They send us back.

We're at a red light. He turns to look at me. Why they do that? He doesn't wait for me to say, Well . . . because . . . He says, Why! hard.

The light changes. We move slowly up traffic-jammed Third Avenue. Silence. Then, Why? Why they let the Nicaragua people come? Why they let Vietnamese come? One time American people want to kill them people. Put bomb in their children. Break their head. Now they say, Yes Yes, come come come. Not us. Why?

Your New York is beautiful country. I love it. So beautiful, this New York. But why, tell me, he says, stopping the cab, switching the meter off. Why, he says, turning to me again, rolling his short shirtsleeve back, raising his arm to the passenger divider, pinching and pulling the bare skin of his upper arm.

You tell me – this skin, this black skin – why? Why you hate this skin so much?

Question: Those gestures, those arms, the three consecutive days thrown like a formal net over the barest unchanged accidental facts. How? Why? In order to become – probably – in this city one story told.

RONALD WRIGHT
Crossroads

PETEN, GUATEMALA, 1985
Army roadblocks every twenty miles or so. I've been searched three times. I write these notes in my worst handwriting, so nobody can read them. I remember what Rod used to say, 'Even paranoids have enemies.' It was a joke then.

'Assassination is the sincerest form of flattery.' – Suzanne Ruta

TIKAL
One hundred per cent humidity, dripping trees, mist hanging like smoke in the branches, rasp of a toucan, a smell of wild allspice.

Dinner was chop suey *generis*. The waiter (black bow tie, white shirt, faded charcoal trousers, elderly) had a collapsed look, like a badly stuffed cushion. Someone said, 'You could regard being president of the United States as the perfect crime.'

Farm Implements for Arid and Tropical Regions FAO Agricultural Development Paper #91. Rome, 1969

Howler monkeys woke me twice last night – a sound like rutting camels, hungry lions, fighting dogs. Monkeys, the Maya believe, are descendants of an earlier race of man which the gods judged imperfect and banished to the forest. The howler is also patron of writing: what a voice!

Accordion prices (for Sulcas): 17 3″ reed $700-800 (used c.$500)
19″ 4 reed, 11 switches. Italian c.$2,500

TARMA, PERU, 1988. DON JULIO
The power fails and the stars come out over Tarma (population 28,933; altitude 10,000 feet). I remember the astronomer and go to see him. Don Julio Rivera is the owner of the Hostal Central, a small hotel with no stars.

He's resting on a cot in his office, hoping for lodgers to turn up.

'So you've come to see my telescope?' (A tweed cap, a stoop, twinkling expression – like a garden gnome dressed as Sid James.) 'First I'll show you *mi telescopio de cartón* – my cardboard telescope!' He goes over to a desk piled three feet high with exercise books. On top of the books is a cardboard disk with degrees and hours marked on its circumference. It has an arrow pivoted in the middle like the hand of a toy clock.

'Let us observe Jupiter and Mars!'

Don Julio chooses a dog-eared notebook and opens it. On each page are columns of figures and ancient astronomical symbols for the planets and zodiac. 'People think I'm crazy, or a wizard, or both. But let me convince you.' He aims his cardboard 'telescope' at a spot on the wall which he says is north; he tilts it to conform with Tarma's latitude and the time of year; he moves the arrow until it rests on a number given in his tables. 'There! At exactly 9.17 p.m. Jupiter will rise from behind that hill in the east.' He points through the window to a small nub on the mountain silhouette. 'Now let us go to the observatory and see if I'm crazy or not.'

Across a dark patio and up several flights of stairs. Rooms leading off balconies; candles glowing behind thin curtains. At last we come out on the flat roof and there, against the dome of heaven, is a darker dome – a mushroom shape about twenty feet high. Don Julio chuckles and unlocks a metal door. The power comes on again, revealing a round space with three large sofas against the walls. 'I built it to seat fifteen,' he says, as if seating capacity was the main consideration in its design. When he removes the canvas cover from his (real) telescope I see that this is indeed the case – the instrument is a four-inch refractor, newer but no bigger than the one I take out occasionally on my back lawn. It looks lost in here, like a shotgun in the turret of a battleship.

'You do a lot of entertaining . . .?'

'One or two people come up from time to time. But nobody is serious. Even though this is the only observatory in Peru!'

'Surely, the university in Lima . . .?'

'I went to see them once, to show them my system, my telescope of cardboard! They have nothing!' He laughs wistfully. 'They even gave me this.' From a box he produces a twelve-inch disk of glass, concave on one side, its reflective silvering as tarnished as a forgotten christening spoon. This was once the eye of a Newtonian reflector on a mountain in Chile. When it became obsolete the Chileans gave it to Peru. Peru gave it to Don Julio. One day he plans to build a better telescope, but he is old now, with no one to help. Besides, there's another problem. 'You can't get mirrors re-silvered here. I'd have to send it to Buenos Aires. Or New York. Imagine the difficulties! Imagine the cost!' He puts away the glass mirror, sadly, like an old maid repacking her trousseau. He rests a hand on the refractor.

'What I'd really like is another like this, only bigger, say six-inch aperture. Perhaps a society in your country has such an instrument they no longer use. We could make an exchange – their telescope, my observatory. They could come here to watch the southern skies. Would you mention it when you get home?'

At 9.17 p.m. we look east towards the mountain.

Jupiter rises.

Tabloid headline: STATUE OF ELVIS FOUND ON MARS.

Spanish Omelette with Quinoa (a nutritious Andean grain of the goosefoot family):

1 cup of cooked quinoa flakes
1 tomato
1 green pepper, chopped
½ an onion, chopped
2 sprigs of parsley
1 stick of celery
1 red chilli pepper, chopped
4 eggs

TARMA PERU. Euhemerism

A newspaper cutting, very yellow – about 1970, to judge from the value of the *sol*. My translation (abridged):

Traffic in Human Flesh in Peru
They Were Hunting Men and Women to Sell as Beef

A traffic in human flesh has just been uncovered by Tarma police in the central Andean region, according to information revealed today. Twenty-six people were attacked in lonely parts of the departments of Cusco, Ayacucho, and Huancayo in order to supply carcasses to an individual identified only as 'The Gringo' . . .

Isaac Martínez and his brother Pedro explained how they killed persons they found alone in the Andes. Afterwards they removed the limbs, as 'The Gringo' was interested only in torsos. These were gathered and delivered to Lima in a van by one known as 'The Fox'.

The Martínez brothers revealed the prices they charged, which were determined by weight: A woman eight months pregnant was valued at

15,000 soles (a little more than 300 dollars), fat men fetched 8,000 soles, and thin ones 5,000 . . .

At first it was believed that the criminals were *pishtacos*, legendary brigands or wizards of the Andes, who attack men and women in lonely spots . . .

LIMA, 1982

Juan Ossio, professor of anthropology, tells me that Indians believe the fat taken by *pishtacos* is used by Max Factor for making cosmetics. Poetic truth: Who wears cosmetics in Peru? Not Indians, but the wives of those who get rich from Indian sweat. At the time of the Conquest, Indians believed that the Spaniards took their fat for curing a great sickness in Spain. Literal truth: 'We dressed our wounds with the fat from a stout Indian whom we had killed and cut open,' wrote Bernal Díaz, who fought in Mexico with Cortés.

In Bolivia, perhaps they have Klaus Barbie dolls.

TAKILI, PERU 1978

Weaving motifs and their Quechua names:

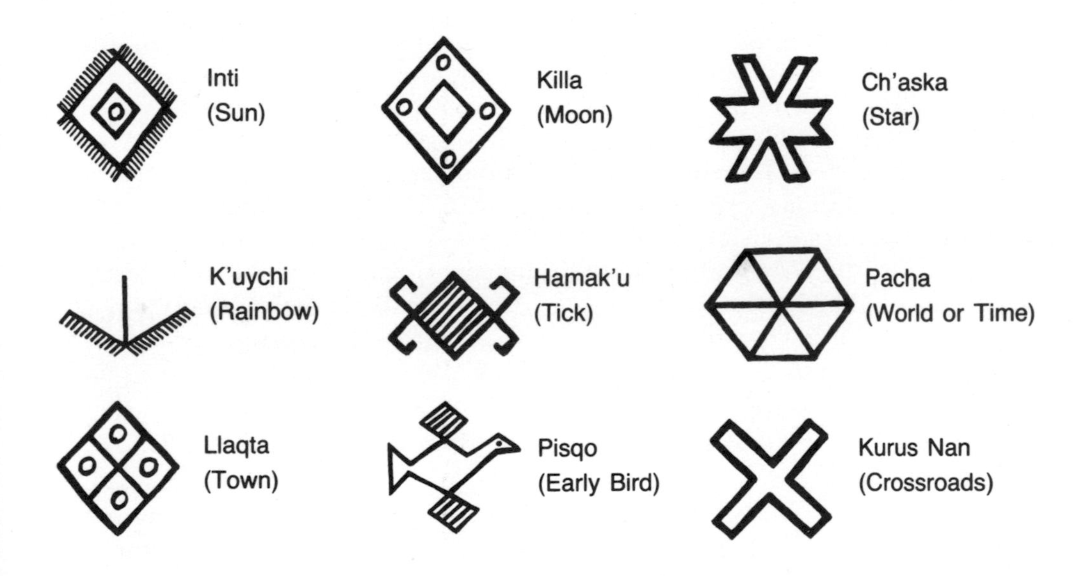

LIMA, 1988
Two sheep, one alpaca, one llama, eating the grass behind Pizarro Palace, where lives the *presidente*. Only the sheep look happy in the thick air of a coastal winter. No sunshine and no rain for months, but plenty of drizzle and fog. A bubble of visibility moves with me through the grey. Police keep people from the Palace walls – to stop them tossing bombs.

A young man seated at a kitchen table in a filthy room with rain streaming down uncurtained windows. A kettle is boiling away on the stove. The young man is plunging a hypodermic needle into his arm. Paint in oils, entitle: *Rain, Steam and Speed.*

MIRAFLORES, clifftop near the roundabout with Wolfie's Grill.
In Vargas Llosa's *Historia de Mayta*, the narrator (V.Ll. himself, of course) describes how the cliffs behind his wealthy suburb – a suburb like this – are strewn with rubbish that nobody ever takes away. It's true. Here's a little park, some threadbare grass, still damp from the gardener's hose, and dusty magueys that get watered much less often. The desert above and the beach below are the same colour: tan. The sea is lead. A dog with foxy ears, elegant in its leanness, picks through a picnic lunch.

Lovers: some standing, some prone; in motionless clinches, unaware of me, of the dog, of apartment windows watching them; lovers wreathed in smoke rising from a rubbish pile on the beach. Burning rubbish smells the same all over the world, and yet this is peculiarly Lima's smell: singed cans, shit, and rancid cooking oil: in hotel towels, in mattresses, on banknotes, in people's hair, in my hair.

A phallic lighthouse, striped black-and-white like a sock, its lens sweeping, stabs into a thousand living-rooms and my two eyes. Below the apartments, in a gravel ravine, there's an infestation of squatters' shacks: a wrinkle of poverty on the fat cheeks of Miraflores. Homes of driftwood and plastic and old doors and zinc sheets held down with stones and hope. A baby wails, a radio wanders on and off the signal (Afro-Andean *chicha* tunes). Breakers roll in from the Pacific fog. Headlands and tall buildings dissolve into the overcast.

The wall of Wolfie's Grill has a scrawled message for Vargas Llosa: PERU IS NOT A NOVEL.

'Though God cannot alter the past, historians can.' – Samuel Butler. A traveller in a foreign jail amuses himself by reworking memories to create a world of malapropisms: The Crime of Miss Jean Brodie; St Augustine the Hippo; The

Naked Brunch; The Adventures of Shylock Holmes; Onan the Barbarian; The Pleasure of the Puta Madre; Troilist and Cressida; Dildo and Aeneas.

When the universe stops expanding and time flows backwards, novelists will take dictation and prophets will be archaeologists.

The future isn't what it used to be.

Comercio de Carne Humana en Perú

Cazaban Hombres y Mujeres Para Venderlos Como Reses

LIMA, 19 de junio. (AFP) — Un comercio de carne humana acaba de ser descubierto por la policía de Tarma, en la zona central andina del Perú, según informaciones dadas a conocer hoy. 26 personas, dicen "Correo" y "Ojo" de hoy, fueron asaltadas en lugares solitarios de los departamentos de Cuzco, Ayacucho y Huancayo, para proveer de cadáveres a un sujeto identificado como "El Gringo" (nombre que se da en el Perú a los extranjeros o a los nacionales cuando son rubios).

(Por Favor Pasa a la Pág. 5)

now that you've got the COMMANDMENTS I'd like to give you the ADVICE, the SUGGESTIONS AND the HANDY HINTS..
thanks awfully but we're only interested in the Bottom line... these days

AMPARO DÁVILA
Welcome to the Chelsea

I arrived in New York on the night of Hallowe'en. Following a suggestion of my friend Erica Frouman-Smith, Lori Carlson had invited me to read my stories at the Center for Inter-American Relations. When Erica asked me at what hotel I'd like them to reserve a room, I immediately said the Chelsea. For many years I had wanted to see what that hotel looked like; I had heard so much about it and about the characters who had stayed there: poets and novelists I admired, painters, bohemians. My friend Francisco Zendejas always stayed there: 'An ideal place for intellectuals; some of them have lived there for years.' I had envisaged a beautiful turn-of-the-century building, or maybe of the 1920s, with a romantic atmosphere pleasing to artists, conducive to writing and painting. There is no doubt that people leave behind, in the places they have inhabited, something of their spirit; the Chelsea, having provided shelter to so many artists, would certainly possess a beautiful melancholy atmosphere. I was thinking all this in the taxi that drove me from the airport into Manhattan.

There was movement everywhere, people in costumes coming and going on the streets, music, noise, happiness, groups of children with lighted pumpkins trick-or-treating their way from door to door, but in Manhattan itself there were even more people and more movement, and the car could hardly get through some of the streets. Chelsea Street itself was a *fiesta* – people running, dancing, singing, shouting.

'There's the hotel,' the driver said. 'I don't think we can reach it . . .' And he pointed out a severe building, several storeys high, with beautiful wrought-iron balconies. I begged him to try and reach the door because I've always been terrified of crowds.

The taxi slowly managed to creep up to the hotel. The driver carried my bags to the door, leaned into the lobby, and called out something I didn't understand, probably that someone should come and get my luggage. Then he left. I waited. The bell-boy never came. Instead, a burly man in shirtsleeves, looking like a crook or a dock-worker, took my bags, and, without a word, led me into the hotel.

I followed the man and froze in fear. If the street had frightened me with all those people in disguise, the lobby was a coven of ghastly masks: hideous witches, one-eyed monsters, hunchbacks, Frankensteins, Draculas, Jack the Rippers wielding red daggers, sinister women with hair standing upright as if electrified, others with white faces and long tresses as if only just risen from the grave, all laughing out loud in an atmosphere heavy with smoke and alcohol fumes. There was little light, the walls were painted grey, and in the centre of the lobby a blackened fireplace and large pieces of furniture covered in black leather worn out by the years made the place even more lugubrious. The man carrying my luggage stopped at the reception desk – which looked more like one of those news-stands out on the street – behind which the clerk asked for my name and started to hunt among hundreds of bits of paper.

'Yes, here's your reservation. Sign here.'

(My God, my God, where have I come to? I moaned to myself.) I asked the clerk if I could call long-distance from my room.

'Better do it from down here. Sometimes it's difficult from the rooms.'

I followed the man carrying my luggage to a small old-fashioned elevator in which he, I and my luggage barely fitted among the empty beer cans, cigarette boxes, paper bags and the rest of the rubbish. The elevator stopped on the third floor, worse lit than the lobby. In front of us was a large iron staircase, dabbed in black. On either side of the elevator long and dark corridors slithered out into the gloom. The man stopped in front of a door with a recent coat of paint under which the grime could still be seen glittering, put the key in the lock and turned it several times. Unable to open it, he muttered something between his teeth and then gave the door several hard kicks. The door opened, he turned the light on and . . . the sight before my eyes could not have been more deplorable. The rug was stained and dirty, the bed was badly made, the sheets wrinkled and showing obvious signs of use; there were a table and chairs covered in dust, a cooker smelling of gas and a sink with rusty taps dripping unceasingly. I pointed to the leak. 'I'll see to it tomorrow,' he said, and left.

I felt like crying in this ruin of a place, so depressing, so painful. This was the hotel I had longed to know, which I had imagined and idealised: it was impossible, impossible. And it hurt deeply, like all beautiful things hurt when they are broken or destroyed, when they come to an end. But I had to call Mexico and let them know that I had arrived safely. I tried opening the door of the room but it was useless. I tried again and again. I put the key in, I took it out, I pulled at the door handle, I tried the key once more, nothing, the door wouldn't open.

Then terror: I was locked up in this disgusting room, locked up, unable to leave . . . I ran to the phone and called the front desk: nothing, no answer. Again, still nothing, five, ten times, many more . . .

'Yes?'

'I can't get out, I'm locked in, I can't get out . . .'

'You can't get out?' (I heard him laughing.) 'What's stopping you?'

'I can't open the door.'

'You must have locked it.'

'No, the key's not in. But it won't open and I want to get out, please, come and open it.'

'There's no one here, they're all in the street having fun. If someone comes along, I'll send him.'

'Please, I beg you, open the door.'

I collapsed on a chair, exhausted. After a long while I heard knocking on the door.

'Take the key out!'

'It's not in.'

The man started to kick the door and hit it with his fists. Finally I heard him scraping with something like a screwdriver. The door opened.

'It stuck with the paint.'

'I'm going down to phone,' I said.

'Leave the chain on and hang the lock on the outside so that it doesn't get stuck again.'

In spite of the racket, the music, the laughter and shouting, I managed to phone home. As soon as I was finished, I went back to the third floor. As I left the elevator, a screeching sound came from one of the dark corridors. Count Dracula, and his mate in a white tunic and long flowing hair were coming towards me, almost running. Was it to catch the elevator or to catch me? I no longer knew whether this was the real Count or a perfect disguise, it no longer mattered. I stepped back into the elevator and closed the door before they could reach it. Trembling, I returned to the lobby. Behind me the couple had managed to come down and were laughing and saying things to one another in a language I didn't understand.

'What is it?' asked the man at the desk.

'What is the time?' was the first thought that crossed my mind.

'Ten to three.'

I thanked him and went back to the elevator. On the third floor I made sure there was no one else in the corridors and then ran to my room. I put the chain on as the man had told me, so that it would not get stuck again. There was a gap left, of about twenty centimetres, but no one would be able to get in. It was three in the morning of that long and crazy night. I would have to wait for dawn before leaving. I was extremely tired, both by the voyage and the nervous exhaustion; I was cold and longed to slip under the sheets of a clean and welcoming bed. I sat down on a chair and did not even take off my shoes. I tried reading, but it was useless. I could hear steps in the corridor, steps reaching the room, a muffled breathing and the never ending drip of water in the sink.

At seven in the morning I decided to go out and find a place for coffee. I would call my friend Erica at eight-thirty to ask her what other hotel she could recommend. If the lobby looked grotesque at night, in the light of day it looked more sombre than a funeral parlour, with its grey walls and its black furniture. There was dust everywhere, piles of old newspapers and empty bottles and beer cans. I went out into the streets, very empty except for huge quantities of garbage. I walked for several blocks until I found a Chinese café where I had a cup of hot coffee that lifted my spirits.

I called Erica and told her briefly about my impressions of the Chelsea Hotel.

'I thought it was strange that you should ask to go there,' she said. And she recommended another place at which most of the guests of the Center were put up.

When I asked for my bill at the desk, the clerk said, 'I thought you were going to be with us for several days . . .'

'I changed my mind,' I answered.

'Didn't you like the suite we gave you? Other guests have always loved it.'

'No doubt,' I said.

And left.

Translated by Alberto Manguel

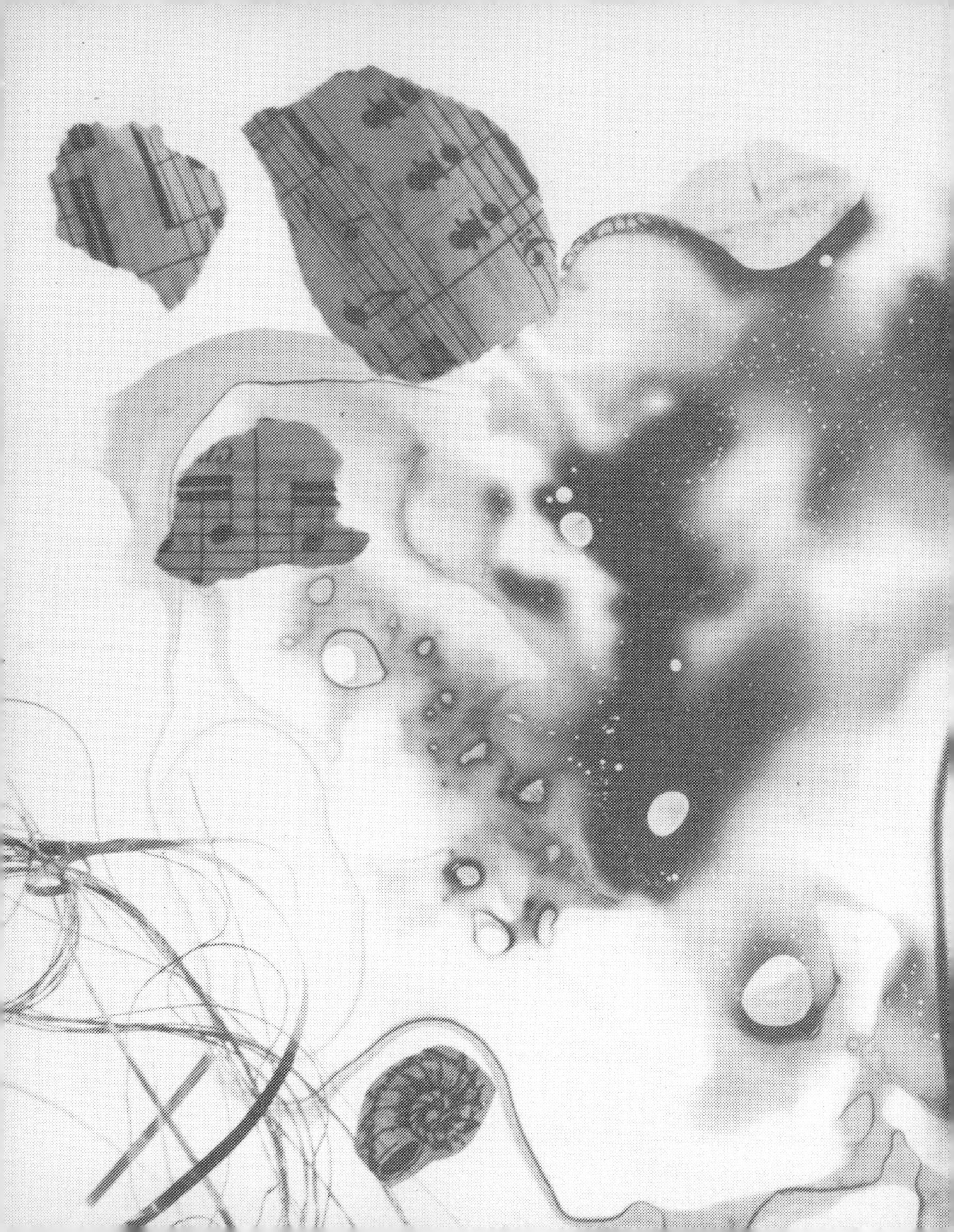

SUSAN SWAN

Meeting Your Reader

(or incidents in the aftermath of a novel)

I knew I was in trouble the afternoon my dentist, Dr C., lowered my pneumatic chair and said in a breathless voice, 'I've just bought your novel.' He hovered over me, smiling in excitement, as my head slowly sank back and downwards and the attendant snapped on my blue bib. Now, I should say that Dr C. is a courtly Japanese man with a sensitivity to pain that borders on telepathy. I'm used to his shy, bespectacled face floating over me like an attentive balloon, picking up the smallest grimace at the same time as his hideous instruments jam my mouth, sending me into torment. Without saying much, he and I have always communicated perfectly.

But that afternoon, as he froze my gums for – groan – a root canal job, he wouldn't stop talking. 'I saw you on TV,' he said, holding his high-speed drill just out of the periphery of my vision. 'Uh-huh. It was very interesting.' His drill began to whirr discreetly. 'At first, I couldn't believe it was you.' He moved the drill up towards the ceiling, testing its speed. 'You were very good. Not like a real television professional, of course. But who would expect that? No. Very, very good.'

I closed my eyes. 'You thought so?' I asked, trying to ignore the sound of the descending drill.

Unexpectedly, he began to giggle. 'And when you asked that literary critic to resign – hee, hee! It was unbelievable!'

'Yes – ah . . .' (and here the attendant began packing my left cheek with cotton). 'You know,' I confided a little anxiously, 'I was only trying to point out a problem with contemporary criticism. Most – Argh! uh . . .' (I had begun to gag as the loathsome saliva ejector was suddenly deep in my mouth) '. . . critics only understand literary realism.'

Dr C. nodded enthusiastically. 'Yes, yes.'

'Critics who slam a writer . . .' (now the drill started to spray metal filings everywhere) '. . . for not being true to life misunderstand the nature of fic –' I spluttered and Dr C. politely withdrew his drill. 'Would they criticise Walt

Disney for making *Mickey Mouse*?' Phew! I'd managed to get one sentence off my chest with the saliva ejector still in place. 'You see, Dr C., we all know real mice don't talk or wear shoes . . .' The drill began heading back again to my lower molar. 'Even literary realism is a construct of the imaginat –'

'I agree – yes, yes. A construction of imagination! Hee, hee, hee. Very good.'

The drill whirred and the saliva ejector bubbled enthusiastically and for a moment I felt safely babied by Dr C.'s technology. I wondered, though, if Dr C. really knew what he was getting into with a novel like mine. Perhaps he was one of those innocents who can't abide strong language or ambiguous endings. So I took a deep breath and looked up into the lenses of the hapless Dr C. 'By the way, you should understand there are some very frank – ah, explicit sexual passages in the novel . . .'

I didn't finish. Something bore into my gums with a psychotic force. And Dr C. jumped in the air, coming down just near his office door. He stared blankly in my direction as his attendant removed the drill (still doing its dirty work) from my gums. 'You scared me,' he said finally. He took a small step towards me. 'Do you mean I will have to change my mind and think badly of you?'

I sighed as the attendant began daubing my bloody mouth with a Kleenex. 'I hope not,' I said.

I know getting my gum drilled by my ordinarily reliable dentist is nothing like what happened to Salman Rushdie. 'Stop complaining,' a friend said when I told her about the incident. 'At least you're meeting your reader.' But there are places where I don't want to meet my reader. That's the problem. I don't want to meet my reader in the dentist's chair. Or in the bedroom either. For instance, the subject of fiction recently ruined a romantic encounter. Snuggled close to the man in question, I became aware of a strange, crunching sound. The sound went on for a minute or two, long enough for me to be sure I wasn't imagining things in my state of post-coital relaxation. Slowly, I heaved myself on to my elbows and looked around. And there was the culprit – his toes snapping and unbending with the dexterity of fleas jumping through miniature hoops at a novelty circus. He was already watching them in admiration, and, slowly and somewhat thoughtfully, I began admiring them, too.

At last, he spoke. 'I bet you've never slept with a man who can crack his toes before.' He smiled hopefully. 'Am I going to read about this in the next novel? You know, maybe one of your characters will meet a man who can do death-defying stunts with his toes.'

I laughed a little nervously. 'I didn't have writing on my mind just now,' I said.

He laughed uproariously. 'You can tell that to the marines.' He quickly crunched both sets of toes for good measure. 'I don't mind, you know. I'm not one those hypocrites who can't face the truth about themselves. Or the opposite. The ones who find themselves in every character a novelist writes – no matter how preposterous.' He put an arm out and drew me close. 'I mean, I don't mind being used as material. Do you get my drift?'

'I do,' I said.

Some of my readers have been phoning.

'Guess who this is?' they often begin. I don't want to complain, but isn't there another way to start a telephone conversation? Sure, I was game the first time I was asked to guess. It was titillating enough and then the voice on the other end turned out to be an old admirer of my mother. Sixty or so, he said, an ex-Argo tight-end with . . . ahem, good family references. He could tell I was a lady who liked a good time. Did I want to go out for a drink? The next time it happened I found myself talking to my old boyfriend from grade four. He reminded me about our snowball fights on the way home from school. But he never thought of me as especially tall. Wasn't I exaggerating my height for effect? And then I had a request to get together over Christmas from a woman who shared a cabin with me once in Florida.

Can you understand why the question, Guess who this is?, is starting to make me nervous? Not that I'm annoyed by these calls. Of course, I'm grateful for the interest. But I've had a few rough ones. Like the case of an old acquaintance who started off with the guessing-game bit and then accused me of passing myself off as something I'm not. 'Postmodern – where did anyone ever get the idea that you were postmodern?' she snarled. 'Your fiction's not even real fiction. It's linear, like Margaret Atwood's. You're both a pair of fakes.'

'Do you know what the term postmodern means?' I asked, trying to get to the heart of the problem.

'Yes,' she said. 'Not a blinking thing except showing the reader you're a smart alec.'

'Well, that may be . . .' I began.

'Laurence Sterne did it with *Tristram Shandy*. So I don't know why you think you're getting away with something new.'

'I think postmodern doesn't just mean being very self-conscious about the way you tell a story. It's got something to do with irony and a certain twentieth-century awareness – about the way we're shaped by our sociological and political beliefs . . .'

'There you go. You're talking like one of them. Haven't you got any shame?'

Maybe I don't, I thought, after she hung up. That same afternoon a house plant arrived. From a teacher of business administration at a local university. He wanted to thank me for my novel which, as he put it, he found so true to life. So that made me feel a little better, if you know what I mean. Although lately I've been thinking of writing to him and maybe explaining about how literary realism boils down to just scratches on the page and all . . .

KESELAMATAN
KWC

UMBERTO ECO
Tales From the Past

As the end of the millenium approaches, I, Minervino, monk of the Saint Caracciolo Abbey, wish to set down on this parchment, in all its horror, the indubitable signs which announce the decline of the century. The food we eat seems poisonous, the grass wilts, and a terrible plague, inexistent until yesterday, has spread throughout the known world felling both the innocent and the sinners, as if their bodies can no longer offer resistance to the noxious vapours which infest them.

Our cities are falling apart among the venomous gases created by alchemists labouring under the cursed fame of gold, and beautiful Vinegia is about to disappear beneath the waves she yearly weds. Yesterday she was invaded by gangs of followers of Dionysius who covered her ground with excrement, and the Holy Mother Church weeps over the deeds of a few fleeting sinners who wish to renew the rites of Bacchus on the beaches of Ravenna. The arms of the sea, once deep-blue, are today black with a viscous mud which seems to have been vomited from the depths of hell, and news has reached us that mobs of warrior maidens from the Northern Extremities, avidly seeking violence, are now, terrified by so much danger, returning from the valleys into which they had descended with such proud self-confidence. The air has become rarefied, as if a vengeful hand had caused a rip in the sphere of gaseous elements, and the earth suffers from sudden fevers, and the rhythm of the seasons has changed. The last woods, which used to lend beauty to our hills, now burn during the summer like sinister bonfires.

And yet, would anyone dare to walk the wooded slopes infested with tattered thieves who fall upon the travellers, keeping them prisoners in inaccessible caverns, demanding gold and silver for their ransom and sending their relatives lobes or larger sections of the ear, as witness of their power which mocks the power of the Empire? Barons, vassals and imperial proconsuls are only concerned with their fratricide battles, and I have seen with my own eyes men assembled under the very Cross of Our Lord injure one another in atrocious intrigues. And the Empire cannot even guarantee the departure and arrival of the horse messengers all along our post stations.

The inquisitors themselves do nothing except try to imprison other inquisitors, and the Empire has lost every right to administrate Justice. Not long ago, when the Abbot of Alba murmured against Jubilus, the City's ex-proconsul, the latter addressed himself to the Papal Court, considering God's tribunal superior to the dignity of Caesar's. And I hope and I pray that at least the Holy Roman Tribunal orders Jubilus to prove his own innocence by submitting himself to the Ordeal of walking over burning coals, in order to bring peace to our Christian family.

The faithful are perturbed by the pretension of the infamous Jews who, blaspheming, consider themselves the beloved children of our same God. Our pontifex Jagellone the First did well in reminding them that they lost this right through their own treason and deicide. This blasphemous race is certainly worse than that of the Saracens, and, God willing, Jagellone will follow the example of the Caliph who threatened with death the greatest of his enemies (who had blasphemed against the Caliph's prophet), demanding from his faithful that they persecute this enemy wherever he went.

All sweetness has vanished from our little earthly garden. Only yesterday we heard that the Emperor of Cathay, after having trampled with chariots the children of his children, and wishing that the Normans build for him many swift Drakkar, offered them as a reward the labour of his other children, reduced to slavery.

Oh! Our grandchildren and the grandchildren of our grandchildren will not be at fault if they call Dark Ages the times in which we now live. They will have seen, in the imminence of the second millenium, the dawn of a Third Age, holier and better than this one, and they will remember us, poor sinners, as the victims of these fierce times, dark and devoid of reason.

Translated by Alberto Manguel

Ouftikour
Khacour-shir
Krobar
el oued-delahr
Boukèr
Afoukir
Rasta-Couèr
Blok
vers Oukkbe
Rabhad
Bouktâr
Ribhud
Plan de la grande porte dorée d'Abou-Houed

Plan du Château de Grez-la-touille (Haut-Lardon)

ROBERT FULFORD

Gotcha! The Literary Imagination in Our Time

In the course of a Shakespearian production in Toronto in 1988, there was a moment that briefly illustrated why contemporary society desperately needs literature and the literary imagination. The moment came just after the scene in *Henry V* in which some soldiers, about to leave for war, tearfully said goodbye to their wives. As soon as the women were safely out of sight, martial music poured from loudspeakers, the men shouted with joy, and patriotic signs were paraded across the stage. One sign held a single word: GOTCHA!

What was remarkable about that little piece of modernised Shakespeare was that it placed, in the middle of a work from the greatest literary imagination of the ages, a graphic reminder of the twentieth-century imagination at its meanest and most degraded. Not everyone in the Canadian audience understood why GOTCHA! was there. This was the English Shakespeare Company, and the reference was to something that happened in England six years earlier. On the afternoon of 3 May 1982, west of the Falkland Islands, torpedos from a British submarine hit the *General Belgrano*, an Argentine cruiser. Almost immediately, the ship began to sink. When the news of this victory reached London, the *Sun*, a hugely successful tabloid, put a one-word headline on the next morning's front page: GOTCHA! This quickly became famous as a symbol of blind jingoism, but it was also a spectacular instance of failed imagination. The people who put that headline on their newspaper were victims of the peculiar callousness that afflicts all of us to some degree. What they did was hideously inappropriate, but it was also in a sense consistent with their training, and consistent with the atmosphere of this historic period.

During the sinking, about three hundred sailors, many of them teenaged conscripts, choked to death on smoke, burned to death in oil or boiling water, or sank to the bottom of the sea. The rest of the crew, eight hundred or so, spent thirty-six hours floating in rafts on icy water, praying for rescue. The appropriate response to any such event is pity and terror, but the response of the people at the *Sun* was boyish glee. The *Sun* had already been treating the Falklands War as a kind of video game, a clash of abstract forces with no human meaning. The ships, the submarines, the helicopters and the people on them were no more consequential than flickers of electric light on a screen.

Flickers of light are the problem – perhaps the greatest mass emotional problem of our era. Flickers of light on the television screen, or the movie screen, have become our principal means of receiving information about distant reality. Television brings us close to certain forms of reality, such as war, but it also separates us emotionally from whatever it shows us. The more we see, the less we feel. Television instructs us that one war looks much like another, one plane crash much like another, one famine like another. Presented each night with moving images of disaster, we lose our sense of the human meaning of disaster. Mass communication deadens rather than enlivens us.

In the movies, as well, we learn that the death of others is unimportant. For a quarter of a century the movies have been teaching us that people who die by gunfire are usually only extras anyway, or simply deserve to die.

Those who defend violence in entertainment are quick to point out that it's always been part of drama and literature – there's violence in the Bible, in the Greek tragedies, and of course in Shakespeare. But until our time, violence in drama and literature was given its proper meaning. It was given weight. It was set in a context that made the appropriate response – pity and terror – possible. In Shakespeare, no one dies without a purpose. One moral of the Shakespeare history plays is that those who kill their kings will live to rue it; certainly those plays tell us, again and again, that the results of killing are never negligible – and that they will be felt for generations. On the other hand, the editor who wrote: GOTCHA! later said, 'I agree that headline was a shame. But it wasn't meant in a blood-curdling way. We just felt excited and euphoric. Only when we began to hear reports of how many men died did we begin to have second thoughts.' There speaks a sadly crippled imagination, desperately in need of literature.

The future of literature is in question. The novel is no longer, for most people, the central means of expressing a culture. Poetry is read by only a few. Literary studies no longer stand at the centre of the university curriculum. Certain of literature's tasks, such as social observation, are often accomplished better by movies and TV programmes. Even in the bookstores, literature is often pushed aside by journalism, how-to manuals and cookbooks.

But literature remains the core of civilised life precisely because it is the only reliable antidote to everything in our existence that diminishes us. Only the literary imagination can save us from the deadening influence of visual news and visual entertainment. When it works as it should, literature takes us beyond our parochialism of response into other minds and other cultures. It makes us know that even our enemies, even anonymous Argentinian sailors, are as humanly diverse as we are.

If we let it, literature can also save us from the narrowing effect of politics. Politics teaches us to see the world in functional terms, defined by power blocs and national borders and pressure groups. Pretending to offer freedom, politics asks us to identify ourselves by ethnicity or gender or class or nationality. Literature, on the other hand, dares us to feel our way across all boundaries of thought and feeling. One of the most beautiful stories I've recently read was written by an Asian Trinidadian Canadian man, speaking in the voice of a Japanese woman: the writer, and his grateful readers, simply refused to be contained by the limits the world regards as normal. This is the immense power that literature puts in the hands of all of us.

In the same way, literature offers us the opportunity to escape the two most pressing forms of bondage in our normal existence: time and ego. Emotionally and intellectually, literature dissolves the rules of time and beckons us towards Periclean Athens, Tsarist Russia, Elizabethan England and a thousand other moments in the past; by lengthening our sense of time it saves us from the maddening urgencies of the present. And when it succeeds on the highest level it breaks the shell of our intense and tiresome self-consciousness. It forces itself inside the egotism fostered by the pressures of our lives and links us with human history and the vast ocean of humanity now on earth. By taking us into other lives it deepens our own.

Our clear task, if we hope to realise ourselves as a civilisation, is to cherish the writers who have done their work and nourish the writers who are still doing it. The literary imagination is not a grace of life or a diversion: it is the best way we have found of reaching for the meaning of existence.

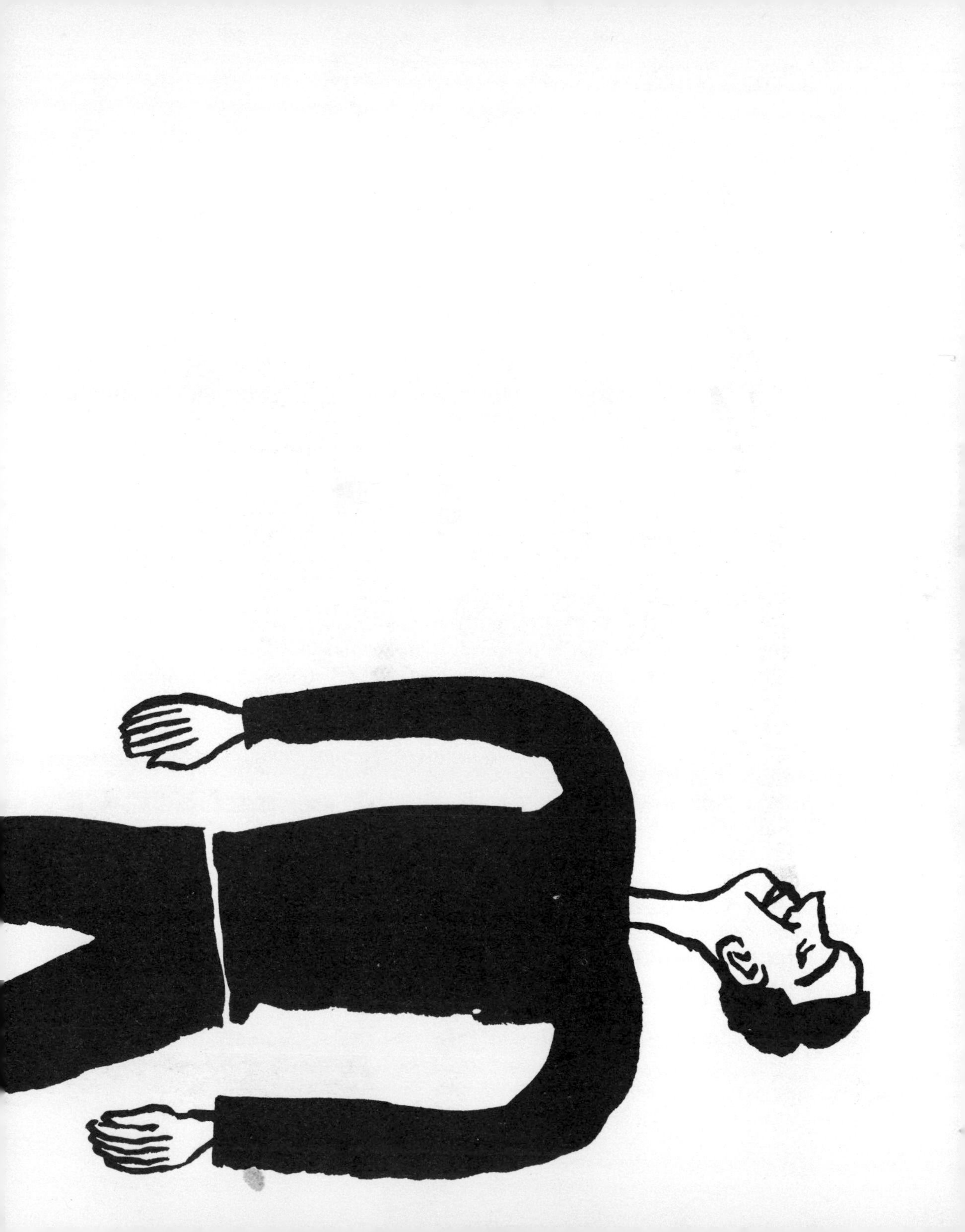

Contributors' Notes

Margaret Atwood (Canada): her seventh novel, *Cat's Eye*, was published last year.

Julian Barnes (UK): his latest novel is *A History of the World in 10½ Chapters.*

Yves Bonnefoy (France) is the author of several volumes of poems.

Jorge Luis Borges (Argentina) died in 1986.

Robert Bringhurst (Canada) is the author of several collections of poems.

David Brooks (Australia): his *Book of Sei* was published in 1988.

Bonnie Burnard (Canada) won the Commonwealth Prize for her first collection of short stories, *Women of Influence*.

Don Coles (Canada) has published several books of poems, including *K in Love*.

Michael Coren (UK) is the author of a biography of G.K. Chesterton.

Julio Cortázar (Argentina) died in 1984. *Hopscotch* was published in 1963.

Amparo Dávila (Mexico): two of her volumes of short stories are *Tiempo destrozado* and *Musica concreta.*

Anita Desai (India): her latest novel is *Baumgartner's Bombay*.

Marguerite Duras (France): her latest book is *La pluie d'été.*

Friedrich Dürrenmatt (Switzerland): his latest novel is *Justiz.*

Umberto Eco (Italy): his latest novel is *Foucault's Pendulum.*

Timothy Findley (Canada): his collection of short stories, *Stones*, appeared last year.

Jeff Fisher (Australia) works in London.

Mary Flanagan (USA) now lives in London. Her new novel, *Rose Reason*, will be published in 1991.

Robert Fulford (Canada) was for many years editor of *Saturday Night*. His autobiography is called *Best Seat in the House.*

Ted Goosen (Canada) teaches Japanese literature at York University in Toronto.

Günter Grass (Germany) is the author of *The Tin Drum.*

Ursula K. Le Guin (USA) is the creator of the Earthsea series, of which the fourth volume appeared this year.

John Hawkes (USA): his latest novel is *Whistlejacket.*

Liliana Heker (Argentina) won the *Premio Municipal* with her latest novel, *Zona de Clivaje.*

Isabel Huggan (Canada) lives in Kenya. She is the author of *The Elizabeth Stories.*

Guillermo Cabrera Infante (Cuba), exiled in London, considers himself the only English writer writing in Spanish.
Izaak Mansk (Romania) lives in London. His collection of short stories, *Forbidden to Grow Old*, was published last year.
Tomás Eloy Martínez (Argentina): his 'factual fiction', *The Novel of Perón*, appeared in English in 1989.
Rohinton Mistry (India) now lives in Canada. He has published a collection of short stories, *Tales of Firoszha Baag*.
Mary Morrissy (Ireland) won the Hennessy Award for short stories in 1984. She reviews fiction for the *Irish Times* and is currently at work on a first collection of short stories.
Haruki Murakami (Japan) is the translator of Raymond Carver into Japanese. His novel *A Wild Sheep Chase* was published in English this year.
Richard Outram (Canada) has published several volumes of poetry. His *Selected Poems 1960–1980* appeared in 1984.
Cynthia Ozick (USA): her latest book is *The Shawl*, a story and a novella collected in one volume.
Grace Paley (USA) is the author of several collections of short stories.
Alejandra Pizarnik (Argentina) died in 1972. Her books include *Arbol de Diana* and *Extraccion de la Piedra de Locura*.
Joseph Roth was one of the greatest writers of the Austro-Hungarian Empire.
Joseph Skvorecky (Czechoslovakia) lives in Canada.
Susan Swan (Canada): her novel *The Last of the Golden Girls* was published in Canada in 1989.
Anne Szumigalski (Canada): the pieces which appear here will form part of her next book of poems, *Rapture of the Deep*.
Craig Thomas (Canada) is a Toronto lawyer and translator.
Rose Tremain (UK): her latest novel, *Restoration*, won the *Sunday Express* Book of the Year Award and was shortlisted for the Booker Prize.
Jane Urquhart (Canada) is the author of *Changing Heaven*.
Marq de Villiers (South Africa) is the editor of *Toronto Life* and the author of *White Tribe Dreaming*.
Ronald Wright (UK) lives in Canada. His latest book is *Time Among the Mayas*.

oho
the end